Journey to the Sun

Journey to the Sun

by
Pierre Boitard

Translated, annotated and introduced by
Brian Stableford

A Black Coat Press Book

ISBN 978-1-61227-517-8. First Printing. July 2016. Published by Black Coat Press, an imprint of Hollywood Comics.com, LLC, P.O. Box 17270, Encino, CA 91416. All rights reserved. Except for review purposes, no part of this book may be reproduced or transmitted in any form or by any means, electronic or mechanical, including photocopying, recording, or by any information storage and retrieval system, without permission in writing from the publisher. The stories and characters depicted in this novel are entirely fictional. Printed in the United States of America.

TABLE OF CONTENTS

Introduction 7
PARIS BEFORE HUMANKIND 21
JOURNEY TO THE SUN 123

Introduction

"Voyage au soleil" by Pierre Boitard, here translated as "Journey to the Sun," was first published in four parts in the *Musée des Familles* in the issues for December 1838, February and November 1839, and February 1840. The second, third and fourth parts do not carry that title, being content with the rubric "Étude astronomique" and chapter titles, but the narrative is continuous and it was obviously planned as a coherent project. At any rate, whatever one care to call it, the *étude astronomique* in question is a sequel of sorts to a work in a different scientific genre, "Paris avant l'homme," here translated as "Paris Before Humankind," which appeared in the same magazine in two parts in the June 1837 and November 1837 issues.

Both of these stories were ground-breaking in terms of their subject-matter and their narrative strategy, and although both now seem very primitive in both respects, the subject-matter and narrative strategy in question having been very elaborately developed in the interim, they are works of considerable historical interest, and their exhumation is an interesting exercise in literary archeology. The second item was never reprinted, and although the author began work on a revised version of the former before his death in 1859, its subject-matter had made such vast advances in the previous twenty years that only small fragments of the original text survive in a far more elaborate text, which was posthumously published, without the final polish that the author planned to give it, as *L'Univers avant l'homme* [The World Before Humankind], in 1861.

Pierre Boitard was born in 1789. His early publications were in the field of botany, his first book being *Traité de la composition et de l'ornament des jardins* [Treatise on the Design and Ornamentation of Gardens] (1925), and most of his

7

later ones were concerned with the relevance of botanical knowledge to the planning and maintenance of gardens and to the planning and maintenance of agricultural endeavor. Because of his interest in botany he also became fascinated by the nascent field that would nowadays be called paleobotany: the study of extinct plants and the sequence of their development over time, by means of the fossil record. That led to a more general interest in paleontology, including the development of animal fossils over geological time, and hence to an interest in cosmogony, the history of the Earth as revealed by the geological record, and what that might imply regarding the nature and development of the entire solar system in the course of cosmic time.

Partly because of that direction of approach, Boitard had no difficulty at all in becoming a believer in what would then have been known as "transformism"; it seemed obvious to him that plants had originated with simple forms that had, over long periods of time, developed into more complicated ones. That pattern was very obviously set out in the fossil record and relatively easy to comprehend. It was, therefore, natural enough for him to transfer the same kind of thinking to his contemplation of the record of fossil animals, where it was much more controversial.

The development of geological studies had long made nonsense of the chronology inferred from *Genesis*, which suggested that the world was only six thousand years old and had been created in six days; the realization that the Earth contained a large number of rock strata laid down by successive processes of sedimentation made that account utterly incredible. Some people therefore considered geology—and science in general—to be a dire threat to religious faith, and one to be opposed at all costs. Others took the view that it made no difference to the real foundations of religious faith, but merely required the six days of creation to be construed metaphorically. Some geologists even took the trouble to divide geological time up into six periods that conserved the same number—an adjustment with which Boitard was quite happy to go along.

There was, however, an additional and particular problem with regard to the sixth day of *Genesis*, which included the creation of humankind. By 1837, paleontological discoveries had begun to suggest, although the crucial evidence was still rather thin, that humans had first appeared on Earth a long time before six thousand years ago, which cast the rest of the chronology of *Genesis* into the same rubbish bin as the six days of creation, without there being any readily available metaphorical shift to save its essence. Worse than that; if it were accepted that animals as well as plants had developed over an exceedingly long period of time by virtue of a complex pattern of transformations, then the possibility arose that human beings were a product of that process too, and not a special and unique creation. That, for many devout believers, was a line that could not and must not be crossed.

Some scientists saw no particular problem there either. For them, transformism simply became God's painstaking method of creation, and the truth of transformism—even if it included the origin of human beings, supplying them with relatively recent ancestors that they had in common with the great apes—need not challenge belief in God as the creator of the world. Boitard apparently belonged to that camp too. There was, however, a considerable difference in 1837 between being prepared to believe that and being prepared to say so publicly. Most geologists and biologists were extremely diplomatic in writing, if only in the interests of avoiding persecution, of which there was still a real danger. (There are, of course, places in the world where it still is.)

Even in esoteric publications directed at an academic audience, it was still advisable, in France in 1837, to be very careful of what one said, and how, about transformism, especially where its relevance to humankind was concerned. That diplomatic risk was, however, magnified very considerably when it was a matter of addressing a popular audience. For more than a hundred years in France, "philosophy" had been virtually synonymous, at least in the minds of philosophers, with atheism (which set them against theism but not necessarily against deism—i.e., against theology and the Church but not necessarily against the idea and possible existence of God), but dogmatic religion was regarded as a necessary means of keeping the populace in order.

Religion was, therefore, generally seen by those early nineteenth century Frenchmen who considered themselves learned and wise as a gigantic confidence trick, whose purpose was to counsel the poor to be content with being poor, while the rich enjoyed themselves, and anyone who opposed that function was, by definition, dangerous to the existing social order—all the more so if he what he said was true. The Revolution of 1789 had abolished all the Church's privileges for precisely that reason, and the Restoration of 1814 had only turned the clock back partially; the general attitude among the French upper classes in general, and the Church in particular, to geology, transformism, and anything else that might weaken faith, was that if it were true, on no account were the underprivileged to be informed, lest 1789 should happen all over again.

The *Musée des Familles* was, as its title declared, a "family magazine" whose sole *raison d'être* was the education and enlightenment of the underprivileged, specifically including women and children. Its subtitle was *Lectures du Soir* [Evening Reading], emphasizing that it was intended, in an era when most women were still illiterate, for the husbands to read aloud to their wives and children in a family gathering. In that context, far more than any other, the beliefs that Pierre Boitard held were ideological dynamite. To parade them in its pages was an act of courage, and of provocation, and to parade them in a manner calculated to make them easily digestible, and even entertaining, was, in the eyes of the disapproving, to add insult to injury. The fact that Boitard did it is therefore surprising; perhaps more surprising still is the fact that he was not prevented from doing it at the editorial level, and almost certainly not merely allowed but encouraged to do it.

It seems probable, in fact, that it was not Boitard's idea to do it; one thing of which we can be certain is that he never did it again while he was alive, although he did prepare an even more provocative text, in the revised and expanded version of "Paris avant l'homme," for posthumous publication—a common tactic among timid rebels who want to make their point without having to suffer the fallout. It seems likely, therefore, that the idea of publishing "Paris avant l'homme" and then following it up with the even more ambitious and equally provocative "Voyage au soleil" did not originate with Boitard, or, if it did, that the idea must have been wholeheartedly endorsed by the editor of the *Musée des Familles*, S. Henry Berthoud. Whether or not he originated the idea for the two serials, however, we can be certain that Berthoud had much to do with the narrative strategy they adopted, which was something else that Boitard never did again—and nor did anyone else for the next two decades, although subsequent writers have certainly made up for the delay since then.

The *Musée des Familles* was one of a number of publications founded by Émile de Girardin (1802-1881), an important pioneer of the popular press in France. His newspaper, *La Presse*, launched in 1836, was the first one of its kind aimed specifically at the lower orders of society, with an educational mission in mind, and it had been preceded by other publication with the same didactic purpose in mind, of which the *Musée des Familles*, launched in September1833, was the most important. Girardin's wife, Delphine, was the daughter of Sophie Gay, whose salon had been one of the cauldrons of the French Romantic Movement, and when she started her own salon after the marriage in 1831 many of the younger members of Sophie Gay's salon transferred their primary allegiance. It was there that Girardin found editors for his publications, including Berthoud and Jules Janin, and it was there that his editors found contributors to help them fill their pages; thus, the *Musée des Familles* published important early work by many of the younger members of the Movement: Honoré de Balzac, Alexandre Dumas, Théophile Gautier, Léon Gozlan, Joseph

Méry, Eugène Sue, "P.L. Jacob the Bibliophile" (Paul Lacroix) and Paul de Kock.

During the first few months of its publication, the *Musée des Familles* followed a format not dissimilar to other magazines of the period, featuring a miscellany of short articles on various subjects, with the occasional short story. When Berthoud took over the editorship in April 1834, however, it did not take him long to adopt very different tactics, running longer stories—mostly novellas, but including some novels—in two, three or four episodes of between 10,000 and 20,000 words. The bulk of the magazine's contents, and the core of its didactic mission, was transferred to these items, which Berthoud labeled "Études." Most were "Études historiques" [Historical Studies] or "Études morales" [Moralistic Studies] but he made an evident effort to gather as many of the topics covered by the magazine as possible under that banner, in obvious pursuit of the theory that educational material was more palatable if it were enclosed in a narrative that had all the conventional reader-appeal of popular fiction.

That is, of course, easy enough to do with history, which is, in a sense, already narrativized, and into which individual dramas can easily be slotted. Indeed, all individual dramas have to be slotted into history in some sense, and the temptation to slot them into interesting periods of history, involving important events and well-known people, is considerable even without any additional informative mission. Berthoud led by example in that regard; he was by far the magazine's most prolific contributor of *études*, many reflecting his own particular fascination with the history of arts, and historical legends. There can be no doubt, however, that he also encouraged his other contributors to narrativize their contributions too, making them into stories rather than essays.

That is not easy to do with regard to science. In 1837, of course, there was no such thing as "science fiction," and it would be more than thirty years before the term "roman scientifique" changed its meaning to refer to a kind of fiction rather than to scientific theories that the user of the phrase thought absurd. The simplest way to do it was simply to carry on a tradition long established in scientific reportage, which was to embed scientific ideas in a dialogue; that is what one of Berthoud's scientific contributors, Auguste Bertsch, did in his series on "Le Monde invisible" (1839), which presented early discoveries in microscopy is the context of a series of dialogues between the narrator and his doctor. Boitard employs dialogue too, but chooses a more interesting interlocutor—a choice partly forced by his subject-matter.

Paleontology and cosmogony are inherently narrativized sciences, which set out fundamentally to tell stories, but the stories in question necessarily extend over very long periods of time and treat large-scale events with no human involvement. It is, therefore, not easy to blend their inherent narrativization with the kinds of narrative that fit so readily into the context of historical depiction. Indeed, in order to for a human viewpoint to be introduced into them, the narrative strategy requires at a minimum, the invention of some kind of time travel, and, in the latter case, space travel as well. In 1837, there was only one previous literary work that had done both: Restif de La Bretonne's unprecedentedly bizarre *Les Posthumes* (published 1802 but written 1787-89)[1], which was not a model that any reasonable writer would have thought it desirable to follow. Very few people had read it, although there is one episode in "Voyage au soleil" that suggests that Boitard might have been one of them. Without going to Restifian extremes, however, there was one narrative device readily available to fulfill either or both of those functions, and that was dreaming. Naturally, that was the one that Boitard adopted.

Dreaming can supply interlocutors as easily as it can supply visions of elsewhen and elsewhere, but a far-reaching scientific dream of the kind envisaged by Boitard requires an interlocutor of a special kind, not only in terms of what he

---

[1] tr. as *Posthumous Correspondence* (3 vols.), Black Coat Press, ISBNs 978-1-61227- 513-0, 514-7 & 515-4.

13

knows, and can therefore discuss, but also in terms of what he can do within the dream to guide it and steer a course through it. When Dante had to go to Hell he naturally chose Virgil as a guide and interlocutor, because Virgil had (unwittingly) done so much to help shape the Christian notion of Hell in the *Aeneid*, but the choice of a cicerone to guide Boitard's dream-self through the labyrinths of prehistory and the heavenly bodies of the solar system was not so obvious. Given its provocative nature, however, and the attitude that those hostile to it were bound to strike, there was one very appealing contender available in French literary tradition, and that was the one that Boitard selected.

It is nowadays considered, quite rightly, that dreaming is not an ideal device for dealing with awkward imaginative materials, partly because it is by definition the work of the unfettered imagination, but mostly because it is inherently and essentially anticlimactic, having only one possible denouement, in which it is hard to avoid a suggestion of bathos. Boitard's evident awareness of that fact is amply demonstrated by the denouement of his second novella. In 1837, however, it would have required an exceptionally intrepid leap into the unknown and the implausible to come up with anything different. That was not the only difficult decision he had to make, however, and two of them were bound to create even bigger problems for the attitude that posterity would be bound to take to his endeavor.

The first of those problems is, of course, the woeful inadequacy of his data. Paleontology was in its infancy in 1837; the vast majority of its discoveries were made subsequently, and inevitably produced data that challenged many of the inferences drawn from earlier incomplete data. We now know that many of the inferences that Boitard drew were false, and those that were not have come to seem so familiar as now to seem trivial and obvious, although they did not seem so at the time. Astronomy was by no means in its infancy, having existed far longer than any other science, but it was still dependent on instruments that now seem primitive and limited, so in that regard too, Boitard's description of the worlds of the solar system now seem equally primitive and limited, and we know that some of his hypotheses—most obviously the manner in which the Sun produces heat on planetary surfaces—are utterly false. Those limitations and errors should not, however, make modern readers overlook the extent of the imaginative effort that Boitard was compelled to make, or prevent them from admiring his enterprise.

The second problem is that neither of the sciences that Boitard was attempting to popularize is independent and self-contained, because no science is or can be. He was as polymathic as it was possible for a man of his epoch to be, but his knowledge of sciences other than his most intensely specialized interests was weak and somewhat flawed. In an essay, such difficulties are routinely avoided by the simple strategy of sticking to safe ground, but fiction inevitably aims for concrete and coherent depiction, and omissions and fudges tend to stand out more obviously to the informed eye. It is improbable, therefore, that any modern reader will be able to peruse the texts in this volume without spotting errors, including some that would pass today for "schoolboy howlers." Again, however, those errors should not cause modern readers to overlook the fact there are also aspects of Pierre Boitard's thought that were unusually sound for his time, and that, at the final analysis, in taking the side of the apes in the transformism debate, and striving hard and ingeniously to prove and dramatize his position, he was on the side of the truth, and was not the least of that army's heroes.

By virtue of the nature of his exercise, and in spite of his use of purely fantastic facilitating devices, both "Paris avant l'homme" and "Voyage au soleil" are attempts to produce what would nowadays be called "hard science fiction": speculative fiction based on accurate scientific data. In the former instance, the scientific basis of the speculative method is provided by the work of Georges Cuvier (1769-1832), the first person to develop the idea that fossils were the remains of plant and animal species that had long become extinct, but which could nevertheless be accurately depicted, even from incomplete skeletal remains, by means of analogical reasoning—although Boitard took leave to disagree with Cuvier with the regard to some of the logical consequences of that theory. In the latter instance, Boitard sought to make use of contemporary data in both astronomy and physics in order to produce an account of the solar system and an analysis of the possibility that its planets—and, indeed, the Sun itself—might be inhabited.

We now know that Boitard got everything wrong—but that was mostly because of the inadequacy of the data available to him and the theories with which he was working. In the case of "Voyage au soleil" his work invites an ironic comparison with its only predecessor as an attempted work of "hard science fiction," Guillaume La Follie's *Le Philosophe sans prétention* (1775)[2]. Whereas La Follie got everything wrong because he based all his theoretical extrapolations on the phlogiston theory of combustion, Boitard got his all wrong because he based them on the theory of "caloric" invented specifically to replace phlogiston theory when its defects became obvious. Alas, it turned out to be equally defective—but that does not alter the fact that Boitard's attempt to extrapolate it was ingenious as well as bold. "Voyage au soleil" also illustrates the perennial problem that writers of that kind of speculative fiction have when they attempt to accommodate their scientific extrapolations and speculations within a work of fiction with a theme of sorts, if not a plot. Nowadays, the strongest temptation is to borrow the formulae of adventure fiction or crime fiction; in his day, it was to borrow the formulae of utopian satire. He did so in a conspicuously half-hearted fashion, but he did so nevertheless—and what else, after all, could he be reasonably expected to have done?

---

[2] tr. as *The Unpretentious Philosopher*, Black Coat Press, ISBN 978-1-61227-136-1.

It is not easy today to pick up echoes of any scandal that Boitard's serials caused the readers of the *Musée de Familles*, although we can be reasonably certain that there was some. Some such argument might have been responsible for the gap between the second and third parts of "Voyage au Soleil"; although the narrative is continuous, the theme of human transformism, strongly developed in parts one and two, is virtually absent from part four, which seems a trifle truncated and tokenistic.

S. Henry Berthoud was removed as editor of the magazine in 1840, when it ran into further financial difficulties, having already been taken over by a consortium of shareholders in 1838; he was replaced by Pierre Chevalier (1812-1853), better known by the nickname of "Pitre-Chevalier." Berthoud was never published in the magazine again, although Boitard contributed a few orthodox and uncontroversial articles on natural history. The magazine continued to experience financial difficulties, and the title changed hands twice more before the revolution of 1848. It was, however, resurrected thereafter and eventually became a venerable and cherished institution, although Girardin's involvement had long ceased.

Because Boitard died in 1859 he did not live to see the furor awakened by the publication in that year of Charles Darwin's *Origin of Species*, nor did he live to see the remarkable boom in the popularization of science that took place in France in the 1860s, although *L'Univers avant l'homme* attempted to be a significant early contribution to it, or the emergence of *roman scientifique* as a genre due to the efforts of Jules Verne—all of whose early fiction was published in the revamped *Musée des Familles*. S. Henry Berthoud, however, did live to see all of that, and to participate in the boom in popularization.

In fact, although Berthoud did not make any contribution to the popularization of science in the *Musée des Familles* while he was editing it, his journalistic activities in the 1850s consisted mainly of a long series of articles, mostly published under the by-line "Dr. Sam," popularizing natural history and new scientific discoveries, in much the same vein as Boitard's work, but very frequently employing narrative methods of presentation, in accordance with his own theory. That work enabled him, when the boom began, to take rapid advantage of by issuing a four-volume set of his own *Fantaisies scientifiques du docteur Sam* (1862-63), which included some of the historical fiction he had written for the *Musée des Familles* as well as more recent items.

Berthoud was also able to publish a portmanteau collection of stories entitled *L'Homme depuis cinq mille ans* (1865), which included his own account of "Les Premiers habitants de Paris," following up on Boitard's "Paris avant l'homme." The similar portmanteau collection *Contes du docteur Sam* (1866) included "Le Château de Heidenloch,"[3] a story whose protagonists are enabled by clever artifice to take a metaphorical trip into times past and witness various prehistoric scenes, including a vision of a plesiosaur and an ichthyosaurus very similar to the one included in "Paris avant l'homme"—in fact, other visions of prehistory, including the one in Jules Verne's *Voyage au centre de la terre* (1864; tr. as *Journey to the Center of the Earth*) very often include the same pairing.

S. Henry Berthoud never wrote an interplanetary fantasy, evidently feeling that such an endeavor lay beyond his imaginative scope, but Pierre Boitard's studies in natural history are an obvious model for many of his studies of insect and avian life, and he obviously retained good and productive memories of their brief association. Boitard's indirect contribution to the development of *roman scientifique* was, in consequence, more considerable than the fall of his own work into near-oblivion might suggest.

As interplanetary fantasies go, Boitard's now seems crude, and markedly eccentric, not least in reversing the pattern most authors of such fantasies followed. Instead of starting with the Moon and progressing from there to the planets,

---

[3] Included in the S. Henry Berthoud collection *Martyrs of Science*, Black Coat Press, ISBN 978-1-61227-229-0.

usually missing out the Sun on the grounds of is presumed inaccessibility, Boitard starts with an accessible Sun and leaves the Moon until last. His was by no means the first interplanetary journey to employ a helpful "genius" (in the sense of spirit) as a means of transport within the context of a dream—indeed, such helpful genii had become a common device in imaginative fiction in the course of the previous century—and the one he recruited was an even earlier literary invention, but his genius has the additional twist of being a devil's advocate fully briefed to plead the cause of transformism in a show trial.

The fact that Boitard did that, in the context of a work that consists partly of educational lectures and partly of argumentative hypothesis before finally relaxing into satirical comedy, does entitle him to some credit for the judiciousness of his selection of narrative agents, and helps to reserve a special place for his outlandish contribution to the exceedingly awkward early development of *roman scientifique*.

These translations were taken from the versions of the relevant volumes of the *Musée des Familles* reproduced on the Bibliothèque Nationale's *gallica* website. Because of the difficulty of opening the pages in the bound volumes, some of the type closest to the margins is occasionally lost in the scans, requiring improvisation. A few errors might have crept in because of my incorrect inferences, for which I can only apologize. The splitting of the two texts into chapters and the titling of the chapters is uneven, differing between episodes, and some chapter breaks and titles might have been omitted in order to fit the available space. I have omitted some numbered chapters from the second part of "Paris avant l'homme" because the first part had none, and have only supplied text breaks in the translation. In the latter parts of "Voyage au soleil," I have added some extra chapter breaks, and have revised the titling system to comply with the pattern employed in the first part. I have also revised some passages that refer to diagrams included in the text in order to try to make them

19

comprehensible without the diagrams, Apart from those technical amendments, and omitting a few of the author's footnotes, which seemed to me to be superfluous, I have stuck as closely as I could to the original text.

Brian Stableford

PARIS BEFORE HUMANKIND

PART ONE

It was cold; the north wind was blowing swirls of hard, dry snow violently against the windows of my study; my fire was crackling, putting out bright and lively flames, and eight o'clock in the evening had just chimed.

No, I said to myself, *I won't go out.* Without removing my two feet from on top of the fire-irons, and without setting down the tongs I was holding in my hand, I stretched myself out in my old armchair and changed position in order to day-dream more comfortably.

Soon, my reveries turned naturally to my habitual studies, and gradually, half-asleep and half-awake, a vague desire to know the various phases of nature took possession of me and preoccupied my vacillating imagination.

Alas, I thought, *why are we no longer in the times of enchantresses and genii? Perhaps I'd find one kind enough to tell me what the world as like—or only France, even just Paris, or the garden of the Tuileries—eight or ten thousand years ago, more or less.*

Suddenly, I heard something like the rustle of paper on my bookshelves. I saw three or four quarto volumes and as many octavos agitating, without an apparent motive force, emerge from their places, extend their double-fold illustrations like wings and fly in a single streak to my desk, within arms' reach. But there was a further prodigy! They arranged themselves in a pile, from which thick smoke emerged, which hid them from view. Then the smoke evaporated, and instead of my quartos I saw Lesage's lame devil.[4]

"I heard you," he said, "and here I am.

"Much obliged, Monsieur Demon."

"The ignorant and the stupid often want to read the future, and very easily find people who, in return for a modest sum, explain clearly what they want to know. Learned people try to collect the scattered shreds of the past, and sew them together to form a usefully useful picture. They're essentially book-dealers and dreamers, but that isn't sufficient, and as you said just now, they need a genius who will aid them. Now, a genius is a very rare thing today!"

"No one knows that better than me, Monseigneur, for I have the honor of belonging to several Academies."

"I've come to get you out of difficulty, because, fundamentally, I'm a good devil."

"What!" I replied, transported with joy. "You'll tell me what there was in Paris four, eight or ten thousand years ago?"

"Yes, and better still; I'll enable you to see it. Although I can't advance an hour into the future, I can go back several thousand years into the past. Come with me—and let's go right away, because it will be a long voyage even though we aren't going far."

---

[4] i.e. Asmodeus from *Le Diable boiteux* (1707; tr. as *The Devil on Two Sticks*) by Alain René Lesage

First Period

The genius passed a finger over my eyes, and I found myself sitting beside him in a small boat floating on a vast ocean.

"I could have gone back several more centuries into the past," he said, "but I wouldn't have anything to show you in primordial ages but inanimate brute matter, obedient without exception to the eternal laws of physics and chemistry, and all that wouldn't have appeared very clearly to you, so we'll take things a little less remote. In order that you to understand fully what you're going to see, it's necessary that I give you a general idea of the globe you inhabit.

"Firstly, its exterior envelope is aeriform, and is named the atmosphere."

"It's said that that first layer is fifteen leagues thick?"

"I don't know," said the genius, and continued: "Secondly, the mass of waters or liquid envelope covering about three-quarters of the surface of the globe, continuously changing place, in such a way as to cover and uncover the continents by turns."

"Is that by the effect of spontaneous inundations, like the deluge?"

"I don't know."

"It's claimed that if the mass of the waters were spread uniformly over the Earth, its thickness would be a thousand meters. What do you think?"

"I don't think anything at all, because I don't know the depths of the oceanic abysms, and it isn't you or me that will fathom them. Thirdly, the solid envelope or mineral crust, is what you're going to see being modified, formed and populated during our short stroll of a few thousand years."

"Do you know its antiquity, dating from chaos—for the Chinese, the Indians, the Egyptians and the Jews aren't in accord with regard to the age of the world?"

23

"It won't be me, at any rate, who will bring them into accord. Fourthly, the central part or the internal mass..."

"I'd very much like to know of what that consists."

"Me too."

Here's a devil who must be veritably knowledgeable, I thought, *for he doesn't pretend to know everything.*

"Your study is in the Faubourg Saint-Germain, isn't it?"

"Yes."

"Rue du Cimetière-Saint-André-des-Arts?"

"Yes."

"Well, stick your nose in the air and look."

I raised my head, but I only perceived a pure azure sky, and, toward the Orient, the first rays of the rising sun.

"You can't see anything else?"

"No."

"We are, however, three hundred meters directly beneath the house you inhabit, and on a sea three hundred meters deep."

"How is that?"

"It's quite simple; I've transported you abruptly to the primitive period, and at that time, the ground surface where Paris stands was nearly six hundred meters lower than in 1836, that's all. You're going to see that surface rise up progressively by virtue of new formations. This sea, on which we're floating, reposes on the primordial soil, or primitive layer, enveloping the entire globe. It's homogeneous everywhere and composed of crystalline schistous terrain: granite and ordinary syenite.[5] One doesn't find rolled pebbles here, nor organic debris. Its layers, sharply inclined, compose the great massifs of mountains. Plants and animals don't exist yet. If you like, we can wait here for a few hundred centuries, until the waters

---

[5] The "syenite" to which Boitard refers is not the igneous rock nowadays known by that name but a species of granite to which the name was once applied because it was identified in Syene (now Aswan) in Egypt.

have flowed away, and I'll be able to show you what I told you."

"No thank you, Monsieur Lame Devil."

"In that case, let's pass on to the second period, the one where sedimentary soil commences—which is to say, the one in which the waters have deposited more or less thick layers on the primordial soil."

Second Period

The genius touched me with his crutch; then, everything had disappeared, both the sea and the boat. We were sitting on gray rock covered with mosses and lichens. The land was almost entirely devoid of verdure, and a frightful silence reigned over that bleak solitude.

"This," the genius, "is the second great period in the age of the Earth. It commenced at the moment when we quit the boat, and since then, a number of centuries have accumulated. Look, here's that primitive schist rock again, showing its bare head above new layers of sedimentary rocks that are only piled up on it. Only a little sand and vegetable detritus furnish the few meager tufts of verdure we can see scattered here and there in valleys, like oases in the middle of the desert. But come on, let's follow this bank, and perhaps we'll find a few of the first inhabitants of the Earth."

I stood up and followed my guide.

"Look," he said. "Nature, as if she were trying her strength, has begun the organization of matter with the simplest beings; no bird flies as yet in the air; no mammal has yet caused the echoes of its cries of amour or anger to resound; no reptile, no vertebrate animal has yet trod this desert. No being exists that has an aerial respiration, a voice whose sounds can trouble the silence of creation. Through the transparent waves you can see a few zoophytes or animal-plants, the majority of them attached forever to the submarine stone that saw them born. Some resemble long floating feathers, others flowery bushes, of which they have the bright colors and the singular faculty of reproducing by means of buds; oysters, madrepores, corals and millepores still have several stony parts, as if to indicate that they still retain something of the nature of the minerals that preceded them. A few mollusks are opening their bivalve shells and dragging themselves with difficulty over the sand."

"What! That's the whole of animality?"

"No; since there are weak beings there also ought to be stronger ones to oppress them; that's the general law. In fact, examine the predatory worm that is sliding insidiously between the stones to seize those that are going to become its victim and its pasture. Can you see it? Well, in this century that's the unique tyrant of living nature; it's the most redoubtable being that the Earth has yet engendered."

"But what about other countries?"

"Nothing; nothing but what you see here. Creation is slow, it moves one step at a time; but it's uniform over the entire Earth, because it's submissive to a uniform and invariable rule, without which it is impossible. That rule consists of proceeding from the simple to the composite, first double, then triple, then quadruple, and all the way to the most complicated organization.

"Cast your eyes over the vegetation; you'll see that it only consists as yet of the most simply organized plants. Those of an entirely cellular consistency showed themselves first; the vascular plants are beginning to appear, but the Earth only possesses a single dicotylenous species as yet."[6]

"Even so, the vegetation doesn't seem to me to be much more advanced than animality."

---

[6] Author's note: "Cellular vegetables are those whose entire organization consists of tiny membranous cells juxtaposed; they have no leaves or roots, and no sex organs—mushrooms, for instance. Vascular vegetables are those that have vessels and, in consequence, a more or less complicated organization. Among them, the monocotyledons are the most simply organized, such as grasses, for example. Dicotyledons are the most perfect; including our fruit trees and the great majority of the trees in our forests. Those named agamic plants or cryptogams are sometimes cellular and sometimes vascular; as they have no sex organs—stamens and pistils—one can regard them as the first drafts of the vegetable kingdom; they are also the ones that appeared first."

"That's inevitable. Vegetables nourish themselves on mineral substances, so they have to be born first, for they alone found the most essential condition of existence, nourishment. Animals, only living on matter already organized, could only appear after the plants that furnish it for them; thus, you'll see their number increase in proportion to the abundance of vegetation. The families to which the mud of vegetal detritus can serve as an aliment have already appeared, such as the mollusks and the zoophytes; then the petty carnivores that can aliment themselves on worms and mollusks, the crustaceans. Herbivorous reptiles will come next—tortoises, for example—and among them the saurians or lizards will accustom themselves to devouring one another. Then the great herbivores such as the pachyderms will appear. The great carnivores—tigers, lions, panthers and bears—will show themselves, declaring war on all the others. Finally the most devastating species, humankind, which will subjugate, kill and devour all of them, will appear last."

We penetrated into one of the rare oases of verdure scattered here and there.

"Here," I said, "are algae and wracks, whose long stems sway in the waves. Here are mushrooms displaying infinitely varied forms and colors. Here are mosses, lycopods, ferns and horsetails. A liliacea[7] is opening its pretty corollas to the gentle influence of the zephyrs, and if I'm not mistakes, I can see a clump of palm trees over there!"

"You're not mistaken."

"But have you transported me to the tropics?"

"We're still directly underneath your apartment, but we're thirty or forty meters closer—which is to say, the entire

---

[7] When the family *Liliaceae* was first described in 1789 it was a kind of catch-all term for monocotyledonous plants that did not fit into other groups rather than the more specific family nowadays described by the term (which did not appear in the fossil record until the Cretaceous), so it was imagined to contain the most primitive flowering plants

thickness of the layer of terrain that the sea has left on the primordial soil since the first period."

"Palm trees in Paris!" I exclaimed, admiringly. "Oh Heavens, how I regret not having brought my thermometer, bought from the skillful Monsieur Delamarre;[8] I'd know what degree of heat there was when palm trees grew in Paris."

"I can tell you that. Your Réaumur thermometer would indicate twenty-six degrees above zero in summer and twelve degrees of frost in winter, in an average year."

"But Monsieur Demon, that's not possible, for palm trees only grow in the hottest regions; and besides, our scientists say that the atmosphere was as warm in those days as Turkish baths, and the waters as hot as a consommé at Véry's."[9]

"Your scientists! Your scientists!" the demon replied, going red with anger. "What the devil are your scientists to me? Learn, Monsieur, that I'm not a scientist, that I detest hypotheses, that I'm a devil who only believes what I can see, that I'm showing you palpable facts, and that I don't like preposterous arguments, devil though I am![10]

"Forgive me if I've annoyed you, but..."

"Don't you know that beings are modified in accordance with the climates and environments they inhabit? Who has told you that the palm trees of that period, and the animals of that period, inhabiting the place where we are, weren't organized in such a way as to support without inconvenience a cold of twelve or twenty degrees Réaumur? Who obliges you to believe that the earth has jumped on its axis because it re-

---

[8] Chollet-Delamarre was the leading supplier of scientific instrument in Paris in the early 19th century.

[9] Madame Very, who owned restaurants in the Palais Royal, the Jardin des Tuileries and the Rue Rivoli, was sufficiently famous to be featured in a print by Thomas Rowlandson. Her menu can still be read on-line in early 19th century guidebooks to Paris.

[10] Asmodeus is punning on the word *cornu* [figuratively, preposterous], whose literal meaning is "horned."

ceived a swipe from a comet's tail in passing, to make the globe a cooled ball, the atmosphere a steam-bath, the sea a hot consommé, and other nonsense of the same sort?[11]

---

[11] Author's note: "The Earth, according to some geologists, was a spark launched by the sun into space. Originally, it was entirely composed of boiling liquid substances. Those substances would still be liquid and hot in the interior of the globe, and the crust, solidified by cooling, would only be fifteen leagues thick. In the globe's primal state of incandescence, water, entirely in the state of vapor, formed an atmosphere impenetrable to the sun's rays, but that atmosphere was itself luminous. As the globe circled in space the heat evaporated, the vapors condensed, the liquids solidified, etc, etc. All was going well and the Earth was already populated when a comet arrived, I don't know where from, struck our poor globe obliquely and changed the position of its axis. That comet broke off a piece, which became the moon. 'The Earth,' says Monsieur Boubée, 'having stopped momentarily during the impact—or rather, its velocity having momentarily slowed, the waters and everything that was not attached to the ground, conserving theirs ordinary movement, which, at the equator is eight leagues per minute, were obliged to launch themselves en masse over their shores, pass around the paused globe, crossing the summits of the highest mountains, battering and ripping the points that offered most resistance to their passage, broke off huge blocks from the rocks and dragged them into the plains, dispersing debris uprooted from everywhere, and finally, opening and hollowing out great valleys and profound basins everywhere that their imperious course dug furrows.' If all that isn't true, its at least well imagined."
The quotation is from *Géologie élementaire à la portèe de tout le monde* [Elementary Geology within everyone's range] (1833) by Nérée Boubée, an elaboration of the cometary theory of deluges, popular at the time and memorably dramatized in fiction by Restif de La Bretonne in *Les Posthumes* (1802; tr.

"So, to get back to the facts, for I need facts myself, how can you explain the history of the mammoth found in 1799,[12] with flesh and hide, in a block of ice thirty or forty feet thick, on the edge of the Glacial Sea? And the rhinoceros with the head of a pig, similarly found in its flesh and hide in the ice of the river Wiluji?[13] Do you think that when it was surprised by the cold that the atmosphere was as hot as a steam-bath? And yet that icy land was populated, as it is today, with mammoths and rhinoceroses; there were, Monsieur, many other animals and vegetables that can only exist today in the tropics because their constitution has changed as they have moved nearer to the equator."

Genii are ordinarily very irritable, as everyone knows; so, although my devil's arguments had not entirely convinced me, I let it seem so for the sake of prudence. Then he calmed down and observed that I was mistakenly confusing true scientists with makers of theories, the romancers of science. Then he took me by the hand, amicably, and transported me to the third period.

---

as *Posthumous Correspondence*). Boitard's own cosmogony was (and remains) far more unorthodox.

[12] The so-called "Adams mammoth" was discovered in 1799 by an Evenki hunter, but the remains were only collected in 1806 by the botanist Mikhail Adams. It was the first complete skeleton of the woolly mammoth to be found.

[13] The rhinoceros skeleton in question was reported by Peter Simon Pallas as having been found in Yakutsk in 1770, and Georges Cuvier—from whom Boitard presumably took the datum—classified it as *Rhinoceros tichorhinus*, presumably without ever seeing it

Third Period

We were in the middle of a vast forest, whose extraordinary aspect did not resemble anything that I had ever seen or imagined. There were no majestic oaks, nor birches with dangling branches, nor picturesque elms, such as shade the woods of Boulogne and Meudon today. We were walking through gigantic ferns whose trunks five feet high, were only surpassed by that of horsetails that rose up as bare as Italian poplars. Cycads, zamias, palm trees and a few other trees whose very genres are unknown today swayed their strange foliage in the air. Through the mosses and lycopods whose long stems carpeted the ground or launched forth in green garlands around the trees, a host of liliaceae spread their brightly-colored corollas. Everything presented itself to my sight with a gigantic aspect and an absolutely strange bearing, to the point that, far from believing that I was on the soil of Paris, I imagined that the genius has transported me to one of the great planets of the solar system.

He read my thought. "No," he told me, "you're really in Paris, except that we've changed location slightly, for we're now strolling in the garden of the Tuileries, and since the previous period we've risen up by a hundred meters. The primordial soil, a few rocks of which can still be perceived here and there, is entirely covered by successive layers of red sandstone, Penean sandstone, variegated sandstone, Conchylian limestone, iridescent marl and lees deposited by the waters. Those layers are stratified—which is to say, regularly laid down in beds one atop another, in the order of their deposition. But look over here, and you'll begin to recognize an individual whose numerous generations will survive the frightful catastrophes of the globe and populate the forests of your homeland."

I looked, and saw a pine, *Pinus defrancii*, laden with cylindrical cones and concave at the base. I wanted to get closer to that tree, whose roots were bathed by water; I was already advancing my hand to pluck a leaf that I destined for the natural history museum, when a shrill and menacing hiss became audible in its foliage. I recoiled in fear on perceiving the scaly head of a horrible reptile gazing at me with flamboyant eyes. Its open mouth, garnished with sharp teeth, menaced me with a double dart; its neck was prodigiously long, similar to a cable, or rather, a great serpent. Its massive body, covered with large yellow-tinted scales, bore some resemblance to that of an enormous fish, but it had four short legs, the extremities of which were enveloped by a thick membrane, which gave them a resemblance to those of a sea-turtle. A short, stout tail like that of a crocodile served as a rudder.

"It's a plesiosaur," said my genius. "Its body is organized for swimming, not for walking, and yet its respiration is aerial; it breathes with lungs, which forces it to stay close to the shore. Its prodigious neck, surmounted by a small head, permits it to reach out to seize its prey, which consists of mollusks and small reptiles, not only from the bed of the waters but also from the foliage of the trees bordering the bank. It commonly grows to thirty or forty feet in length, but what will astonish you more is that, like chameleons and a few anolis lizards, it has the singular faculty of changing color instantaneously by reason of the passions that agitate it.

Suddenly, the sea started seething a few paces away, and we soon perceived another monster of gigantic stature approaching that of a whale came to run aground near the shore. It uttered frightful hissing sounds, while it strove to get back to deep water. Its body closely resembled the other, especially in its cetacean feet; it was similarly covered with scales like those of an alligator, but its lizard-like head was not borne by a long neck; its tapering muzzle was prolonged in front like that of a dolphin, and its long jaws were armed with tightly-packed and trenchant teeth. My genius told me that it was an ichthyosaur.

"These two animals," he said, "belong to the class of saurians, or lizards.[14] The latter preferentially inhabits beaches where marine turtles, on which it feeds, come to graze algae and fucus; it also hunts the fish with which the sea is beginning to be populated. Do you want me to take you to visit the islands comprising that archipelago? You'll see a similar nature everywhere and living beings showing themselves more or less in the order of the complication of the organs. Among the vegetables you'll only find very few dicotyledons, and the plants that are dominant belong to the family of cycads. Among the animals, the species of the previous period are still very numerous; there are more gryphaea, ammonites and belemnites, the latest arrivals. There are crustaceans, saurians with monstrous forms, turtles and fish; but the boscage doesn't yet resound with the melodious song of birds; none of those animals has yet cleaved the air with light wings; no mammal has trod the mosses of these forests.

I was in haste to see nature developing before my eyes; on the other hand, I confess that I wanted nothing better than to quit a place where I saw plesiosaurs and ichthyosaurs swimming, of scarcely attractive appearance.

My genius divined that, and passed his finger over my eyes.

---

[14] The term "saurian," coined in 1802, originally included lizards and crocodiles; it was subsequently refined. The term "dinosaur" was not coined until 1842.

Fourth Period

A magnificent valley opened before us, and a vast horizon was discovered, limited to the south by a girdle of blue-tinted and very high mountains. Toward the north a fresh water lake extended, the shores of which were intercut by pools and marshes. The vegetation was almost the same as in the preceding period, except that the horsetails were not as tall. The cycads were less numerous and scarcely furnished a third of the vegetation; ferns and conifers furnished the other two-thirds. In the shade of the woods there was still a host of mushrooms, lichens, mosses, lycopods and other vascular cryptogams. The large yellow or white corollas of nenuphars could be seen swaying gently over the waters of the marshes, while their large varnished leaves, extended over the surface of the waves, served to shelter the first fresh-water fish, and a host of snails moving over the algae and developing their retractile horns.

"Look," said the genius. "The inflexions of that immense lake snaking northwards already indicate the general form that the basin of Paris will take when the sea has laid down its foundations of white chalk; but it's necessary for many centuries to go by yet."

"This," I exclaimed, "is a charming landscape, and cool boscage in which one would love to stroll while meditating!"

"Be careful of judging before knowing! At any rate, the lias, the last superior layer that we saw during the previous period is covered today with oolithic formations and stratifications that are more often inclined than horizontal, separated by beds of clay or marl. It's to that formation that the mountains of the Jura are due, and those that form the blue-tinted girdle that you perceive on the far limit of the horizon; it's also to that formation that your daubers of Paris owe the best calcareous schist, on which they lithograph their witty concepts and, more often, their calumnious caricatures."

At that moment a soft and reedy voice became audible at the edge of the nearby marsh; I drew nearer.

"Stop," said the demon, "or perhaps you'll find something you weren't looking for."

Then, setting his crutch down beside him, he sat down tranquilly on a stone at the summit of the hill. I paid no heed to him and continued taking long strides toward the marsh. How terrified I was when I found myself ten paces away from a horrible caiman, which, on perceiving me, opened a maw capable of swallowing an ox. My disturbance did not prevent me from observing that its jaws were very short, which gave its open mouth the form of a circular gulf. Without making more ample notes, I turned on my heel and started fleeing at top speed. The animal pursued me, but as I knew that its course could only be rapid in a straight line because of the long distance between its two pairs of legs. I made a thousand turns and detours, and it soon lost track of me.

I thought that I was saved when, as I traversed a clump of reeds, I saw a gavial even larger and more formidable than the caiman; this one had narrow jaws, but six feet long and armed with teeth larger than a lion's. If the first had seemed to threaten me with being swallowed whole, this one seemed to be able to slice me clean in two with the first snap of its teeth. I therefore started running harder, while tacking, and darting supplicant glances at my demon, who, with an admirable tranquility, was watching me run without bothering to quit the comfortable attitude he had adopted.

While I fled, running out of breath, I was racing along the edge of the lake momentarily when I saw a megalosaurus swimming toward me, a lizard whose body, stouter than that of an elephant, appeared to me to be at least eighty feet long. I launched myself toward the hill, and found myself face to face with a geosaur, another lizard of colossal size, which raised its horrible head above the reeds.

I uttered a cry of distress and begged the genius to come to my rescue. Alas, he only replied to my distress with a long burst of laughter, and, without disturbing himself, he started placidly whistling a galop by Monsieur Musard.[15]

I was breathless with fatigue and terror, when a dense clump of pines and firs appeared before me; their straight and mossy trunks were so tightly packed that only a human, at the most, could slip between them. I immediately threw myself into the trees, thinking that the monstrous reptile could not pursue me there—and, indeed, I could no longer see it. I was beginning to reassure myself when a strange sound made me shiver again. I heard the sound of two powerful wings cleaving the air above my head rapidly. I looked up and saw a formidable flying dragon soaring above the trees that protected me.

Its membranous wings, similar to those of a bat, had a span of five or six feet; its livid yellow body was covered with a scaly armor and terminated in a long tail; it's head resembled a crocodile's, but its jaws, strong and well armed with teeth, were extraordinarily prolonged in the form of a beak. As the membrane of its wings was sustained by one of its fingers, prodigiously elongated, when it settled on the ground it could not easily make use of its forelimbs to walk, which obliged it to adopt the attitude of a kangaroo—which is to say, to raise the anterior part of its body vertically and lean on its tail in order to maintain that position. That vigorous tail also served to launch it into the air, as if by the effect of a spring, when it deployed its wings in order to take flight. It was a pterodactyl.

I crouched down in the moss and allowed the monster to pass; it soon elevated its flight like an eagle and disappeared into the clouds. Several other pterodactyls of different species were fluttering around me, but they did not frighten me because they were no bigger than a crow. I even saw some that were no larger than canaries and had short muzzles.

---

[15] Philippe Musard (1792-1859) was a prolific composer of dance music; a galop (shortened from *galopade*) was a rapid dance, a forerunner of the polka.

Finally, I climbed the hill, disputing my passage with tortoises, lizards, frogs and monstrous toads, and came to fall, drained by fatigue and emotion, at the feet of my guide, who was still whistling his Musard galop with an imperturbable calm.

"I warned you," he said, finally, "but you didn't want to listen to the voice of your genius. You set off like a fool and frightened yourself like an idiot."

"Like an idiot, you say? I'd like to know how the most intrepid man would have come through it!"

"It's not a question of the other stupidity that you call intrepidity, which, more often than not, consists of gambling for something trivial—a stupid prejudice—the only real wealth that a man possesses: his life. Only an idiot can play a game in which he has everything to lose and nothing to gain. It's a question of very simple reasoning. How could I have found you in your study in 1836 if you'd previously been devoured by a crocodile? All those animals didn't even perceive you, because you only belong to this antediluvian period in the invisible and impalpable form—if it is a form—of a spirit, and, just between us and without wanting to annoy you, a rather poor spirit.

After that brief rebuke the genius recovered all his good humor and went on: "This period only offers, by way of animals, zoophytes, madrepores, sea-urchins and crinoids; among the shelled mollusks, ammonites, belemnites, oysters, terebratula, trochus, etc.; a few crustaceans; and finally, among the vertebrates, fish, and a prodigious quantity of reptiles of various forms, mostly gigantic. But birds and terrestrial mammals have not yet been seen to appear."

"One moment, Monseigneur Genius. It seems to me that I've read somewhere one thing that doesn't accord with what you're saying. Mammal bones, and even birds, have been found in the Stonesfield schist, and yet that schist belongs to the formation of the fourth period."

"That's true—but you'll notice that Stonesfield is the only locality where that anomaly is observed, and it only proves that the portions of terrain in which those bones were found had not been modified by the waters since the epoch of their original formation. If you don't mind, we're going to leave this period when the reptiles, principally the lizard, dominate the animal kingdom."

"Gladly—but before then, give me the pleasure of telling me where we are, for I'll be very pleased to see once again in Paris the place where I was so terribly frightened."

"Very well; I was sitting in the main pathway of the Luxembourg, while you were running from the railings of the Observatoire to the palace of the peers of France."

Fifth Period

The sea had once again taken possession of valleys of palms and pines; everything was swallowed by the waters. Only one spur of chalky rock rose above the surface of that immense ocean, and we were sitting on top of it.

"It's three or four thousand years at the most since we quit the fourth period," said the genius, and yet, in that short interval of time, which is scarcely equivalent to half the life of a baobab, *Adansonia baobab*,[16] the globe has experienced several upheavals, if we can judge by the great diversity of composition offered by the formation of new layers of terrain. These layers present themselves in the form of raised plateaux or hills with steep slopes, and are less inclined than those of preceding terrains. They're composed, in the order of their superposition, of ferruginous sands and green sands, inferior or green chalk, median or gray chalk, and superior or white chalk. It's probably in this period that it's necessary to place the formation of our principal mountain chains."

"You think that the butte of Montmartre...?"

"Let's be clear. I'm not talking here about our low hills, composed of more of less horizontal layers of sediments; they were obviously formed by tranquil waters that initially deposited them and then by running waters that degraded their terrains and hollowed out valleys therein. It's not the same for the high mountains whose immense chains furrow the globe in various directions."

"To what can you attribute their formation?"

"The primordial crust of the globe is composed of granite and syenite in massive rocks devoid of stratification, and then of gneiss, mica schist and clay schist, but the latter distinctive-

---

[16] Author's note: "Baobabs are easily found in Africa whose trunk, cut transversally, offers six thousand ligneous layers, and it is well known that trees only acquire one per year."

ly stratified. Now, if you examine the interior of high mountains, you'll see those same superior layers, once continuous, dislocated and broken into a multitude of fragments, no longer offering anything but massifs of disrupted stratifications, presenting such disorder that it's necessary to attribute the dislocation to an upheaval. If you start from low plains, heading toward those massive chains, and examine attentively the superimposed layers of sediments over which you're walking, you'll see them lose their horizontal position as you get closer to the heights, rearing up more or less abruptly and taking an oblique position; you'll see them pierced, torn and lifted up on the flanks of the mountains. It's necessary to conclude that the masses of the great chains have been formed by elevation or eruption, and that they have emerged from the bosom of the earth, breaking violently and lifting up the superior crust, and piercing the sedimentary layers. That explains why you see granite exhibiting itself nakedly on their frowning crest, as well as in the profound valleys."

"What interior agent could have lifted up such masses as the Cordilleras, the Pyrenees and the Alps?"

"Caloric,[17] the elastic gases resulting from chemical decompositions and, in brief, all the agents that occasion earthquakes and volcanic eruptions, whose source of activity is situated beneath the mineral crust. Their action no longer has, at present, the frightful energy that it once had, but it's true nonetheless that it still exists. It usually announces itself by subterranean noises, shocks that succeed one another with varying rapidity and force, and which, with incredible celerity, make themselves felt over immense distances. If the mineral crust breaks and splits, it gives passage to materials that are pushed out—hence volcanoes spitting flames, vomiting lava,

---

[17] "Caloric" was a hypothetical subtle fluid, the substance of heat that allegedly flowed from hot bodes to cool ones, invented by Antoine Lavoisier in 1783. It became redundant when the mechanical theory of heat was introduced in the mid-19th century.

hurling scoria or ashes, giving issue to torrents of muddy water, etc., etc. Hence solfataras, or sulfur-pits; salsas gushing salt-water and mud; lagonis impetuously exhaling gases and boiling water vapor; ardent fountains emitting jets of gas that can be ignited by a candle or catch fire naturally; and firewells that the Chinese are able to use in their factories.

"But if the mineral crust presents an equal resistance in all its parts it is lifted up *en masse* and overturns the layers of sediment that are superposed on it—hence a granitic mountain. The last century, and even this one, have furnished us a few examples. In 1759, in Mexico, following an earthquake, a plain three or four miles square was suddenly lifted up and metamorphosed into a mountain five hundred feet high. In 1707 a new island suddenly rose from the bosom of the sea near Santorini, and its birth was unaccompanied by any volcanic phenomenon; in 1822, during the earthquake that destroyed several towns in Chile, it was observed that the coast was raised in a sensible fashion over an extent of more than thirty leagues; finally, modern observations prove conclusively that the level of Sweden is gradually rising, by virtue of causes that are still acting.

"One very singular thing follows from what I've just told you, which is that you can judge the approximate age of mountains by the observation of the layers that girdle them. The layers that have been pierced by the elevation of the granitic crust will be inclined and backed up against the mountain, because they have been lifted up by it. On the contrary, the layers deposited after the eruption will have taken the horizontal position usual to terrains of sedimentary deposits.

"During that fifth period, as the sea has constantly covered the soil of Paris, with the exception of a few islands no bigger than this one, you can understand that animals and terrestrial vegetables could scarcely multiply, so you won't perceive any. Around the islands that have some verdure however, lizards are still hidden that have a physiognomy as unbecoming as those we've already seen. Look, there's one gliding through the marine algae; it's a mesosaur, whose size attains at least twenty-five feet in length. In that pool behind us you'll find crocodiles; in the clumps of sedge, from which the Egyptians made the first paper, there are iguanodons; quantities of turtles are grazing the focus on flat beaches.

"If the class of terrestrial animals has made little progress, in recompense, that of fish could not have multiplied more, and the sea contains sharks compared to which those of your modern era are mere minnows. If you like, I'll take you to see one of those whale-sized animals at close range."

"Morbleu, no!" I replied, with a certain vivacity. "In spite of the strength of your arguments, I don't have any appetite for risking the role of Jonah. Tell me instead where we are at present."

"Underneath the École Militaire."

"At a great depth?"

Exactly twenty-nine meters underneath the École's well—which is to say that we're placed on the white chalk that forms the inferior bed of the Paris basin. We're going to pass on to another period, during which you'll see the Earth change its face completely."

Sixth Period

I opened my eyes in a charming woodland, the vegetation of which already differed a great deal from that of preceding periods, for dicotyledons showed themselves for the first time in more considerable numbers than the monocotyledons. Meanwhile, a few palm trees raised their beautiful heads here and there like parasols. The slopes of hills were covered with pines, firs and other conifers of species that I had not seen previously. I recognized several trees bearing catkins. I also saw a nut-bearing tree whose fruits were a trifle angular and pointed at the summit. I noticed a maple, a willow and an elm. What surprised me extremely was a coconut palm laden with fruits rising up in the midst of a cinnamon laurel bush whose flowers perfumed their air with their aromatic perfume.

Aha! I thought. *My devil must be right, and it's the organization of beings, not the atmospheric temperature that has changed, for coconut palms, cinnamon bushes, fir trees and elm trees wouldn't grow well together today wherever one placed them; some dread warmth as much as the others detest cold. Then again, how can one explain the association in bone caves of tigers of the torrid zone and pikas, inhabitants of the icy poles; hyenas from hot countries and gluttons from northern Siberia; Russian reindeer and African rhinoceroses? All that can't fail to appear singular to a man who believes in the infallibility of scientists. Could we not, reasoning on the same principles as them, sustain precisely the contrary, and conclude that the temperature, instead of being high, was then much colder than today, since pines, elms, pikas, gluttons and reindeer are beings that can only live in icy climates?*

A plain of vast extent was designed around me as far as my eyes could see; however, by virtue of a few hillocks distributes here and there, it was easy to see that it was slightly hollowed out in a valley, and that we were occupying the lowest part, very nearly.

"You see," said the Lame Devil, "the basin formed by the white chalk, of which a layer of siliceous pudding-stone, one of sand and one of plastic clay mixed with lignite has already accumulated a few inequalities. This immense basin extends toward Beauce, Perche, Basse-Normandie, Orléanais, Gâtinais français, etc. etc. As it's going to be subjected to several major changes, I'll show you all its evolutions. We'll follow them by eye as one follows the changes of scene at the Opéra. There's more; with my magic crutch, I'll play the part of the showman in a traveling menagerie; I'll show you and name the extraordinary animals that populated the earth in these remote times and left their bony fragments buried in the quarries of Paris and its surrounding areas.

"We can divide this period into five quite distinct epochs.

First Epoch
Five meters above the zero
of the Pont de la Tournelle.[18]

"That's the one in which we are at present, the one in which the fresh waters have retired and left a layer of plastic clay on the chalk basin: the one, in sum, when we've finally reached the level of Paris. You see that little sandy valley; it's precisely at the height of the zero of the Pont de la Tournelle, and it's from that zero, marking the low waters of the Seine, that we'll depart henceforth to measure the thickness of the soil as we rise up with it."

"In that case, we won't rise much, because the cellar of the house in which I live is only a few feet above that zero."

"Well, my dear friend, there's your poor science in default again, for here, eight or ten thousand years before you'll cover your fire and put on your night-cap in order to go to bed,

---

[18] The scale installed under the Pont de la Tournelle in 1719 was used to measure floods and droughts in terms of the height of the Seine.

45

I'll place you in a boat propelled by sails on a beautiful freshwater lake five hundred meters above your dwelling. But here's the sea invading us. See how it's rising, how rapidly it's gaining. Already, one can no longer see the ground. It's just like the Opéra, isn't it?"

"Absolutely. It's like a change of scene, and in all probability, even the blast of the whistle won't be lacking."

"I'm showing you in five minutes what happened in several hundred centuries. It's only slowly that the sea has successively abandoned its vast beaches and its profound abysses to cover and uncover the continents. Otherwise, nature would be horribly disrupted and all organized beings would have perished in those frightful catastrophes. Can't you see, on the contrary, that the creation of animals follows a regular and successive march, analytically, if I can make use of that expression; that it commences with the simplest and passes on to the complex, and from there to the even more complex, and that it will eventually conclude with the most perfect, humankind.

"Has it been observed that the march in question has recommenced several times? Has it been observed that it has recommenced with unique formations of simple beings after being halted in the formation of more complex ones? And besides, are not water and air, those ever-active agents sufficient to explain everything in a simple and natural manner without having recourse to instantaneous and general catastrophes? Air and water decompose and disaggregate superficial rocks incessantly; rain and frost degrade sheer mountains, ice undermines them at the base; hence landslides and detritus, which, constantly carried away by streams to rivulets, and by them to rivers, and by rivers to the sea, must eventually fill in the basins of the Ocean.

"The abysms filled up in one place are opened in another by currents and tempests, from which a continual change of location results. The deltas, the tongues of land that form at the mouths of great rivers, are a striking proof of it; it's known that the promontories formed by the mouths of the Po advance

46

into the Adriatic by some two hundred feet a year; it's known that the Nile deposits five inches of sediment every hundred year on the floor of the Egyptian basin; it's known that the dunes of sand raised by the wind on the shores of the sea would gain nearly sixty feet a year on the continent if barriers weren't opposed to them; it's known..."

"Ah! I understand. You think that the sea has only covered the continents so many times one after another; that while we were observing the first period of formation in Paris, we might have been observing the second at Port Jackson; that the same causes ought to have produced the same effects, albeit in different epochs; that if the layers of sediment have been superimposed in the same way all over the Earth, it's because the mass of the waters, sliding around the globe, so to speak, like a slug circling an orange, has left the same traces everywhere even though it hasn't been everywhere at the same time. You think..."

"What?"

"Some of our geologists, however, place in the same epoch the formation of analogous layers in all parts of the world, which would prove..."

"Eh! Who the devil was talking about your geologists, you pitiless chatterbox? Have I said a single word to you about your geologists?"

Out of prudence, I cut the dissertation short, for I could see that my demon's face was beginning to take on tints of red and violet, like a salmon-trout from Lake Geneva. He calmed down, though, and continued.

"The Ocean that you see is populated by an immense quantity of cetaceans, fish and mollusks. Among the latter one can already count more than twelve hundred species, but the dominant genres are those of cerites, milliolites, nummulites, turritellas, volutes etc."

47

Second Epoch
Thirty-eight meters above the zero point
of the Pont de la Tournelle

The sea had retired as quickly as it had come. The vegetation seemed to me to be very nearly similar to that of the preceding epoch.

"This formation," said the genius, "is composed of an inferior layer of glauconite, enormous banks of gross chalk and a bed of marine sandstone. It's from that formation that the material were extracted from which the whole of Paris was built.

Third Epoch
Eighty meters above the zero point
of the Pont de la Tournelle

"The marine sandstone," said the genius, "has been covered again by the fresh waters of a vast lake, which has deposited the thick layer of siliceous chalk, inferior lacustrian chalk and gypsum, in which numerous quarries of plaster and green marl will be opened."

The landscape was charming, but so intercut by lakes, pools, marshes and streams that one doubted whether one was on firm ground or an island forming part of a vast fresh water archipelago. The vegetation had changed little; however, it seemed to me that the palm trees were more dominant, and I could easily distinguish three species. One of them, *Culmites nodosus*, which closely resembled a rattan, had a thin, flexible, articulated stem of prodigious length, extending from tree to tree in the fashion of lianas, twisting around their branches, dividing at the summit into two sections, each terminating in a beautiful tuft of foliage. Another palm tree attracted attention by virtue of its magnificent fan of leaves, several ribs of which were fused at the base for a part of their length. I also saw *Nerium* laurier-roses, *Phyllites nerioïdes*, displaying their lovely flowers in groves of cinnamon.

As I stretched myself out limply on a bed of moss in the shadow of a coconut palm, my ears were agreeably struck by the joyful song of a warbler.

"There," I exclaimed, "is the first bird that creation has engendered!"

"Yes," said the genius, "but it's not the only one. You'll see the water of the lakes rippled beneath the heavy bodies of pelicans, while ibises and sea-swallows run lightly along the strands. Woodcocks inhabit the rushes of the ponds in the woods; owls hide in the cavernous trunks of old elms, and huge buzzards soar in circles in the air, watching out for quails whose size yields nothing to that of your homing pigeons. If you lend an attentive ear, you'll also hear the monotonous song of the cicada, the cricket and the grasshopper. Superb butterflies, larger than a hand, suspend their vagabond flight momentarily to pose their delicate feet on the petals of flowers. Silently slipping under the moss are numerous families of coleopterans, whose wing-cases are ornamented with the brightest metallic colors; finally, bees are buzzing around perfumed corollas to collect the honey that will nourish them in winter. Those are the first insects.

"Scarcely have they been born than nature has placed enemies in ambush in the hollow trunks of trees and holes in ricks, ready to pursue them in the air to seize and devour them. The class of Chiroptera has just appeared to replace that of pterodactyls. They're no longer winged lizards but bats. Those animals, like humans, apes and elephants, have teats on their breasts.

"In that pond, Sciaenes are swimming, of which, by virtue of the course of the centuries, analogues can only be found in salt water: amia calvia, but which have two fins; mormyrids, trout, cyprins, carps, pikes, living like freshwater fish, having very nearly the same habits, but nevertheless only resembling them in general form.

"There's one of those animals you dread so much, a crocodile, crawling in the marshes seeking to seize its prey. It has lost its colossal size, and its aspect ought to astonish you less, for, in its form, especially that of the head, it has a great deal of analogy with the crocodile of the Nile and the caimans of America." The genius pointed with his crutch. "Close by, there are two freshwater turtles; the one with the soft carapace belongs to the genus *Trionyx*, the other to *Emys*.

"Finally, the mammals have been created. What is very remarkable is that a family that will occupy a comparative small place in 1836 is, in this antediluvian century, the most generally distributed over the surface of the globe. That is the family of pachyderms. All the species composing it lack a clavicle; they do not have the faculty of spreading their fingers, which are all entirely enveloped by a nail in the form of a hoof. All of them live on vegetables, but some ruminate and others do not. Here's one of the former."

Indeed, I saw an animal passing by that had the stature of the largest horses, with the most bizarre physiognomy, It was a great palaeotherium, *Palaeotherium magnum*. Its nose terminated in a rather short muscular trunk, similar to that of a tapir; its muzzle was shrunken under the base of the trunk; its eyes were small and as stupid as a pig's; its head was enormous, its body short and thickset; its legs were short and massive, its feet terminated by three fingers encrusted in hooves, of which the middle one was much larger than the others. Its entire body was covered in coarse short hair.

"That animal," the demon continued, "nourishes itself on grains, fruits and green herbaceous stems, but more often on the fleshy roots of aquatic plants that it finds by digging in the mud of the marshes and uproots with its trunk. Its character isn't ferocious, but brutal and stupid. In sum, it likes the banks of fresh waters and loves to wallow in the mud.

"There are several species of Palaeotheria, which all have a similar form and habits, but which differ in size. The median palaeotherium, *P. medium*, as a height at the withers of thirty-one or thirty-two inches; it resembles a tapir with thin legs, and among the other animals of its genre, is approximately what the babirusa is among the pigs.

"The short palaeotherium, *P. curtum*, closely resembles the large palaeotherium, but is much smaller. The thick palaeotherium, *P. crassum*, is almost thirty inches tall at the withers, and of all the species that is the one that most closely resembles a tapir. The large palaeotherium, *P. latum*, is between eighty and eighty-six inches at the withers; its head and body are heavy and massive and its legs enormous, which renders it slow and idle. The little palaeotherium, *P. minus*, is sixteen to eighteen inches at the withers, and has the form of a thin-legged and nimble tapir. The very small palaeotherium, *P. minimum*, is the size of a hare and it has the legs and agility of one.

"All these animals, which will soon disappear from the surface of the Earth, are the natural intermediates between hyraxes and tapirs. The general resemblance that exists in their compared bones is sufficiently striking to class them in a single family; however, if one wanted to operate in a classification as modern naturalists do, it would probably be necessary to divide them into two or three smaller genera."

Soon afterwards, I saw an animal every bit as singular as those, which has not left any traces in living nature, The genius told me that it was a common anoplotherium, *Anoplotherium commune*. It seemed to me to be as big as a medium-sized donkey; it stood three feet and a few inches tall at the withers, and was eight feet long, including the tail, but the latter added at least three feet and was very stout at the base. Its light head, of medium size, bore rather long ears;[19] its cloven feet were equipped with two toes, each enveloped in a hoof. Its entire body was covered in long silky hair. It frequented damp places to seek its nourishment, consisting of the

---

[19] Author's note: "Here I am not longer in accord with Georges Cuvier, because I have never been able to reconcile myself to giving the habits of an otter to an animal that has the foot of a gazelle, and even less to place in the same genus an amphibious species with short ears and an alpine species with long ones."

roots and rhizomes of aquatic plants. Sometimes, it took the risk of swimming from one island to another, and then its long tail served it as a rudder. We did not see it dive, and none of the herbivore's habits reminded me of a carnivorous otter.

Another species, the slender anoplotherium, *A. gracile*, launched itself into the plain, which it crossed in the blink of an eye with the rapidity of a chamois, of which it had the size, but its lighter and more gracious form would have made me mistake it for a gazelle if it had had horns. Like all fearful animas, it had long ears that warned it of the faintest sound and the slightest anger. Its body was covered with short and lustrous fur; it nourished itself on aromatic herbs and loved to graze on hillsides.

I perceived a third species, the hare-like anoplotherium, *A. leporum*, which did not differ at all from the previous one in its general form and habits, but whose exceedingly thin legs we even better adapted to rapid running, and whose size was almost equal to that of a hare. My genius told me that there were another three species of anoplotheria in ante-Paris, plus choeropotames, pachyderms forming natural intermediaries between pigs and anoplotheria, and adapis, other pachyderms a third larger than a hedgehog and similarly formed.

"It's singular," I said to him, "that of so many strange animals, not one will still be alive when I go hunting rabbits in the woods of Meudon. I'd very much like to bring back a little anoplotherium in my game-bag, even if only to know whether it's as good as jugged hare!"

"They'll disappear, and the cause is easy to explain; to-day they have their conditions of existence, which are the lack of large carnivores, the rarity of small ones, and, above all, the absence of humans, who will destroy the large carnivores in their turn and will gradually being about the disappearance from the globe of all the species useless to their needs and pleasures."

"What do you mean?"

"Tell me, what has become of the types of dogs, horse and camels? Dead, or submitted to slavery! What has become of the gigantic aurochs that he first French princes loved to hunt in their forests? Dead, disappeared. And the colossal elk whose enormous antlers can still be found in a few peat-bogs? Entirely lost! Even the lion, the king of beasts, which once desolated Greece, Italy, European Turkey and a great part of Asia, has been driven back by humans into Africa, and is becoming rarer every day in the deserts of the Sahara and the Cape, the only places where it still exists. Probably, within a hundred years from 1836, it will only exist in paintings and in natural history museums.

"In any case," the demon continued, "here come the carnivores, which, although of inferior races, are commencing the war of extermination with the pachyderms. The one that you can see traversing the plain, running on the trail of the anoplotherium-gazelle, is the intermediary between the dog and the Arctic fox. It lives in the woods and, like the wolf and the fox, it hunts animals smaller and weaker than itself continuously. In those bushes you'll find a genet the size of a dog and two civets, one of an ordinary size and the other a larger by a third.

"Look at the largest of the carnivores of this era slipping through the rushes of the marsh. It's a mongoose, almost exactly similar to the ichneumon or rat of the Pharaohs, but attained the size of a large mastiff. It's all the more redoubtable because of its trenchant teeth, arming extremely vigorous jaws. It roams incessantly around the waters in order to surprise the larger species of anoplotheria and palaeotheria, which it kills and devours.

"There's a very singular little animal; it's a sarigue the size of a marmoset; it had a membranous pocket on its belly, supported by a bony arch, sand it carries its young in that game-bag of sorts until they're strong enough to look after themselves and their needs. From time to time it takes them out so that they can enjoy the benevolent influences of the air and sunlight, but at the slightest sound it hastens to gather them in and flee, carrying them away. Asia, Africa, Europe, and even less the environs of Paris, will not present you with any creature that has the slightest analogy with that one; it's only in Australia and America that they will be encountered.

"There are several hundred other small mammals here. There's a mouse, but it's the size of a large rat. In compensation, the dormouse eating that fruit is smaller than a *Muscardinus*.

"Since we're on the subject of rodents, I'll point out an animal of which you've heard much mention, because its species has survived the most recent revolutions of the globe and its mores are rather extraordinary; it's the beaver, of which a few isolated individuals are still to be found, living in burrows like otters, along the Rhône, the Danube, the Weser and a few other European rivers. The first voyagers who observed them in North America have exaggerated the accounts they gave of their mores and habits to such an extent that you probably won't be sorry if I show you the truth here.

"Beavers are almost the same size as a large badger, their tail is flattened horizontally, in an almost oval form, and covered with scales. Their feet have five toes linked by a membrane, like those of a duck, which gives them a great facility for swimming, their tail fulfilling the function of a rudder. Their life is completely aquatic for several months of the year.

"They don't live habitually in society, as has been said. From the first fine days of spring until autumn they remain solitary or in couples, in the woods, and they raise their family in burrows that they dig alongside streams. When the first frosts make themselves felt, it's then that they gather together and occupying themselves building the famous dams of which such marvelous tales have been told. They consist simply of a mass of branches, stones and mud, which they accumulate in the bed of a stream in such a way as to block the watercourse and force it to back up in the form of a small pond. As the materials they employ consist of branches of aquatic trees growing on the banks of streams, it naturally happens that they take root in the fashion of cuttings, and the dam, whose thickness increase by the day, is fortified, forming a thick bush that owes its solidity more to nature than to its architects.

54

"As for the lodges, they are constructed on very nearly the same principle. They begin to heap up a large quantity of small branches, stones and mud in a place where the water is between eighteen inches and two feet in depth, and they give that mass the form of a conical mound, of which only half is submerged; then they hollow out a round hole in the mound, at water level, which they enlarge in the middle of the heap of materials in such a way as to give it a form analogous to that of an oven. It's there that they deposit provisions of bark destined to nourish them during winter. They pierce another hole in the dome of that storehouse, and then similarly enlarge that hole in the form of an oven, thus making two rooms one on top of the other, which have only one issue. The latter room is above the high-water mark, and the family and sleep dry there.

"They know how to take full advantage of the current of the stream in order to float their materials to the place where they have to make use of them, but the piles, the trees sharpened at the foot and transported with a kind of artistry, the collaboration in the work, the pretended leaders who force the idle to play their part in the labor, the tail that serves as a trowel, the masonry and the solid walls roughcast with earthen mortar, the kind of police that reigns over each village or even each family, are all as many tall tales with which voyagers have enlivened their narratives.

"In spite of the lodges, the beavers don't neglect to hollow out burrows in the environs, to which they retreat preferentially at the first sign of danger.

"There is, in the waters of this marsh, another species of beaver, the trogontherium, which will no longer be found alive in modern times. It only differs from the preceding one by virtue of its larger size, equaling that of a Siamese pig. Strong enough to defend itself against its enemies, it has no need to protect itself against their attacks by hiding in the middle of the waters, so it doesn't construct lodges. It is a general rule that animals, and perhaps humans, only perfect their intelligence in proportion to their needs, and all possible needs have their source in two instincts innate in all organized and sensible beings: that of self-preservation and that of the conservation of the species.

"Study those two instincts, without which sensible beings would not exist; study as a physiologist the material forms that modify the innumerable ways of satisfying them, and from the sight of their forms you can deduce the mores and habits of animals of which you can no longer even recover all the fragments. Fear and amour: those are the two pivots on which all intelligence is posed; they are the unique source of all the passions, in humans as in animals.

"Here's a hare much less timid than those of modern times, because it has far fewer enemies, walking tranquilly in the plain. Look at its ears; they're not as long because it doesn't make such continual use of the organ of haring. Exposed to fewer miseries than its unfortunate descendants, at has no need to be incessantly alert to ensure that he cruel pack doesn't fall upon it. Its legs are les exercised by fear, so they're not as long and little stouter by comparison with the modern species. As for its other general features and its size, there's hardly any difference.

"There's a rat of a species that will remain completely unknown roaming through the bushes. What is most remarkable about it is its size, which equals that of an average wild rabbit.

"Look—there are other rodents lodged in the cavernous holes of those trees; they're pretty little animals, and above all, very innocent, resembling both muskrats and guinea-pigs, and having all their habits because they have all their weakness and general forms. Those forms are rather remarkable for the animals that can be arranged naturally in the same family. Their hindquarters, much surpassing in height their forelegs, force them to hop rather than run. When they're seated, they carry their nourishment to their mouth with their forepaws, and it's then alone that they develop all their graces. Their eyes are directed sideways; two large incisors arm the front of their jaws and serve to gnaw fruits, plants and bark, even wood when they nourish themselves thereon.

"Here are two species, which, like the beavers, live on the water's edge, but their size attains that of a mouse at the most, and their form likens them to field-mice. They have furry tails almost as long as their bodies, and all the habits of our water voles. Like them they dig burrows in marshy terrain and raise their young families there. They dive and swim well, and nourish themselves on roots.

"It's in peat-bogs and caves that the greatest numbers of rodent bones will be found."

Fourth Epoch
135 meters above the zero-point
of the Pont de Tournelle

The genius said to me: "The sea has passed again, for the last time, over the site of Paris, and has raised it up by some 55 meters. First it deposited a layer of clayey green marl; a bank almost entirely composed of shells, including oysters; an immense thickness of micaceous sand; then sandstone devoid of shells; and finally a superior marine sandstone. As you see, the vegetation already bears a considerable resemblance to what there will be in the modern period. There are still a few rare palm trees to be found, but the zamias and the cycads have disappeared. The forests are composed of walnuts, elms, oaks and other trees mostly belonging to the class of dicotyledons. Even the animals are beginning to take on forms analogous to those they will have in modern times."

We saw a mammoth walking slowly along the edge of the marsh where the channel of the Ourcq now passes; its height surpassed that of the largest Indian elephant, of which it otherwise had the general form; but its body was heavier and more thickset. Over its neck flowed a long black mane, prolonged over the dorsal spine; the rest of its body was covered in dark brown hairs fifteen inches long, hiding a fine, silky wool nine or ten inches long, slightly curly, especially toward the thick root, tawny in some places and red in others. Its trunk was very similar to that of an elephant, but its tusks, enormously longer, where curled back in a spiral and directed outwardly. It had an elongated head, a concave brow and ears garnished with dense tufts of hair. Its inferior jaw was neither pointed nor advanced, but short and truncated in front. I also noticed that the soles of its feet overlapped the toes somewhat.[20]

"Several animals exist, in the epoch to which I've transported you, that have an analogy with that one," the genius told me, "and which are similarly herbivores—the mastodons, for example. The large species, which inhabits America, is very similar to the elephant; it has the same height, but is more elongated; it has a thinner belly and thicker limbs. The narrow-toothed mastodon is a third smaller; it lives in Europe, as do the small mastodon and the tapiroid mastodon."

At that moment a rhinoceros passed close to us, heading toward the location of Montmartre. Like that of India it only had one horn on the nose, but of enormous size; its head was longer and narrower, smooth and without calluses; its eyes were set further back, placed above the last molar and not the fourth; it lacked incisors. Its limbs were very short, from which it resulted that its belly as almost trailing on the ground. Its feet terminated in triple hooves. A very abundant fur, especially on the legs, covered the entire body, and its skin did not form any folds. Furthermore, it had the stupid and ferocious gaze of animals of its genre, and it loved to wallow in the mud of marshes.

"In a country not far from here,"[21] the genius told me, "there's another species of rhinoceros that only differs from

---

[20] Author's note: "This description is based on the individual found by a Tungus peasant in the ice on the sea shore. Tell me why the Siberians, who encounter its remains very frequently, call it an 'earth-mouse' and think that it lived in the fashion of moles! Is it because the debris is most often found in bone-caves?"

[21] Author's note: "In the département of Tarn-et-Garonne, at Moissac."

this one in having incisors. If you know the African rhinoceros, you can judge for yourself that it doesn't resemble it at all."

"Indeed," I replied. "I not only know the African, but the Indian and the Sumatran. The first has two horns on its nose, and can't, in consequence, be compared to it; that one has a skin without folds, but bare; in the Sumatran rhinoceros it's almost devoid of folds, but it also lacks fur and has a second horn placed behind the first; finally, the Indian rhinoceros has only one horn, and its skin is remarkable for the profound folds that form behind and over its shoulders; that thick armor is so hard that it not only resists the Indians' arrows and spears, but also the bullets of our best rifles, so hunting that untamable animal is very dangerous.

"Rhinoceroses are not cruel, but their brutality and natural stupidity render them very redoubtable to hunters bold enough to go after them. They flee at first, like all animals; then, in the end, harassed by the dogs, the noise, the horses and he gunshots, they become furious, turn round and charge head down at all the objects that disturb them, knocking over and trampling underfoot the horses and hunters unfortunate enough to get in their way, and only falling under the redoubtable blows of their enemies when a bullet strikes them in the had close to the eye, where there is a chink in their impenetrable armor. It's neither their courage nor the instinct of their power that makes them brave danger thus and hasten toward death, but rather a blind fury that calculates nothing, comprehends nothing and often, in captivity, develops for no reason and against anything.

"At any rate, those formidable animals flee inhabited places and seek the solitudes of marshy and wooded deserts, where they nourish themselves on grass, reeds and young tree-branches. If, in its nocturnal roaming, chance leads one into a cultivated field of sugar cane, maize or bananas, it breaks and overturns everything, and spoils ten times more produce than it would need to nourish itself. Lured by a nourishment that pleases it, it withdraws during the day to sleep in a nearby

59

forest, and for several nights it returns to inflict similar damage.

"As soon as the Indians perceive its disastrous visits, they follow its tracks from the place where it has broken the bamboo fence to get into the field; experienced hunters know that where it has passed the day before it will pass again that day and the next.

"Immediately, a ditch between twelve and fifteen feet wide and deep is dug and the opening hidden by extending bamboo canes and date-palm leaves over it, which are covered with dry leaves, moss and a little earth. Then the owner of the field, hidden in the branches of a tree a few hundred paces away, waits for the redoubtable but not very cunning animal to fall into the trap.

"The rhinoceros arrives; it believes it can pass over, but the false floor collapses under its massive feet; it falls to the bottom of the hole, from which its efforts cannot extract it..."

I was in full flow and I was about to relate how the Indians who come running kill the monsters with arrows, but I perceived that the genius was no longer listening to me, and I cut my narration short.

We had come, while walking, to the place where the waters have since hollowed out the plain of Grenelle. I heard a singular kind of snorting coming from a nearby pool; it was a hippopotamus expelling water from its nostrils every time it raised its head above the surface. Soon, I was able to examine it. Its stature was prodigious by comparison with the African hippopotamus, from which it was distinguishable, at first glance by its head, narrower and longer at the back, an its abrupt forehead. I perceived several others, one a little smaller than our living species, a third the size of a wild boar, and finally, a fourth no larger than a Siamese pig.

From time to time I saw camels passing in the plan, along with horses, buffaloes and other large ruminants, all having something strange about their form and bearing no resemblance to species living today.

But what astonished me most was an aquatic salamander that I saw sliding slowly through the reeds. Its head was as big as a man's and its body was proportionate to that enormous dimension; its total length was no less than six feet. Its skin, covered with tubercles, was dark brown, marked on the back and sides with several long interrupted parallel stripes in a beautiful orange yellow.

"There," said the genius, smiling, "is an animal that will put scientists in a difficult position when they find its petrified debris. Its poorly-conserved carcass, discovered in a quarry at Oeningen, will be mistaken for an anthropolith or fossil human, and will exercise the pens of Scheuchzer, Gessner, Vogel, Blumenbach and Karg, all of whom will see it as *Homo diluvii testis*—the human who witnessed the deluge—and then a Silurian, *Silurus glanis*, until Messieurs Jaeger, Kielmeyer and Cuvier, after a long and serious polemic, have proved definitely that it was nothing but a gigantic salamander.[22]

"Another hideous crocodile!" I exclaimed, shivering.

"Ha ha! You're always afraid of crocodiles," mocked the devil, "And yet, of all the dainty children of nature, they're the ones of which she's fondest, doubtless because they were her first-born, the oldest of the great family of pulmonary animals. Since the formation of the first sedimentary terrains they've existed, and alone from those epochs they'll exist in modern times, so much has she favored them. They'll survive all the revolutions of the globe, and the fossil debris of their numerous species will cover France, England, Italy, Germany and

---

[22] The fossil misidentified by Johann Jakon Scheuchzer in *Lithographia Helevetica* (1726) as *Homo diluvii testis* became rapidly notorious. In 1758 Jacob Gessner challenged Scheuchzer's identification and suggested that the fossil was that of a giant catfish, Silurus. Cuvier examined the specimen in the Teylers Museum in Haarlem (where it is still displayed) in 1811, and was allowed to clear away more of the matrix containing the fossil, exposing the limbs and permitting its identification as a salamander.

the entire Earth. The gavials, principally, will be found everywhere. One found in Caen is twenty feet long; its muzzle forms a slender and very long beak, and its body is strongly armored by two rows of longitudinal rectangular scaly plates, very hard and very thick, but thinner toward the edges, with an exterior surface pitted with little demi-spherical dimples the size of a lentil, closely packed together. Every scale has its anterior edge covered by the posterior edge of the preceding one.

"The Jura gavial resembles it very closely. One from Le Mans is thirty feet long; the four species from Honfleur are smaller. The Meudon crocodile reaches forty feet, as does one from Auteuil, and there are very similar ones at Blaye and Mimet in Provence. Those of Argentan form several species, one of which has a muzzle compressed at the sides and very elevated on top. Those from Montmartre belong to the genus of caimans, whose living analogues are found in America.

"With these reptiles live other privileged children of nature, born at the same time as them, and which will exist as long: they're the land, freshwater and marine turtles. Their fossil bones furnish more than fifty species whose living analogues will no longer exist in modern times but will be replaced by others. As I speak, it's the genus *Trionyx* that is the most numerous in species and individuals. Their body is only covered with a soft skin and lacks the carapace or scaly shield; their feet are palmate, but not elongated; the horn of their break is covered with fleshy lips; their nose is prolonged in a little mobile trunk, and, what is not the least singular thing about them, their anus is pierced by the end of the tail. The emydes or freshwater turtles are quite common in the marshes of Montmartre; they only differ from land tortoises by virtue of their carapaces, generally flatter.

"All these animals favor the water's edge and swim of dive with great facility, which will make the first humans who occupy themselves with natural history think that they're amphibians—which is to say that they can live both under water and on land.[23] But in our century that error will be rectified, thanks to the work of anatomists. They will prove that all vertebrate animals respire either by means of gills, like fish, in which case they can only live and breathe in water; or by means of lungs, in which case they can only live in air.

"Naturalists will nevertheless leave the name of amphibian to a class of carnivorous mammals whose feet are so short and so enveloped in the skin that they can only serve them on land to crawl, but as the intervals between the digits are filed by membranes, they are excellent oars.

"A few leagues from here, on the edge of the Ocean, I can take you to see, among others, a seal twice as large as those of the living world. It's a beautiful animal, which spends the greater part of its life in the sea and only comes on to land to repose in the sunlight and nurse its young. Its head is rounded, its eyes are large and shiny, but nevertheless soft and expressive; its body is elongated, very supple, almost cylindrical, diminishing uniformly in girth, terminated by a short tail placed between the two hind feet, which are engaged under the skin all the way to the heel, and are somewhat imitative of the forked tail of a fish. Its skin, tight, fine, smooth and lustrous, is a yellowish gray, whitened when it gets old. It swims with as much grace as facility, raising its head, neck and a part of its torso above the waves.

"The first humans who saw seals playing in the waves from a distance mistook them for marine humans, and the fable of tritons was invented. Perhaps the story of the sirens is similarly owed to the sea-cow that is seen grazing marine algae and sometimes raising the anterior part of its body out of the water. Its teats placed on its breast will suffice, and be-

---

[23] Although the taxonomic distinction between *Reptilia* (reptiles) and *Amphibia* (amphibians) can now be traced back to 1816, it had not yet become standardized in 1837, so Boitard is only using the word "amphibian" in its common meaning, thus missing out of his schema what would now be considered a crucial phase of animal evolution.

yond, to heat the imagination of Maillet, Sachs, La Chesnaye Des Bois, etc., etc., and cause them to invent the most marvelous tales.[24] At any rate, the sea-cow, whose bones will be found at Marly and Linjumeau, will only inhabit the torrid zone in modern times.

"Since I have mentioned the sea-cow, which belongs to the class of cetaceans, I'll introduce you to a few animals of the same class inhabiting the sea that covered the soil of Paris not long ago. Let's go closer to the shore of the Ocean, and I'll try to make them pass before your eyes, as a man with a magic lantern does.

"Among them you'll easily recognize the dolphins, for their form differs very little from those of living species. The first is nine feet long; the second is remarkable for its prodigiously elongated muzzle, similar to that of a Ganges gavial. The numerous teeth, large and conical, with which the jaws of all these dolphins are armed, their grim character, their carnivorous habits, and above all their cruelty, will render scarcely credible for naturalists the supposed amity for humans that

---

[24] The first name cited here is that of Benoît de Maillet (1656-1738), author of the posthumously-published and severely censored *Telliamed* (1748; partly restored text 1755; fully restored text 1968), whose geological studies led him to a transformist theory of the development of animal life, including human beings. Maillet did not have Boitard's elaborate knowledge of stratification, however, so he had no way of estimating either the time-scale or the detailed pattern of transformation, and imagined the emergence of humans in metamorphic terms; in support of that thesis he collated ancient and modern reports of numerous semi-human species, including "marine humans" (i.e., mermaids). The other references are to physician and natural historian Philipp Jakob Sachs (1627-1672) and the prolific François-Alexandre de La Chesnaye Des Bois (1699-1784), who translated early German works on marine fossils and added his own commentaries, again without the benefit of Boitard's far more elaborate data.

Aristotle, Pint, Seneca and the ancients in general attributed to them. They will be obliged to relegate to the number of historical fables the story of the dolphin of Lake Lucrino that, having conceived an amity for a poor child, came twice a day to lend him his back in order to cross over to the other side of the lake. Pliny adds that the animal, in order not to wound the child, took care to lower and hide the spurs of its dorsal fin. Unfortunately for Pliny's veracity, dolphins have never had bones or spurs in the dorsal fin.

"Among the cetaceans that inhabit the seas that cover France today there are three that will be lost entirely, the genera of which will remain unknown in living nature. They are the long-beaked, flat-beaked and hollow-beaked ziphius. They are the natural intermediary between cachalots and hyperodons. In modern times, in 1779, a wine-merchant in Paris dug up the bones of an unknown species of whale, at least sixty feet long, in his cellar in the Rue Dauphine.[25]

"Since we're on the edge of the Ocean, let's cross it to see the two most singular beings to which antediluvian nature gave birth. Both belong to the family of dentate mammals—which is to say, those whose jaws lack incisors when they have teeth, which isn't always the case.

The megalonyx seems to have been formed from fragments accumulated from ant-eaters, armadillos, cabassous and sloths. Nevertheless, with regard to size, it has no analogy with any of those animals, for it surpasses that of the largest ox. Its ears are long, its muzzle somewhat pointed, its jaws armed with cylindrical teeth like hose of the armadillos; its legs are exactly like those of an ant-eater. But they terminate in the feet of a cabassou. It has two short squat fingers armed with exceedingly powerful nails, and can suspend itself beneath them like a sloth; the index finger is thinner, armed with

---

[25] This find was reported in an *Essai de géologie* by Barthélemy Faujas de Saint-Fond first published anonymously in 1803 and reprinted several times, which was frequently cited thereafter, although its authenticity is open to doubt.

a less powerful nail. Its gait is also as slow as that of the two-toed or three-toed sloth; it nourishes itself partly on vegetables and partly on carrion; it has teats on its breast and only has one infant, which it carries on its back. It lives in lairs in rocks.

"The megatherium is even more extraordinary. It has the head of a sloth, but its muzzle is elongated into a kind of short, muscular trunk adapted to dig in the ground in the manner of a pig's snout. Its lower jaw is equipped with an enormous bulge imitating a tumor or goiter, but placed close to the chin. It has the shoulders and general form of a sloth. Its legs bear a close resemblance to those of pangolins, but they're excessively stout; the hind legs are almost as thick as the body. Its feet are oblique and enormous, almost as big as its head; the forefeet, like those of the giant armadillo, are composed of five digits, two of which are hidden beneath the skin, while the other three are very large, armed with powerful nails adapted for digging. The hind feet have a close analogy with those of sloths, but they only have one single claw, very large and very long. Its body is as large as that of a medium-sized elephant, massive, and covered like that of armadillos with scaly bands, but interrupted and intermingled with hairs. Its belly is stout; its tail very short and very thick, also has scaly pads, but they're not in the form of rings or whorls. Like the megalonyx, it has a very slow gait; its teats are placed under its breast and it only has one infant, which it carries on its back. It lives in caves and lairs in rocks. With its enormous nails it opens the earth, into which it digs with its short trunk to tear up the roots that are its habitual nourishment.

"But why should I go so far in search of monstrous beings when the soil of France is covered with them? Let's return to the environs of Paris and look.

"Here's the giant pangolin, belonging to the same family of edentates. It has no teeth, but its slender, tapering tongue, eight feet long, is extensible, and permits it, when darted at insects and the other small animals on which it feeds, to seize them and trap them at long distance Its body is no less than twenty-five or thirty feet in length; it is covered, including its tail, with large flat trenchant scales, disposed to cover it like the tiles of a roof. All its feet have five digits. In sum, apart from its size and a few other slight differences, it closely resembles other pangolins. When it fears danger it bristles, rolls its body into ball like a hedgehog, and presents the trenchant edges of its scales to its enemy in every part.

"Soon," he continued, "all the tusk-less species will disappear, because tigers hyenas, bears and other large carnivores will multiply greatly in the forests.[26] The most singular of those animals is a wolf surpassing the size of the largest horse, with a body eight feet long from the muzzle to the root of the tail, and no less than five feet tall at the shoulder. Fortunately, it's very rare. The carnivores, for the most part, live in profound caverns hollowed out in the rocks by the waters, and gradually fill them with the bloody bones of all the tusk-less pachyderms. Those masses of partly-gnawed bones will be a subject of astonishment for the scientists of the nineteenth century.

Fifth Epoch
150 meters above the zero-point
of the Pont de la Tournelle

"Look," said the genius. "We've arrived in the modern epoch, and you ought to recognize it."

I cast glances around me, and indeed, I did seem to recognize, not the country where I was, but the vegetation of my time. I no longer saw the coconut palms and other palm trees, and the cinnamon bushes, which had surprised me so much. But oaks, elms, birches and, in general, all the plants I had included my guide to the plants of the environs of Paris compiled over the last few years.

---

[26] Author's note: "The species of great liger, or lion, was nevertheless very rare in France. Only two fragments have been found in France, one in the Rue Hauteville, while digging a well, and the other at Abbévile. They are common in Bavaria."

A few animals passed close by; there was no longer anything strange about them and I recognized them all for having encountered them several times during my hunting parties. There were foxes, wolves, badgers, roe deer, fallow deer, red deer, hares, rabbits, etc. etc. no different from those of today.

"Ah!" I exclaimed. "Now my century is approaching. Show me, I beg you, beings of my species, for I'm very curious to see the first humans. Are they giants or pygmies? Are they white, red or black? Do they walk on two feet or four? Do they live solitary in the woods like bears or do they gather in herds like gazelles? All these things are extremely important to now, and I shan't fail to make a fine book in which the arguments will be supported on..."

"On a dream, as usual," said the genius. "At any rate, I can't satisfy you because there aren't yet any humans on the entire surface of the globe, not even an ape, which is the grimace of them or, if you like, the caricature. Wait another few thousand years.

"Several centuries ago," he continued, "the island on which we're standing was not separate from the one you perceive a short distance away, and formed a vast plain with it, covered with woods. That plain had been formed by freshwater deposits superimposed in the following order: a bank of millstone flint devoid of shells; a bank of lacustrian millstone flint sometimes replaced by a superior lacustrian limestone; then layers of gravel and mud, and finally vegetal earth composed of mineral, animal and vegetable detritus. It is noticeable all over the world that those layers present themselves in situations such that their mass, far from being augmented by the water of the present epoch, which often doesn't reach their level, tends to diminish every day by a degradation that is the necessary consequence of several causes. The principal causes in question are rain, frost, the succession from warmth and cold and from cold to warmth, chemical reactions, gradual decomposition, etc., not to mention the more or less rapid flow of the streams, torrents and rivers that furrow it to a greater or lesser depth."

"The island we're on is charming; where is it located?"

"We're on the Butte Montmartre. Look this way," he added, directing the tip of his crutch westwards. "You can see the woods of Saint-Cloud, Ville-d'Avray, Marly and Les Aluets, forming an island separated from others by the strait where Versailles will be, the little valley of Sèvres and the large valley of the park of Versailles. That other island in the form of a fig-leaf that you can see a little to the left will bear Bellevue, Meudon, and the woods of Verrière and Châville; it's separated from the continent by the strait that follows the valley of the Bièvre and the hills of Jouy. One can also perceive a few islets distributed here and there in the great lake that forms the Paris basin, but you're sufficiently orientated to recognize them yourself."

"My study must be terribly damp at the present moment, for, if I understand you correctly, it's at least twenty or thirty meters under the surface of the waters of this lake."

"That's true, but let's sit down, and in five or six thousand years—I mean five or six minutes—I'll show it to you dry."

In fact, the waters of the lake retreated through a valley that they hollowed out while snaking northwards, via Saint-Cloud, Saint-Denis, Epinay, Argenteuil, Croissy, Saint-Germain, etc., and I saw the Paris basin forming, as it is today, as they flowed away, taking with them large portions of the layers that had formed since the first epoch of the sixth period. The hardest parts, which resisted the current, formed numerous hills, on the summits of which the most charming and most fortunate habitations of Paris are now located.

In the bottom of the basin, when it was uncovered, ran a wide and beautiful river whose cheerful banks were covered with forests. A group of three islands, which I recognized easily as the Île Louviers,[27] the Île Saint-Louis and the Cité ena-

---

[27] The Île Louviers was not connected to the right bank of the Seine until 1847, so it was still an island when Boitard wrote this story.

bled me to identify the exact location of Paris, although I could see neither the palace of the Tuileries, nor the drinking-dens of Courtille, nor the Opéra, nor the Salpêtrière, nor beggars in rags, not elegant carriages, nor railways, not steamboats; I only perceived a few settlements of beavers, another industrious people, whose lodges rose up in the bosom of the watercourse.

"Master," I said to the demon, "I can see that the end of our excursion is approaching; before concluding it, could you tell me how long it has lasted?"

"There were six periods."

"And those periods each consisted...?"

"Of three, four, six, three, four and five epochs; twenty-five remarkable formations in all."

"That's very good, but how many centuries of interval were there between each formation?"

"Make an estimate of the time that has elapsed since the last, and by approximation you'll know the duration of the others."

"If I had a basis for that, but..."

"Do you not have the duration of the life of certain individuals?"

"What?"

"Admit that all the beings living today have originated by way of generation."

"Of course; that's certainly necessary; for I don't suppose that there's a single organized being in nature that is the first of its species, the same individual that emerged from the hands of creation."

"How long do you think can reasonably be accorded to the degrees of genealogy of the being that has the longest life?"

"It seems to me that it would be very little to have it preceded by only twenty generations."

"Let's start from that basis. I won't cite you the linden of Fribourg or that of Villars-en-Moing in Switzerland, because they're only a thousand years old at the most; they're infants.[28] I won't talk to you about the yew in Braburn cemetery in the county of Kent measured by Evelyn, because it only dates back 3,000 years.[29] I'll pass over in silence the baobabs seen by Adanson and later by Monsieur Perrottet in Cape Verde and the Senegambia,[30] for, although I'm certain that they're at least 6,000 years old, one can't be sure that they're very old relative to the longevity of their species. But I will mention the bald cypress of Oaxaca in Mexico, under the foliage of which Fernard Cortez put himself in the shade with all his little army, because it was at least 7,000 years old.

"To begin with, we shall only take half its age, 3,500 years, as the average term of its generation..."

"Why even take half? A bald cypress can reproduce its species before that age."

"It can reproduce seed, yes, but individuals, no. It is not only necessary that it sows its seed, but also that it cedes its place, that it does in order that the seeds can develop to replace it. The place that each species occupies on the surface of the globe necessitates it, for half of the mass of individuals arrives while the other half departs. But as I don't want to frighten you I'll only take half of 3,500, which is 1,750 years. Now, 1,750 years multiplied by twenty gives 35,000 years for each epoch of formation. Then we'll multiply that number by that of the epochs—which is to say, by 25—and we'll have for

---

[28] The 1834 tourist guide from which Boitard apparently picked up this dubious datum actually refers to "Villars-le-Moine," meaning the Bernese canton of Villars-les-Moines.

[29] This reference to the Brabourne yew, derived from Hasted's 1799 History of Kent, is also dubious, the supposed antiquity relating to local legend rather than any measurement.

[30] The references are to observations made in *Histoire naturelle du Senegal* (1757) by Michel Adanson and *Souvenirs d'un voyage autour du monde* (1831) by George Samuel Perrottet, but those sources contain no hard data to support Asmodeus' supposed certainty.

a total the age of the globe, starting from the first period: 875,000 years."

"That calculation surpasses my imagination; I have difficulty believing that it is accurate."

"Poor mite! What is a duration that one can calculate with numbers, by comparison with eternity without beginning or end? In any case, reassure yourself: for the immortal principle of everything there is neither space nor duration."

I made a reflection. "Why, I said to my genius, "have you divided the time of creation into six epochs, which, in truth, are very well characterized and self-evident?"

He shivered at my question, did not reply, and darted a sinister glance at me.

"Aha! I understand. You wanted to make me remark the conformity between the order assigned by *Genesis* to the various epochs of creation and those of the geological periods that the observation of nature has recognized, for in fact, everything has been created in six times."

The demon made a horrible grimace. He became crimson with anger, and I saw fiery sparks scintillating in his eyes. "In fact," I continued, "if one makes a facile comparison, one sees that..."

The Lame Devil, at the peak of his fury, raised his crutch and struck me a heavy blow on the ears; his body became all flames and he disappeared, exhaling a strong odor of burned horn.

The pain caused me to raise my hands to my head, and it was just in time; the candle had set fire to my cotton night-cap, and my hair was beginning to singe when I woke up. I had gone to sleep on the works of Cuvier, Brongniart, Lindley and others.

"Alas!" I said, shaking the sparks from my night-cap. "What a pity I only saw all those beautiful things in a dream!"

When I was fully awake, I thought that I ought to relate to my readers the means that I employed in being able to describe in their entirety animals whose living analogues are completely unknown. I owe them that account in order to inform them of the exact degree of confidence they ought to have in the descriptions they have just read.

"For many years naturalists have been struck by the prodigious quantity of fossil bones that have been found buried in caves or in the grounds while digging wells, quarries, etc., and a few memoirs were published on that interesting matter. But all the scholars initially wanted to relate the bones to analogous living species and that prejudice, resulting from a lack of anatomical knowledge, closed before them an area that was as new as it was singular. Baron Georges Cuvier, who combined vast knowledge of natural history with profound studies of anatomy, was struck by an idea that had escaped his predecessors: that the majority of those bones could only have belonged to species, or even to genres and families, that were entirely extinct.[31] In consequence, he dared to undertake an immense labor, succeeding in combining fragments and restoring entire skeletons, and he thus opened up an entirely new field of study. His work caused a great stir in the scholarly world, and several scientists of the first order followed in his footsteps in Italy, Germany, England and even in America.

---

[31] It was, in fact, Cuvier's *Essais sur la géographie minéralogique des environs de Paris* (1811, with Alexandre Brongniart) that first popularized the idea that animal and plant fossils belonged to species that were now extinct, and the data of those essays formed the principal basis of his generalized theory of the Earth's evolution, featuring a series of "epochs of creation" interrupted by catastrophes. Cuvier insisted, however, that there had been a series of separate creations and refused—at least openly—to believe in transformism; Boitard still seems to be hesitating at this point between Cuvier's interpretation and the transformist thesis that all Earthly life belongs to a common sequence of descent, but the subsequent episodes in the series bring him down firmly in the latter camp.

Geologists joined in, and from that fortunate association resulted the knowledge of an exceedingly singular fact, which is that is every country, analogous layers of minerals contain the same species of bones. That astonishing discovery served to date in a certain manner the series of epochs in which each species of organized being, animal or vegetable, had appeared for the first time. It is to Messieurs Brongniart in France, Lindley and Hutton in England, Schlothen and von Sternberg in Germany, Nilson in Sweden, etc., that science owes the most in the latter regard, particularly that of vegetable fossils.

I have taken advantage of the works of Baron Cuvier and a few other scholars to do something that, thanks to them, no longer offered any great difficulty. I have put muscles on the skeletons that they had restored, and, rigorously observing the size of the imprints that those muscles have left on the bones, it was easy for me, at least approximately, to discover their thickness. It only remained to cover them with skin, and for that I had nothing to guide me but analogy. But it seemed certain to me that an animal belonging by the majority of its characteristics to the great saurians must have, like them, a body covered with scales; that another, belonging to the class of carnivorous mammals, must have been covered in fur, etc., etc. Subsequently, to render them the appearances, graces and movements of life, I have had recourse to one of the best artists of natural history in Paris, Johann Theodor Susemihl. As for the mores of the animals, it was even easier for me to divine them, and I can that say with complete certainty because I have two means to do so, which lend one another mutual support: firstly, analogy, which brings us naturally to conclude that an animal having, for example, the size, forms and weapons of a tiger would also have the general habits of a tiger; and secondly, the inspection of teeth, which always characterize with a great deal of precision an animal's way of life. That general rule in living nature is, I believe, without exception.

Thanks to the works of Adolphe Brongniart[32] and the authors cited above, I have been able just as easily to group around each animal the vegetables that existed in its time.

---

[32] Adolphe Brongniart (1801-1876), the son of Cuvier's collaborator, was the great pioneer of paleobotany; he had not completed his *Histoire des végétaux fossiles* (1828-37) when the first part of "Paris avant homme" was written.

PART TWO

Sixth Geological Period

I had just returned, sad and thoughtful, from the Rue Vivienne, where I had been to see the gigantic remains of an antediluvian animal. An enormous head, four feet long and three wide—which is to say, larger than that of an elephant—and then, tusks placed, contrary to any analogy with what is known of living or fossil animals, not in the upper jaw, but the lower one; not in the place of canines but that of incisors; not in a position pointing toward the sky but downwards, toward the ground; not projecting from the mouth but having to emerge through two holes pierced in the lower lip.[33]

Truly, I said to myself, *that's enough to embarrass a man more learned than me. It will be impossible for me to write an article for the* Musée des Familles *on that monster, which seems to have been found expressly to confuse scholars.*

While making these annoying reflections, I went back to my lodgings; I stretched myself out in the old armchair that I have already mentioned, and remained plunged in meditation for a quarter of an hour.

---

[33] The skull in question had been found in Eppelsheim in Hess-Darmstadt in 1836. The strange tusks cause a great deal of dissent as to what kind of animal the skull might belong to, and a severe test of Cuvier's method of reconstructing images of an entire animal on the basis of incomplete fossil skeletons. Thanks to further discoveries, modern paleontologists now feel confident in asserting that *Deinotherium giganteum* was, in fact, an elephant, as Henri de Blainville, (1777-1850) contended, thus rendering Asmodeus' hypothesis and the subsequent description of the animal entirely false, but at the time, it qualified as a fair, if somewhat fanciful, guess.

"Oh well!" I exclaimed, suddenly, "the die is cast; in spite of all my reluctance it will be necessary to make this *Dinotherium giganteum* a walrus or seal, as Monsieur Buckland has said, or an elephant, as Monsieur de Blainville presumes, a tapir or a pangolin, as Cuvier has written, or a whale, as some German authors think—and yet, the animal has not the slightest analogy with them. Come on, let's decide; it will be...."

"A mole!" said a shrill and mocking little voice, accompanying those words with a long burst of laughter.

I shivered, and turned swiftly in the direction from which the singular voice had come. I perceived... you will have guessed that it was my lame devil.

"A mole! But Monsieur Demon, a mole hasn't the slightest resemblance to a tapir, a whale or an elephant. What would the authors I've just cited say?"

"Your authors can say what they like, but I maintain, personally, that the carcass you've just seen belonged to a mole."

"That's not possible! Look, here are the engravings that I was given at the door; judge for yourself."

With a nimble bound, the devil leapt on to my desk; he sat down gravely on a pile of quarto volumes, placed his crutch between his legs, set his spectacles on his nose, and took my pictures between the thumb and the other fingers of his left hand. Then, passing the index finger of his right hand over the design representing the head of the animal, he said:

"To begin with, my dear pupil you see that this skull is three and a half feet long at its greatest extent, and two feet six inches wide; from which it follows that if it were covered with muscles and skin, it could not have been less than four feet long and three wide; now, the medium size for the head of a quadruped mammal, is a quarter of the total length of the body. The dinotherium was, therefore, sixteen feet long, which is the size of the largest elephants. I'm being very modest in fixing those dimensions, for I'm supposing that this carcass, found on the bank of the Rhine by Professor Klipstein, is the largest that the entire species of dinotheria has been able to furnish, which is improbable, since there are other fragments proportionately larger, which suggest that the animals might have been eighteen feet long."

"And you conclude from that that it must be a mole?"

"One moment. Notice the enormous cavity designed to receive the muscles of the nose."

"Yes, of the trunk."

"Who mentioned a trunk? Where do you see a trunk?"

"The scientists..."

"Why do you want to see a trunk instead of a nose? Take the skeleton of a pig and that of a mole, and you'll find, in the same place, enormous impressions of muscles. Do you conclude from that that the pig or the mole has a trunk?

"So, the dinotherium had a nose, but a large, elongated, mobile and powerful nose, adapted for digging in the ground—in brief, a mole's nose. Will you deny that? Is it more improbable that an animal has a nose like any other than having a anomaly like the elephant?"

"It's true that in calculating the probabilities coldly, one ought to believe more easily in analogies than anomalies; that seems more logical to me...but a mole!"

"Notice, my dear, that the holes of the eyes are extremely small by comparison with those of all known animals, and that they don't close in the posterior part; and, in fact, why should the dinotherium have eyes proportionately larger than those of a mole, since, living in the obscurity of a subterranean habitation, those organs would be no more use to it than they are to a mole?

"As in all animals that are obliged to push earth forward while digging through it with the head, the frontal bones are short, but strong and very broad; the face of the occiput, enormously wide, forms an angle with them of 139 or 140 degrees, which is only seen in whales. The prodigious muscles that move that colossal head give it an crushing force. Only the chrysochloris or golden mole of the Cape can offer any analogy with the dinotherium in that regard. You can imagine that an animal obliged to fray a subterranean passage ten or twelve feet in diameter needs that prodigious force in its neck muscles—a force that can only be compared, as I said, with that of a whale.

"And in spite of that, it must often encounter obstacles, stones, and stout tree-roots. It would have been stopped dead in its digging if nature hadn't given it a pick-ax to uproot those obstacles; there is that pick-ax: the tusks that emerge from the lower jaw, directed downwards. They resemble, I think, those forked hoes that vine-growers use in stony or newly-broken ground. Look: they must have a terrible strength, to judge by the enormous fossas hollowed out in the temporal bones to lodge the muscles that move and direct the lower law. Furthermore those tusks or fangs offer, in relation to their form, and above all their position, an example of structure unique in all creation.

"As for the other teeth," the demon added, moving his finger to the drawing representing them, "you can see that they're five in number. The first in trenchant in its anterior part, the third has three projections and the others two—from which one ought to conclude that the animal lived on roots, rhizomes and tubers that only grow in the soil. Now, I ask you, how can a trunk have been any use to it? It would certainly have been very cumbersome, and that's all."

"I agree that the head is well-adapted to digging in the ground, but that doesn't prove that the animal had a subterranean existence."

"Let's examine the other fragments," said the demon, placing his finger on another drawing. Here's the scapula; it's long and narrow, and closely resembles that of a mole; observation has proved that all the animals that have it employ their anterior feet in constant and difficult movements, requiring great muscular force. Also, that form of scapula, rare in mammals, is very common in birds, because they need great wing-power to sustain themselves in the air.

"Let's pass on to the second phalanx of the front foot. You'll notice that the articulatory facet of the bone presents a disposition completely different from that remarked in other animals. It follows inevitably from that very superficial articulation that the dinotherium could not walk on the ends of its digits and had to drag itself with the external edges of the hand, like a mole. The latter animal is again the only one that presents an analogy of form in that phalanx with our fossil monster.

"But here's a fourth fragment even more conclusive; it's the first or ungual phalanx of the same front foot. Look how profoundly indented it is in its anterior part. That incision only exists, in mammals, in three kinds of animal, all three of which dig in the soil and lives in burrows; it gives their nails the prodigious strength they need. The pangolin, the chrysochloris or Cape mole and the common mole are the only living animals that offer the same conformation, and, remarkably, the characteristic is less pronounced in the mole than in the dinotherium.

"Now, my dear, what ought one to conclude from all that? Given that, as our naturalists admit that the dinotherium has no analogy with any other animals than those I've cited, and it has the head of a mole, the scapula of a mole and the hands of a mole, it seems to me to resemble a mole more than a whale."

"I confess, Seigneur Demon, that the majority of the analogies are in favor of your opinion; however, there are the teeth, which..."

"Don't resemble those of a mole, I agree, for its jaws lack incisors and canines; but they're nevertheless adapted to crushing roots, and even mollusks and insects that it encounters in its digging. In any case, my dear, that anomaly, if it is one, has numerous examples in living animals. For example, if you ever undertake a voyage to New Holland, you'll find a numerous family of mammals whose species have so much analogy that it's impossible to separate one from the group they form, but which nevertheless differ as much as possible in their dental system.

"Among those species with heterogeneous dentition, the sarigue—the only genre that is not Australian—represents the insectivores, such as tenrecs and moles; the kangaroo-rat has teeth appropriate to a frugivorous diet, like the hedgehog; the giant kangaroo lives on grass, lacks the superior canine that characterizes the previous species and only has transversal projections on its molars and premolars, which make it very similar to our herbivorous pachyderms; finally, the wombat is, like the hare, a veritable rodent in its teeth and intestines—and yet, no naturalist has been tempted to separate those marsupials to remove them into the major divisions in which their teeth rigorously classify them. I therefore hold to making the dinotherium, if it isn't a mole, at least belong to a neighboring genre, in which I place it with desmans, *Scalopus*, *Chrysochloris* and tenrecs, all similarly subterranean animals.

"Anyway, if you're not content, you can place it elsewhere—but in that case, you'll be obliged, in accordance with your principles, to create, not a genus, a family or even an order, but a class apart, which it will occupy on its own, and that necessity will be the bloodiest criticism you could make of the supposedly natural method of your scientists."

In spite of the high opinion that I had of the merit of my irascible demon, I had a head so full of pangolins, seals, tapirs, whales and elephants that I could not accept his mole at all, and a slight smile of vanity and disapproval brushed my lips.

He perceived it, and cried: "Aha! I can see, Monsieur Incredulous, that it needs something more than reasoning to convince you. Well, damn it, I'll convince you by means of your own eyes or I'll lose my devilment trying."

He launched himself upon me, seized my by the arm, pulled me behind him astride his crutch, and we both departed like a crossbow bolt through the window. The rapidity of our journey stunned me to such an extent that I can't say for sure how long it took us to travel the route, or which way we went, but what I'm sure of is that we traveled much faster than by steamboat or railway carriage, because, so far as I can judge, it was less than a minute after we departed when we arrived several hundred leagues away.

I found myself lying full length on a bed of moss, under a tree that was at least a hundred feet high. When I had recovered from my confusion I asked the genius where I was.

"We're in the region," he said, "that will be called, in a few thousand years, the Rhenish province of the Grand Duchy of Hesse-Darmstadt. The great lake that you see over there to the east will have dried up, and one of the most beautiful rivers in Europe, the Rhine, will traverse its ancient bed throughout its length. The place where we are will be the town of Eppelsheim, and further away, the city of Alzei. If you remember the first voyage we made together, you'll recognize from these palms, becoming rare, the absence of zamias and cycads, and finally, this walnut tree under which you're lying, that we've gone back into past time as far as the beginning of the sixth geological period, the one in which the extraordinary animals you talked about in your account of that first voyage will disappear, and in which humans will make their first appearance on the Earth."

A muffled but horrible roar caused me to shiver all the way to the marrow of my bones. I darted my frightened gaze around, but I could not see anything. Suddenly, the cry resounded in my ears a second time, and I felt the earth tremble beneath my feet. The idea of the subterranean sounds that are heard before an earthquake came to mind; fear took possession of my heart; I got up precipitately and started running away as fast as I could—but I had not taken two hundred paces when my demon grabbed me by the arm, made me sit down on a fragment of rock and pointed with his finger at the place where the most extraordinary scene was unfolding. It was directly beneath the tree where I had paused.

The earth was convulsively agitated, and its movement was communicated to the foliage of the tree, which quivered and swayed, as if a whirlwind had plunged into its thousand branches. The ground was lifted up, roots snapped with a frightful noise; the carpet of moss opened up; the tree oscillated five or six times in the air, and then finally fell noisily; and the earth, raised up in an enormous cone more than twenty feet high, opened up at the summit of that singularly-formed mountain.

"Parbleu!" I aid to the genius. "I didn't think that you were going to show me the formation of new Pyrenees in miniature!"

"Miniature!" he replied. "My word, it's nice, your miniature! Look what's emerging from its hole."

In fact, I saw a monstrous head the size of a barrel suddenly emerge from the abyss that that was hollowed out in the height of the cone, then a neck even thicker, a massive body more than eight feet in diameter—which is to say, with the girth of the largest elephant—and finally, a strange animal sixteen or eighteen feet long, frightful in appearance, dragging itself along awkwardly on four short, stout legs.

Its entire body was covered in long, silky hair, green in color, changing to copper and bronze, offering, like the chrysochlore of the Cape, the most beautiful metallic reflections. Its nose, extremely large, more than two feet long, terminated in a kind of mobile snout, bristling with trenchant and horny tubercles, well-adapted for opening the bosom of the earth. Beneath its nose was an enormous lower jaw, prolonged in front in a long downwardly-directed chin. At the end of that chin, two two-foot-long tusks, touching at the base, emerged through the skin of the lip and directed their points to the side of the body rather than in front. I saw that the monster was helping itself to crawl by stretching its head, digging them into the ground and pulling its body toward them.

Its eyes were so small that they would certainly have been invisible through the long hair surrounding them if they had not been gleaming with a dark red gleam, like sparks. Its ears were very small, the shells scarcely apparent. Its hind feet were rather short, armed with very strong nails, but the front ones terminated in two enormous hands, absolutely similar to those of a mole, serving to shove earth to the right and the left as it hollowed out a subterranean tunnel with its nose.

The formidable animal came down from the mound that it had elevated; with a great deal of agility it crawled a few toises; then it uttered a cry so shrill, so loud and so extraordinary that I could not compare it to anything ever heard by human ears. The demon saw me shiver, and reassured me by telling me that it was calling to another animal of its species, and that it would draw away from us if it heard a response to its voice.

It continued to utter a shrill cry from time to time, while directing its march toward a vast virgin forest the covered the flanks of a hill, where I perceived a few mounds similar to its own.

Suddenly, it stopped dead, because a horrible voice had responded to its own, but with a cry that was doubtless not the one it expected, for its little eyes became more scintillating than ever; its hair bristled on its back and formed a kind of long mane along its entire body, and it began to beat the earth with its formidable tusks and make stones fly around with its large hands.

At the same time, a bellowing that could only be compared to that produced simultaneously by a hundred bulls made itself distinctly heard, and I turned to look at the forest. Another monster, just as stout but not as long, being eight or nine feet high and ten or eleven long, was advancing at a rapid trot in a furious fashion. It was a narrow-toothed mastodon.

It bore a considerable resemblance to an elephant, but it was essentially different by virtue of its more elongated body, much less stout in the region of the belly; its feet were thicker, its tusks straighter and downwardly directed, in such a manner as to be easily able to dig in order to extract the roots and fleshy tubers on which it nourished itself. My demon told me that its teeth had no analogy with those of an elephant, but a great deal with those of a hippopotamus or a wild boar, and that, for that reason, it lived for preference in marshy terrain on the banks of great rivers, because it found its nourishment more easily in the mud.

"It seems to me," I said, "that it has a close resemblance to the great mastodon you mentioned to me during our first voyage."

"That's true," he said, "but it differs in its size, which is less by a third, by virtue of its shorter trunk, because it lives in Europe, is much lower on its legs, and in a few other slighter anatomical characteristics."

I noticed then that its body, like those of the antediluvian mammoth and rhinoceros, was entirely covered with long hair, which formed a mane over the neck. But the scene of which I had become the spectator soon changed the subject of my observations.

The two monsters hurled themselves upon one another with a terrible fury and commenced a combat that, it seemed to me, could only end with the death of one or the other. The offensive and defensive weapons with which nature had provided them rendered the struggle most extraordinary.

The mastodon attacked its enemy by charging it head down, in order to present the terrible points of its tusks to it, and it held its trunk raised, either to strike or ward off blows. The dinotherium, by contrast, waited for the impact, rearing up on the posterior part of its body. It deflected its antagonist's tusks with its hands; then, when it had avoided the thrust, it brought its gigantic head down like a club on to that of the mastodon, in order to implant its tusks in the skull. But the other was able to avoid its blows with considerable skill by pushing the monster sideways with its powerful trunk, and then the dinotherium only struck the ground, which trembled beneath their feet.

Their howls were terrible, and a cloud of dust, earth and vegetable material that rose up around them hid them from my yes or a few minutes. By the time the wind had swept it away, the battle had ceased and the two breathless monsters, covered with mud and blood, were lying fifty paces from one another, seemingly resting for a moment in order to attack thereafter with a new fury. The mastodon was already waving its trunk in a threatening fashion, and its angry bellowing was making the echoes resound, when I saw the dinotherium set its nose to the ground and agitate its neck rapidly.

Soon, its entire head plunged into the soil; its hands hurled stones and earth more than fifty feet into the air; its body gradually sank; a minute later all that could be seen was its large rump, which suddenly disappeared, and nothing remained in the place that it had occupied two minutes before but a round hole ten feet in diameter, resembling the opening of a large mine-shaft. It had hollowed out a subterranean tunnel with so much rapidity that I seemed to be seeing one of those phantoms of the Opéra sinking from view in order to redescend to Hell.[34]

Then the mastodon got up, showing a kind of anxiety, as if it feared that its perfidious opponent might undermine the earth beneath its feet. I could not doubt its thought when I saw it retreat slowly toward the forest, advancing hesitantly and only putting one foot after another after having tested the ground, so to speak.

"That animal," I said to the genius, "must have a highly developed degree of intelligence, for its precautions suppose thought and prudence."

"There's no need to be astonished by that, because the mastodon is one of the primordial types of the elephant, and you're familiar with the latter's intelligence."

"I certainly am! I know it be heart, and I can prove it to you. One very remarkable thing that has never been noted is that the species of elephants is the only ne, among wild animals, that doesn't have a unique moral type for all the animals of its species. I'll explain what I mean. In the wolf species, for

---

[34] The "special effect" in question had been popularized by its spectacular use in Meyerbeer's *Robert le diable* (1831), which started a vogue for "devil plays" that doubtless helped to inspire Boitard to resurrect Asmodeus. In Edward Bulwer-Lytton's satire *Asmodeus at Large* (1832), the lame devil complains bitterly about the caricaturish aspects of *Robert le diable*.

example, all the individuals are cruel and cowardly; in the fox species they're all cunning; in the lion species all courageous, in the sheep species all stupid and meek, in the goat species all capricious, and in those of the wild boar and rhinoceros, all stupid and brutal, etc., etc. Every individual has the moral character of its family, and never emerges from it, because it cannot.

"Humans and elephants are the only exceptions to that general rule; one finds among them individuals more or less intelligent and more or less brutal; individuals courageous to the point of temerity, and others exceedingly cowardly; one sees some benevolent to the point of stupidity, others malevolent to the point of ferocity, etc., etc. That's doubtless why so many contradictory tales are told about the two species.

"What is certain is that in a state of health, although the most brutal human has an immeasurable advantage over the elephant, the least intelligent of the latter has a great deal over other wild animals. I can cite you in support of that several authentic facts,

"Although elephants are naturally very mild, neither bloodthirsty not ferocious, they conserve the memory of an insult for a long time, and never miss an opportunity to avenge themselves. Thus, in the lands where those animals are often hunted, it's very dangerous to encounter them; those that have been wounded or have escaped from some trap, especially, experience an implacable wrath as soon as they recognize the presence of humans. As they have an excellent sense of smell, a clump of grass trodden by a hunter's foot is sufficient to awaken their attention and put them on the alert.

"The elephant that finds the clump tears it up with its trunk and passes it to one of its comrades in order to have the other sniff it; the latter passes it to a third, and so on, until the whole herd is aware of the enemy presence. Then they set off, marching in battle order—which is to say that the oldest male, and hence the best-armed, sets himself at the head of the column, while the second oldest brings up the rear in order to maintain order and prevent any laggards from falling behind.

The young males and the females form a second front; the pregnant females and those that are nursing, along with the infants, are in the middle. If any of the latter are too young to keep up the pace, their mothers pick them up with their trunk and carry them.

"Whether the elephants are obedient to a leader whose orders they understand, or whether they are content to imitate the actions of the one marching in front, it's certain that they all make, together and spontaneously, the decision to attack, to pass by indifferently, or to flee.

"Those animals do not multiply in captivity, and all those submitted to domestication have previously been wild. Thus, their qualities and defects cannot be in any way attributed to human influence. When they're captured in the forest they oppose the keenest resistance and make prodigious efforts to free themselves from bonds with which they are charged, but as soon as they sense that their resistance is futile, they understand perfect that the best thing to do is to resign themselves and submit, and that is what they do, immediately. This is what the traveler Père Tachard says on page 352 of his second voyage:[35]

"'We had the pleasure, a few days later, of hunting elephants. The Siamese are highly skilled in that kind of hunt, and they have several ways of catching the animals. The simplest of all, which is not the least amusing, is by means of female elephants. When one is in heat, it is taken into the woods of the Louvo forest; the mahout leading it crouches down and covers himself with leaves in order not to be perceived by wild elephants; the cries of the domesticated female, which she never fails to make at a certain signal from the mahout, attracts the elephants in the surrounding area, which hear it and immediately reply to it. The hunter, having taken note of these exchanged cries, takes the road back to Louvo, and goes slowly with his entire retinue, who do not leave him, and goes at a slow pace to an enclosure of stout stakes, made expressly for

---

[35] *Second voyage de Siam* (1689) by Guy Tachard.

the purpose, a quarter of a league from Louvo and sufficiently close to the forest.. They had accumulated a fairly considerable herd of elephants that way, among which there was only large one difficult to master...

"'The mahout leading the female emerges from the enclosure by means of a narrow passage the length of an elephant; at each end there are sliding doors that drop and lift easily. All the other little elephants followed the tracks of the female one after another, several times, but such a narrow passage astonished the large elephant, which always withdrew. They brought back the female several times; it followed her as far as the door, but it never wanted to go in, as if it had some presentiment of the loss of liberty that it was about to suffer.

"Then several Siamese who were in the park advanced in order to make to go forward by force, and came to attack it with long pikes, with the points of which they struck heavy bows. The angry elephant pursued them furiously and speedily, and none of them would have escaped if they had not retired promptly behind the piles forming the palisade, against which the irritated beast broke its tusks several times. In the heat of the pursuit, one of the men, who was attacking it most vigorously, and was most vigorously followed, fled between the two doors, where the elephant ran after him, but as soon as he had gone in the Siamese escaped through a small gap and the animal found itself trapped, the two doors having fallen at the same time, and although it struggled, it remained there. To appease it, bucketfuls of water were emptied over it, while ropes were attached to its legs and its neck.

"Some time later, when it was very fatigued, it was brought out by means of two domestic elephants that pulled it out forwards with the ropes, and two others that pushed it from behind, until it was attached to a large pillar around which it was only free to circle. An hour later it became so tractable that a Siamese climbed on to its back, and the next day it was detached, to lead it to the stable with the others.'

"Now, Monseigneur Demon, the highest proof of intelligence one can give—a proof ordinarily beyond human reason—is to know how to submit with resignation to the inevitable blows of destiny, as elephants do.

"'That animal, once tamed,' Buffon says, 'becomes the meekest and most obedient of all animals; it become attached to the person who cares for it; it caresses him, anticipates him, and seems to divine everything that might please him; in a short time it comes to comprehend signals and even to understand the expression of sounds; it distinguishes the imperative tone, that of anger or satisfaction, and acts in consequence. It does not mistake its master's words, it receives his orders with attention, and carries them out without precipitation, for its movements are always measured, and its character appears to have the gravity of its mass. It is easily taught to bend its knees to give more facility to those who want to mount it; it caresses its friends with its trunk, salutes the people indicated with it, uses it to pick up burdens and assists with its own loading; it allows itself to be clothed and seems to take pleasure in seeing itself covered with gilded harness and shiny apparel; it can be attached to chariots, carts or capstans; it pulls evenly, continuously, and without refusal, provided that one does not abuse it with unwarranted blows and that one seems to be grateful for the good will with which it is employing its strength.'[36]

"A sign of reflective intelligence is rarer in the history of the animals, but here is a characteristic one. The ancient Romans liked to see elephants appear in their spectacles, and emperors often gave that pleasure to the people. But before making those monstrous children of India or Africa appear in the arena care was taken to train them to perform a few surprising exercises, and, if one can believe the ancient authors, one was even taught to walk a tightrope. At any rate, a skillful mahout was charged with teaching several of those animals a certain dance, and as there was one of them that found it more difficult to learn, it received severe reprimands several times,

---

[36] The quotation is from volume 11 (1764) of Buffon's *Histoire naturelle*.

which caused it great chagrin. The mahout perceived that for several nights the elephant left the stable and spent several hours in a small adjacent park; he was curious to know what it might be doing there, and his there in order to spy on it; in the moonlight, he soon saw the elephant repeat for hours on end the lesson that he had given it during the day.

"I won't relate to you the thousand curious facts that one could relate concerning the generosity and rancor of elephants..."

"And you'll do very well," exclaimed the genius, interrupting me, "for you'd be risking telling me old stories. Anyway, I have to occupy your time more usefully. Look where we're going. Look up into the foliage of that walnut tree."

A nut was detached from one of the low branches and fell almost on top of my head. I picked the nut up and saw that it different a great deal in form from those I had previously collected under walnut trees, whether in Europe or America. It appeared to be a third smaller than an ordinary nut; its shell was not as rough, striped longitudinally but with little regularity; its form was more elongated, spherical at the base and quadrangular at the summit, which terminated in a broad and long conical point. In addition, the internal partitions were not thick or ligneous as in some American nut, and the kernel came away easily from the shell.[37] The leaves of the tree appeared to me to be like those of an ordinary walnut, but longer, with narrower folioles.[38]

We were on dry, absolutely sterile ground, as uniform as if the waters had just drained away, greatly resembling a mixture of sand and mud dried by the sun. Several extraordinary

---

[37] Author's note: "I found the fossil nut I describe here in the English gardens of the Château de Soligny, two leagues from Mâcon, in the département of Saône-et-Loire."

[38] Author's note: "Here I suppose that the nut found at Soligny belonged to the species of walnut whose leaves I recognized imprinted in the calcareous stone of the same département."

animals of various sizes had passed that way before us, for the ground was covered with their footprints. This is almost all of what could be observed:

The imprints of forefeet were always light and those of hind feet very deep; one could thus conclude that the animal carried its weight on its rear as it walked, in the fashion of kangaroos and a few other marsupials. It was probably a quadrumane, for the impressions resembled that of a hand whose thumb, especially on the rear feet, was curved backwards in a very strange manner; all the fingers, with the exception of the thumb, were armed with pointed nails; the animals liked in families, for large prints were constantly to be found with medium-sized and small ones. The largest impressions of hind feet were more than ten inches long, which implied an animal larger than a human; others were found of five and a half inches, eight and a half and one and a half, the palm and fingers included. Its gait was rather light, because, in the larger prints, the front foot was nearly one foot ten inches away from the hind foot.

"I'd like to know what that animal was," I said to the genius.

"Well," he replied, "you have only to consult your scientists, who divine everything, and you'll find them in accord on that point as in the case of the dinotherium. At the first glance Monsieur Kaup will tell you that its name is *Chirotherium barthii*, and he's sure of that because he's the one who baptized it; for the rest, he knows no more about it than you do, and yet he conjectures, with Messieurs Barth, Hohnbaum and Wiegmann, that it was a kangaroo, or something similar. Professor Berthold believes, on the contrary, that it was a species of amphibian. A few French naturalists sustain that it was a bear; and here's Messieurs Buckland and Koening, who don't know yet what it is but will soon find out, so they say. As for me, I don't agree with the opinion of any of those Messieurs."[39]

"You think that it was…?"

"The devil, my dear friend! Interrogate the peasants of the vicinity of Darmstadt, and see whether they don't make you that reply. For on many high hills of the duchy, the rain and the alternation of the seasons have laid the rock bare; on one of those rocks several footprints are found similar to those you see here, and the peasants see them as the unequivocal traces of a dance of demons."

"I've already heard mention of that legend, as absurd as it is poetic, but I believe that it wouldn't be accepted without argument at the Académie des Sciences. People are skeptical in the century in which we live."

"That's true; one finds many incredulous individuals, of whom one could make two perfectly distinct classes: those who doubt because of an excess of education, and those who doubt by virtue of ignorance. The former might very well reject the story of the mole that I've just shown you, but to put a seal or a whale in its place; they would recognize the facts and only deny some of the conclusions that you draw from them, especially if they contradict their preferred theories. As for the ignorant, they reject without examination everything that seems extraordinary to them, because it is outside their narrow sphere; they are ordinarily the most skeptical; if you want to convince them, show them the skeletons of antediluvian animals that you have described, and tell them where the bones were found, but some of them will probably still doubt."

---

[39] As with the deinotherium, this passage refers to a recent controversy concerning tracks found in 1834 in Thuringia. We now know that the sandstone in which they were made is Triassic, about 240,000,000 years old, and that they belong to a dinosaur, but Boitard had no chronology to go on and dinosaurs had not yet been invented. The taxonomist Johan Jakob Jaup believed that there was an innate mathematical order in nature, and, like Cuvier, refused to believe in transformism.

"The advice is good, Monseigneur, and I won't fail to follow it."

"You'll do well, for fossil nature is so extraordinary that it's permissible, even for a man of good sense, to demand proofs before making up his mind to believe. I caused to pass before your eyes, during our first voyage, the singular beings that populated the basin of Paris, and four or five other inhabitants of the Earth, but if I showed you them all, your astonishment would be greatly augmented."

"Show them to me, Monseigneur, I beg you."

"So be it. Sit down on that rock that sticks out from the sea shore, and I make the strangest animals of the periods that preceded this one file before you as if in a parade."

In fact, I suddenly saw myself surrounded by fantastic beings that had no living analogues.

"Look at this one," said the genius. "It forms the natural link between the fish and the reptiles; it's still half-pike and half-turtle, and it would be more like the later than the former if it didn't breathe by means of gills. It's a Megalichtys,[40] and as you can see through the transparency of the waves, it has conserved of its former reptile nature the heaviness of its natation and the slowness of movement. Beside it are swimming sauroïdes, half-fish half-lizard, which are characterized by flat rhomboid scales and conical pointed teeth alternating with flattened teeth. Those fish-reptiles only appeared for the first time after the formation of coal-bearing terrains, for before then there were no carnivorous fish—which is to say, none with pointed conical teeth adapted for tearing the flesh of other animals.

---

[40] This designation has long been obsolete; it referred to a number of fossils found in Old Red Sandstone that puzzled vertebrate paleontologists for a long time, but which were eventually classified as "osteolepid" fish; they are not now thought to have played any role in the transition between fish and amphibian.

"On the bed of the sea, dragging itself over the sand, is a mollusk whose petrified shells are found very frequently in layers of chalk and compact limestone. It's an ammonite the size of a cartwheel. It's distinguished from the nautilus that exists today by its partitions; instead of being flat or simply concave, they were angular and jagged at the edge, like acanthus leaves."

I perceived a brightly-colored lizard sliding through the grass, which appeared to be watching out for its prey on the water's edge. By its laterally-compressed tail I immediately recognized that it was a monitor, also known as a sentinel or a tupinambis. It was a little more than three feet long and its head bore some resemblance to that of a crocodile, but its muzzle was very short and its jaws were only armed on each side with eleven trenchant and pointed teeth. Its hind feet have five unequal digits, of which the fourth as the longest.

"That animal," the demon told me, "is the type, or, if you wish, the ancestor of the Ouaran[41] that will one day populate the banks of the Nile, and the first civilized Egyptians will worship it because it will nourish itself on the eggs of the crocodile, another divinity in their way of thinking. He need for protection and gratitude on one hand, hatred and fear on the other, such are the causes that confer divinity in human reckoning. That is why gods were made of Caesar and Nero; why certain peoples have simultaneously worshiped the principle of good and the principle of evil; and why the Egyptians divinized cows and crocodiles—which does not imply and contradiction, as you might have thought. Furthermore, that animal, marked by white spots, which form little oval and irregular, but nevertheless agreeable, compartments on its back, will receive the name of sentinel because, when an imprudent person goes to sleep on the edge of a marsh and a hideous crocodile prepares to devour him, the monitor will not fail to whistle in order to wake him up and save him from that fright-

---

[41] Cuvier's taxonomy gives Ouaran as the Arab name for the Nile monitor.

ful danger. Such, at least, is the tale that will be told to explain the origin of its name."

"And how do you explain the more bizarre name of tupinambis?"

"It comes from one of those blunders so common among plagiaristic scribblers. Margrave said that the sentinel of America was called *temapara* by the topinambu savages, and in consequence he gave the lizard the label *Temapara tupinambis*. Séba who copied from him, mistook the latter word for the animal's name, and all the copyists who have come after him have made the same error."[42]

The waters, the savannahs and the forests were filled with such a large quantity of enormous reptiles that I still shiver when I think about them. At every moment I perceived above the surface of the waves the long neck and serpentine head of ten species of plesiosaurs surpassing the tallest marine vegetation or coiling around aquatic trees. The head of the smallest was eight and a half inches long—which is to say that it was equal to that of the largest boas of today; the largest heads were more than two feet five inches, which is enormous, and supposes an animal of a monstrous size.

I also perceived seven species of ichthyosaurs, between four feet long and thirty or forty. Those animals, living in the sea, where they fed on fish and turtles, had enormous glittering eyes, which permitted them to see clearly by night. They had the jaws of a dolphin, armed on each side by sixty to ninety longitudinally striated teeth, as large and terrible as those of a crocodile, the head and sternum of a lizard, the feet or fins and a cetacean, and the vertebrae of a fish. They lacked external ears and skin passed over the tympanum, as in chameleons and salamanders. Their body was proportionately very stout, and their lizard-like tail not very long. Being furnished with lungs, they breathed air naturally, and were obliged in conse-

[42] This anecdote is quoted from Cuvier; "Margrave" is elusive, although Darwin also refers to his work on the fauna of Brazil, but the other alleged copier is Albertus Seba (1665-1736)

quence often to show their horrible face above the surface of the water.

I saw some that emerged from the bosom of the waves, in order to enjoy the pleasant influences of the sunlight, crawling with difficulty on to the sand in the manner of seals. They slept on the strand during the day, but as soon as dusk descended on the land they woke up, made their frightful voices heard, which had some analogy with the sound of a large organ pipe, and threw themselves into the water in order to attack their prey or surprise it in its sleep.

The shore of the sea was still populated by three species of geosaurs, one of which was gigantic in size. They had a considerable analogy with crocodiles, but their movements were much more agile and their running more rapid, which rendered them very dangerous to animals weaker than them. There was also a species of mastodonsaur, which differed entirely from other lizards by virtue of its teeth bristling with little protuberances, which gave it much milder mores, for it could only nourish itself on fruits, roots and leaves. By the manner in which the other monsters were giving chase to it, I saw that its species would not last long on the Earth, and it was also one of the first to disappear. In any case, that did not astonish me, for I had seen a thousand similar examples among humans; there as elsewhere, weakness and innocence almost inevitably fall prey to malevolence, if one is not careful to avoid its society.

I perceived to species of steneosaurs, which immediately set about giving chase to the mastodonsaur and track it in the grassland in order to devour it. Those animals had a great deal of analogy with the gavial, or Ganges crocodile but their heads were extremely narrow toward the temporal region and their eyes, of enormous grandeur, placed not on top of the head but at the sides, gave them a very strange physiognomy.

Another monster, a teleosaur twenty feet long, had a physiognomy even more extraordinary. Imagine a crocodile with a wolf's head, with the difference that it is covered with scales, like the rest of the body, instead of fur. Finally, we also encountered macrospondyles, pleurosaurs, lacerta, leptorhynchi, streptospondyles, racheosaurs, aleodons, ganthausaurs, salamandroids and metriorhynchi, whose physiognomies were as terrible to behold as their names are terrible to pronounce.[43]

Seven species of pterodactyls were flying overhead, suspending themselves from tree-branches from time to time by their hooked nails, doubtless to rest. One of the largest settled on the edge of the sea, and I could see then what purpose that long beak armed with pointed teeth served; it ran along the strand, hoping on its tail and hind feet in the manner of gerbils or kangaroos, and when it felt the damp sand flex beneath its feet it immediately plunged in its beak, its head and even a large part of its neck, never withdrew it without having seized a fish or a snail, whose shell it broke with its sharp teeth in order to pull out the mollusk and eat it.

During my first voyage I had familiarized myself with that innumerable host of lizards in order to not to be frightened of them any longer, and I remarked to the demon with a proud smile on the calm courage with which I was examining them—admittedly, from a respectful distance. He contented himself, for his own response, with grimacing at me in the fashion of an ironic smile, and at the same time he pointed at the summit of a hill that rose above us.

I looked, but could not see anything except a dense thicket of cycads, yews, ferns and horsetails, which extended like a superb blue-green curtain all the way to the valley in which we were sitting.

Suddenly, I saw the trees stir and bend over one after another in a long line that was drawing closer to us. I heard their branches snapping as if they were breaking effortfully, and I saw the summits of some of them bend over to touch the ground and then straighten again with the elasticity of a relax-

---

[43] I have reproduced the names in this list by Anglicizing those that appear in the original, although *rachéosaures* and *ganthausaures* are untraceable, and might be misrendered.

ing spring. The most enormous beam dragged through a stand of young trees would not have produced such an effect. I froze, gripped by astonishment, and I confess that my cheeks must have paled slightly when I saw that the line of movement was coming directly toward us, like a whirlwind breaking and overturning everything in its path.

The spectacle that offered itself then was not made to reassure me, for a frightful megalosaur emerged from the wood and advanced into the grassland where we were. It was at least sixty feet long, and the largest crocodile would only have been a pygmy by comparison; its legs, although short in proportion to its body, were five feet long, and its body was at least as thick, from which it follows that the tallest man would have had difficulty reaching its back with his hand by raising his arm and lifting himself up on tiptoe. Its jaws were armed with numerous strong and trenchant teeth. Its head bore more resemblance to that of a caiman than that of a lizard, but its entire body was covered with little scales and patches with brown and yellowish green.

The monstrous animal passed us by and went to the end of the valley to throw itself into the sea, from which it had emerged. We saw it seize a crocodile as it went and crush it voraciously between its frightful jaws without slowly its pace even momentarily.

I was not exactly afraid, but I was quite glad to quit a shore populated by such horrible beings. My genius, who perceived that, said: "My dear friend, we're going to quit this place and resume our first voyage where we left it—which is to say, in the sixth period; but as you only know, of that period, the animals that populate the Paris basin, this time, to show you the others, we're going to go all over the globe, and I'll transport you, minute by minute, from Vienna to Peking, from Peking to Saint Petersburg, from Saint Petersburg to Port Jackson, from Port Jackson to Algiers, from Algiers to Lima, from Lima to Constantinople, etc., etc., etc. and the surrounding areas.

We arrived at our first station before he had finished speaking. To recover from the emotion I had experienced, I sat down on a bed of moss are looked around at the charming landscape that extended around me. It was intercut by hills, on the slopes of which a few trees of the cycad family still grew, but they were lost in forests of pines, firs, thuyas, yews and other conifers. Grasslands extended in the plain in beautiful sheets of verdure, and here and there, lakes and pools reflected the azure of the skies.

"What!" I cried. "Yet more reptiles?"

"They're the children of marshes," my guide replied, "and while the great continents haven't yet entirely dried out and come under cultivation, they'll enjoy a major role in animality; but don't worry, it's the last time that I shall show any of them to you, for there are no longer any more than two species that will be lost, and which will only exist as fossil bones when you publish your voyage."

"Let them be lost, then, and thank God it won't take long, for they're waiting for my manuscript at the printer's."

"Look in that freshwater pool, at that iguanodon, swimming gracefully, a sort of lizard fifty-five feet long at the most. Its body is covered in a scaly robe decorated with bright colors; its eyes are ken, but mild, and its mores are entirely innocent, for it limits itself to grazing aquatic weeds and herbs on the shore, which are its sole nourishment. Don't have the slightest fear, therefore, for if by hazard it came to swallow you, it would be entirely without malevolent intention and purely by inadvertence. I don't know what analogy might exist between a government and an iguanodon, but I can't see one without the idea of a good prince occurring to me.

"There's a mosasaur, presenting itself for the first and last time, for the existence of the species will be brief; its appearance on the Earth will scarcely last forty of fifty thousand years.[44] It's twenty-five feet long and its jaws are three and a

---

[44] A specimen of a mosasaur acquired by Faujas de Saint-Fond in 1798 was shown to Cuvier in 1808, and it was one of the

half, which is very modest for the epoch. Its tail, ten feet long at the most, and consequently shorter than a crocodile's, is very thick and very strong, and forms a powerful oar for steering it through the waves; otherwise, it's more like a lizard than a crocodile, which it only resembles in a few partial features."

"Let's go elsewhere," I said, impatiently—and I found myself on the edge of a magnificent lake, in an immense savannah, dotted here and there by clumps of date-palms, coconut-palms and various other picturesque trees. In front of me, a large number of small islets covered in cheerful vegetation interrupted the monotony of the lake, and several shore-dwelling birds seemed to have established their domicile there, for their shrill flocks were wandering along the strand while the females sat on their eggs in the reeds, on the sand, in the brushwood and even in holes in the rocks. I recognized sandpipers, woodcocks, the ibises of which the Egyptians made gods, and cormorants. Buzzards and sea-eagles were soaring in the sky; owls were hiding in clefts in the rocks, and while walking through the grass I saw several quail no larger than sparrows take off, which were the first gallinaceous birds that had appeared on Earth.

In the marshes formed by the arms of the lake between the islets I recognized paleotheria, which I had already seen during my first voyage, but the number of species had increased by two, to wit, the Orléans paleotherium and the Issel paleotherium. Other pachyderm mammals were strolling tranquilly among them, and also recognized, having seen them

---

key examples in persuading him that some animal species had become extinct, but in thinking that it belonged to the modern period he was grossly in error; we now know that it dates from the Creaceous. He had made the same mistake with Iguanodon after samples were shown to him in 1825. It was *Megalosaurus*, *Iguanodon* and *Mosasaurus* that provided the initial grouping for Richard Owen's designation of the *Dinosauria* in 1842.

before, that they were anoplotheria. I saw a new species with a more rounded head, named *Anoplotherium laticurvatum*.

In a little valley covered by aromatic herbs, a *Xiphodon gracilis*—which owed its name to its sharply pointed teeth—was grazing; the gracious animal had the light and elegant form of a gazelle, and its height did not surpass two feet. Its long ears, which titled forwards when it raised its head at the slightest sound, announced that it was timid and fearful, like all animals to which nature has given lightness and agility for their only defense.

A host of other pachyderms of large stature showed themselves, either grazing in the grassland or reposing in the shade of coconut palms. In order not to fill an entire volume with descriptions, I shall limit myself to citing the principal genera and species that struck me most by their singularity.

The lophiodons resembled the palaeotheria, but their inferior molar teeth were bristling with more or less oblique transversal ridges; there were twelve species differing principally in their size. The largest, the giant lophiodon, attained exactly six feet in height and surpassed the stature of the largest rhinoceros; the smallest, the pygmy lophiodon, was no larger than a rabbit.

I heard a grunting in the waters of the lake similar to that of a pig, and I saw an animal swimming, not gracefully but with force and facility; it had the form of a peccary but it was larger, and its habits were those of a hippopotamus, so it had been give the name of choeropotamus.

Several anthracotheria were also swimming in the waters of the lake, and six species were easily recognizable, the largest of which had the stature of a donkey and the smallest that of an otter. They appeared to me to be forming the natural intermediary between the anopolotheria and the choeropotamus.

The animal that surprised me most, however, because of its small size, compared to the pachyderms alive in 1837, was the adapis, whose size did not surpass that of a hedgehog; save for the horn, it resembled a miniature rhinoceros.

We quit the savannah, and after having traveled two or three leagues in haste we rested in the shade of a forest of birches with white and papery bark and pendant green foliage. There we encountered a herd of mastodons. I recognized the three species that I had seen during my first voyage, but I saw three new ones, two of which lived on the present banks of the Irrawaddy in the Burmese Empire and the other in America, France and Switzerland.

All the species of pachyderms that I have just cited, and even the genera to which they belonged, are entirely extinct and have nothing analogous in living nature; they are for us, new inhabitants of the Earth, fantastic beings that have revealed themselves to us by means of a few fragments scattered in the bosom of the rocks; they are phantoms that the magical voice of science has evoked from the depths of the tomb, and forced to make an appearance on the Earth or a second time, with a body devoid of matter and an ideal existence.

As for the pachyderms that are to follow, it is not the same; their descendants still exist among us, except that the centuries that have accumulated since their creation have modified their organization so much that we are forced to make particular species of them today, more or less distant from their extinct types.

I saw, therefore, two species of elephant, three of hippopotamus, rhinoceros and tapirs and two wild pigs that different very little from the living animals of the same genera. The three species of tapirs, especially, surprised me considerably; one was very similar to the American species; it was the size of a donkey, with a brown, almost bare hide; it had a tail of mediocre length, short legs, an arched body like that of a pig and a fleshy neck forming a kind of crest on the nape.

I saw several young tapirs, which wore white livery, like fawns; all of them had large heads and noses prolonged in a short fleshy trunk. They are sad, gentle and timid animals, fleeing all combat and only going abroad at night; they only eat plants and aquatic roots, so they rarely stray far from marshes, the edges of rivers and lakes, into which they plunge at the first sign of danger. If they are pursued they swim for a long distance under water without showing themselves at the surface, and even have the intelligence to remain there for a long time, entirely submerged except for the tip of their little trunk, through which they breathe, and which they conceal under the leaves of a floating plant; they escape the sight of their enemies by that means.

The tapir is now known to the inhabitants of South America by the names of anta and Manipuri, and hunting them is very easy; it is only done at night, and the moment is chosen when the animals, which live in numerous herds, are about to return to the grottoes or dens that serve as retreats during the day. The hunters each carry a flaming torch, whose light they take great care to hide. When the tapirs think they are going into their accustomed dwelling, the hunters suddenly show themselves simultaneously, at an agreed signal, uttering loudly cries and waving their torches at the frightened animals, which panic, knocking one another over and getting in one another's way. It is easy then to kill them with rifle shots or even spear-thrusts. But in countries where the population is numerous, the tapirs have become wary, and in order to capture them it is necessary to dig pitfall traps, into which they fall easily; they can be killed therein without any danger, for the animals never try to defend themselves.

We also perceived two species of horses, which were grazing in the grassland and appeared to live on very good terms with gigantic oxen and sixteen species of deer, some of which surpassed our largest horses in size.

What astonished me greatly, however, when my genius had transported me to the place occupied today in the southern Himalayan mountains of India, two miles from Rampurand six from Pinjore, was to see a camel with two humps, closely re-sembling the species alive today, with the difference that the animal did not have the bloody calluses on its knees that cam-els have even in their mother's womb, which is only a stigma imposed by long domesticity.

The genius transported me to other countries where the pachyderms and ruminants that I had seen so numerously thus far had become very rare. I had noticed that, thanks to the absence of humans, they formed a population almost as large as the land could nourish, and that all the species lived pell-mell without showing the slightest fear or suspicion. Here, it was no longer the same; the small number of grazing animals that I perceived had acquired an anxious and fearful attitude, and they fled as fast as their legs could carry them from the slightest sound they heard. I asked the genius for an explanation of those circumstances.

"We're reaching the end of the third epoch, and carnivorous animals have been created. They have all the power of new and energetic matter; they also have a size and a strength of which nothing you have seen in the living world can give you an idea."

At that moment a mastodon passed close to us, under rocks covered in brushwood.

Here's one species, at least, I said to myself, *that has nothing to fear, for its enormous mass alone protects it from the attacks of carnivores.*

I was mistaken, and did not take long to perceive it. Suddenly, a cat hiding in the thicket launched itself from ambush and with a prodigious bound of at least fifty paces came to fall on the back of the unfortunate mastodon—which was, however, not knocked over by the terrible impact. It uttered a terrible roar, and began a brief but frightful struggle with its horrible antagonist.

The cat was clinging on to its neck, and while it sank its claws into the breast it tried to open the cranium with its jaws. In vain, the mastodon struggled furiously, striking its enemy with its trunk; it ran furiously through the woods, knocking down trees that it found in its path; it rolled on the ground, but the cat did not let go. Finally, I heard a kind of crack similar to that of a breaking beam, and the mastodon fell dead on the moss; the cat had just broken the skull and plunged its long and prickly tongue into the brain.

The battle over, I could consider the victor at my ease. It really was a cat, for I could not see any difference from those living in the gutters of Paris, except that it was nearly six feet tall and twelve feet long, not including the tail, which was a further ten. Its body had almost the girth of the largest ox, but it was much longer. When the animal opened its enormous maw it revealed sharp teeth six inches long, and a bloody tongue bristling all over its surface with thorns similar to those of a rose-bush, with their points turned toward the throat. Its paw would have covered the largest plate, and each of its digits was armed with a hooked and needle-sharp retractile claw, as trenchant as a razor on the underside, seven or eight inches long.

Save for the terror inspired by its grim gaze, it was a very handsome animal with a fine and lustrous skin, with reddish gray fur pleasantly patched with alternative brown and white stripes. My genius told me that it was the giant cat, *Felis giganteus*. He added that the terrible family was fairly numerous in species, and showed them to me one after another.

"Here," he said, "is the medium-sized cat, *Felis media*. It greatly resembles the previous one, but is slightly smaller, its size not surpassing that of an ox. This one is the ancient cat, *Felis antiqua*; its hardy differs at all from the royal tiger, of which it has the size and the stripes. Like the previous two, it attacks mastodons, but as its strength does not correspond to its courage, it sometimes comes of worse in the struggle, so it preys more commonly on cattle, horses, anoplotheria and palaeotheria. It's the type of the Bengal tiger the most terrible of the carnivores living on the Earth today.

"Here, lying in wait for a wild boar in the reeds of that muddy pool, is the Auvergne cat, *Felis arvenensis*, almost as large as the tiger, having all the ferocity without the courage or the strength. It's the type of the jaguar, or American tiger, an animal whose mores are little known in Europe.

"In this bush is a cat, *Felis pardinensis*, whose descendants, submissive to the influences of the various climates in which they will live, will give birth to the American cougar or puma. That animal has a slightly larger statue than the jaguar, but it's slimmer and lighter, and its longer legs give it more agility for climbing trees. Its russet hide, with little patches of darker brown, but which scarcely distinguish it, often causes it to be confused by voyagers with the lion, although it has nothing in common with it except the family to which it belongs. Although weaker and more cowardly than the jaguar, it's as ferocious and perhaps as cruel. It attacks its prey furiously, devours it without butchering it, and becomes idle and retiring as soon as it is sated.

"It rarely attacks humans, unless driven to desperation by hunger and finds one asleep, but if it's hunted and wounded it enters into fury and becomes very dangerous. It likes the shade of forests and hides in the thickest undergrowth, or even in a bushy tree, from which it launches itself unexpectedly at animals that pass within range. By night it emerges from its retreat and wanders around habitations trying to catch dogs, sheep, pigs and other animals of inferior size. Captured young and brought up in domesticity it's susceptible of being tamed and they're sometimes seen following their master and allowing themselves to be beaten like a dog.

"Those forests you see toward the west are populated by *Felis megantereon*, with a bright tawny coat with little black spots, simple and evenly distributed. It's the size of a panther but taller because it has longer legs. That cat, or an analogous species, the cheetah, is trained in India to hunt gazelles and other animals, and seems susceptible to a degree of attachment to its master.[45]

"In the same woods there are also two kinds of cats that will form the types of the European and Canadian lynx. The first that presents itself to you, *Felis issiodorensis*, with pale gray skin spotted with pale brown, will become the Canadian lynx, and the second, *Felis breviostris*, will furnish the common lynx of Europe. The latter is a tawny russet, often with

[45] The Asiatic cheetah is now extinct in India, but it was used in hunting there in the days of the Raj.

black spots; it has a very short tail, which is unusual in the family to which it belongs.

"The lynx is still reputed among uneducated people to have eyesight so piercing as to be able to see through walls, but that is a gross error; it's true, however, that it has bright eyes and a cheerful attitude. It's the size of a fox, but it doesn't run like one; it walks and pounces like a cat, lives by hunting, and pursues its prey all the way to the treetops; wildcats, martens, ermines and squirrels cannot escape it; it also seizes birds; it lies in wait for the fawns of red deer and roe deer, and passing hares, leaps upon them, seized them by the throat, and when it has mastered its victim it sucks its blood and opens its skull in order to eat the brain, after which it abandons it to search for another.

"On that palm tree is another cat, the smallest of the entire family, in which you will easily recognize the type of the domestic cat; it's *Felis minuta*, the geologists' small cat."

We continued our route and entered into the forest, in the hope of encountering a few other animals. In fact, as we were traversing a heath we pursued an opossum, of the family of marsupials or pouched mammals. Thus far we had only noticed giants, so to speak, and I was glad to be able to make further observations of a pygmy, in comparison with everything else we had seen, for it was scarcely the size of a mouse. I recognized it as a *Marmosa*; it was a tawny gray, and a brown stripe designed to either side of its eye slightly augmented the vivacity of its gaze, ordinarily dull and sleepy; its tail, partly bare, wound around the branches of the trees that it climbed, rather slowly; a widely-split mouth, garnished with fifty teeth, and large naked ears, gave it an original but unattractive physiognomy; it gave off a fetid odor, and the genius told me that, like all opossums, it was a nocturnal animal, nesting in trees and nourishing itself on insects and birds that it surprised in their sleep.

A strong odor of musk rose to my nose and warned me of the approach of another animal; it was a genet, but much stouter than the animal presently living. I admired its long, light figure, and its cheerful and cunning physiognomy; its gray coat was pleasantly patched with black, and its tail was ringed with the same colors.

A moment later, a hyena emerged from a thicket and threw itself on the rotting remains of a paleotherium that had probably been killed by a tiger or a jaguar, for its skull was fractured and the brain was missing.

Finally, I also saw two species of dogs, or *Canis*, one of which perfectly resembled a wolf and the other a fox; another hyena; and two bears of species other than the one we had previously seen.

On the shores of a small lake an otter was fishing for fish that were unknown to me, while large beavers transported materials for constructing their habitations, and water voles wandered on the strand; squirrels and dormice leapt from branch to branch in the trees of the forest, and a hare ran away from our feet. A host of birds made the woods resound with their variously melodious singing, but it was impossible for me to recognize the species; they nourished themselves on seeds, berries and insects, and among living birds of prey I only recognized owls, buzzards and sea eagles, which I had seen previously.

Suddenly, we heard the barking of a dog in a nearby forest, loud enough to be heard for a league around. Almost immediately, a singular animal emerged from the dens wood. It was larger than a wolf, but its form was very different and was closer, in terms of mass and bulk, to that of a bear, and like a bear it was walking on the soles of its feet rather than its digits. It had a long, dangling tail, and a singularly elongated nose, as mobile as a little trunk, from which I concluded—which turned out to be correct—that it lived in earths, or at least holes in rocks and cavernous tree-trunks. Its muzzle was brown, its fur a tawny russet, and its tail as alternately patched with brown and yellow rings. Those colors reminded me of the russet coati that presently lives in the hottest forests of America, but its size was five or six times larger, which meant that I couldn't confuse the two.

It was evident that the animal was being pursued by the dog whose voice we had heard, for it was employing all its cunning intelligence against its enemy, putting it off the track by continually passing over its own footsteps, and traversing pools and steams by swimming—in brief, seeking any and all means to hide its trail. But the dog did not allow itself to be deceived, and shortly afterwards we saw it emerge from the wood and hurl itself in pursuit. I was astonished, before seeing it, that a carnivorous animal like the coati, with the strength, or at least the stature, of a bear, should decide to run away from a dog without trying to fight it, but as soon as I saw the latter my astonishment ceased, for at was at least as big as a cart-horse.

I had long read Buffon with a good deal of suspicion, because I had found a host of errors in his nomenclature and his synonymy. Seeing him mistaken, so to speak, every time that he had the objects he had to describe before his eyes, I naturally thought that I couldn't accord any confidence to his opinions when they were only founded on reasoning and analogy. In that I was badly mistaken because, in this case, I was confusing philosophy with nomenclature—which is to say, genius with method. Now I regard him as the greatest naturalist that we have had, and the dog that I saw confirmed my further in that idea.

In fact, it was neither a wolf, nor a jackal, not a fox, as modern naturalists say, but a veritable sheepdog, as Buffon has divined. What distinguished it, and still distinguishes it, from all digitigrade carnivores, which walk on their toes, is its raised tail, upwardly curved when it is devoid of passions. Its hair was long, slightly wavy without being frizzy or curly, shiny black in its entirety; its ears were large, vertical and pointed, and the tip was slightly inclined forwards; it had a keen, animated eye, but mild, expressing neither ferocity, like that of a wolf, nor hypocrisy like that of a fox, nor petulance and covetousness like that of a jackal. As it passed close to us it perceived us and paused momentarily to consider us with a kind of benevolent curiosity; then it resumed its pursuit of the coati and was soon ready to overtake and seize it.

A bushy oak, however—one of the first I had seen—was within reach of the coati, which launched itself toward its enormous trunk and started climbing, thinking thus to escape its hunter. The tree seemed as old as the world, for its trunk, more than ten feet in diameter, was entirely rotten at the core, and thus formed a kind of cavern that had only one opening placed more than thirty feet high. Having arrived at that opening the coati stopped and turned tranquilly toward its disappointed antagonist. The dog, after having made three or four prodigious but futile leaps, sat down at the foot of the tree and contented itself with gazing, while barking, at the prey that had escaped it.

Its cries mingled with a kind of growling evidently coming from the trunk of the tree and announcing the ill humor of the individual whose habitation it presumably was. Then, suddenly, I perceived two red eyes, blazing with anger, shining in the depths of the dark hole, and almost at the same time, a large hair head appeared in the opening. It was a she-bear that was nursing her cubs in that vegetal lair.

It considered the scene that was unfolding outside for nearly five minutes, and it seemed to me that its prudence was making it employ that time in deliberating as to the manner in which it ought to act in the circumstances. Finally, it made its decision, emerged from its hole and set off in pursuit the coati, which fear of its new enemy had caused it climb almost to the summit of the tree. I was then able to consider it at my ease, and I saw that it was absolutely no different from the bears that still inhabit the solitary mountains of the Alps today, except that it was slightly larger.

I admired the prudence of the animal, which never lifted a paw to place it on a higher branch without having made sure two or three times that its other feet were clinging solidly to the bark. In spite of its slowness, I saw that it was an excellent climber, and I had no doubt that it would soon reach the coati, which was trembling in every limb.

As the bear got closer, the other climbed higher; it had soon reached the summit of the tree, however, and its position

111

then became critical; already the bear was no more than a few feet away. It could already feel the humidity of its breath on its fur, bristling with fear, when desperation caused it to make a final decision. Braving the danger of a fall from a height of a hundred feet, it ventured on to a small branch scarcely strong enough to support the weight of its body, and advanced, vacillating, almost to its extremity.

The bear was amazed on seeing it make that maneuver, and did not risk pursuing it any further, but, after having made quite sure of its own position, it put its heavy paw on the branch and started shaking it with all its might, as bears do in the Alps when, climbing a beech, they shake its branches to cause beech-nuts they cannot reach to fall.

The poor coati clung on as best it could with its nails, but it was impossible to maintain its equilibrium for long and it was tipped upside-down; nevertheless, it did not fall, and the dog, a spectator of the singular scene, expressed its impatience by redoubling its barking.

The bear shook more forcefully; the branch gave way and broke; the coati let go, fell heavily to the ground, and the dog, immediately hurling itself up it, killed it, seized it in the middle of its back, picked it up and carried it off into the wood to eat it.

The bear descended again, growling, with the same prudent precautions it had taken while climbing; then, when it saw the hunter decamping briskly toward the forest, carrying its booty, it went back into its hole and disappeared from our sight.

Sixth Epoch of the Sixth Period

"Do you remember," the genius said to me, "in what geological epoch you left the readers of the *Musée des Familles*?"

"Certainly: in the fifth epoch of the sixth period—which is to say, if I'm not mistaken, the very epoch in which we have arrived while traversing this forest."

112

"You're right, so prepare yourself to see how the Earth made arrangements to become absolutely similar to what it is today, in the living world.

"As you can see," the demon continued, "there's no longer any difference between the vegetation of this epoch and that of your time; the forests are composed of oaks, elms, birches, etc., etc., all similar to the ones you know; the grasslands are dotted with the same flowers and the willow, the alder and the poplar shade the streams whose limpid waters flow among the rocks.

"The anoplotheria and the paleotheria no longer exist, but they've been replaced by other animals, the majority of which still exist in your century, after having been subjected nevertheless to a few slight changes of form, such as, for example, the hippopotamus, the rhinoceros, the tapir, cattle, the horse, deer, antelopes, sheep, pigs and a host of others.

"There are also a few that will be lost, and they're the most singular, so let's direct our stroll in such a fashion as to encounter them. You've already seen the dinotherium, of which I make a mole until someone can prove to me that it's a whale; there's a second species of it, *Dinotherium bavaricum*, somewhat smaller than the one you know; I won't show it to you, nor five or six species of elephants, including the mammoth.

"Here's one that is appearing for the first time to your eyes: it's Fischer's elasmotherium; the animal has features reminiscent of three very different species: the rhinoceros, whose stature it has, the horse and the elephant. It has mild mores and only nourishes itself on grass.

"Also grazing alongside that one is the giant sivatherium, which, in its conformation, appears to be intermediate between ruminants and pachyderms; as you can see, its stature surpasses that of the rhinoceros, and the size of its head approaches that of an elephant, but what distinguishes it from all the pachyderms, except the giraffe, are its two horns, covered with skin and hair, placed between its eyes. Its skull is enormously developed at the rear; and its nose, raised far above the face and advanced in an arch over the external nostrils, gives is a physiognomy more stupid than malevolent. Its bones are found in the Sivalik Mountains, extending from the Himalayas, and it's probably for that reason that it was named after the Hindu god Siva.

"Many of the animals of your time are already multiplying prodigiously in the forests. Among the small carnivores there are polecats, weasels, bats, shrews, moles, badgers and gluttons; among the large there are dogs, wolves, foxes, bars, tigers, lions and jaguars.

"Among the birds that populate the woods are vultures, sparrows, blackbirds, thrushes, crows, pigeons and woodcocks; ducks and gulls are floating on the rivers; pheasants, grouse and quail are nesting in the plain, and swallows are attaching their nests to the rocks of shores.

"The landscape that is opening up ahead of you already has the same physiognomy that it will have in your time; there are plains mingled with woodlands, hills covered with forests, and, in the distance, chains of mountains of which rain and frost have already eroded the summits in such a way as to draw away the alluvial deposits that covered them and lay bare the rocks that form, so to speak, their interior skeleton. Once, lakes and subterranean currents undermined their enormous base, but upheavals or earthquakes, dislocating their mass, have let out the waters contained in their bosom. Those waters have precipitated into the valleys through those accidental issues, and their dark and dried beds have formed grottoes and caverns that serve as lairs for monstrous reptiles, dinotheria, tigers, bears and other carnivores.

"Nothing is better calculated to inspire dread than exploring those vast subterranean solitudes, illuminated by the uncertain light of torches, in which one cannot help thinking about the possibility of remaining there, buried by some unexpected landslide, or getting lost there if some accident extinguishes the torch to which you have entrusted your life. Advancing through the darkness and silence under immense vaults, the least superstitious mind is truck by panic; one fears encountering in some remote corner of those somber labyrinths one of those fantastic and terrible beings that once lived, and might have escaped the destruction of time.

"Soon, however, a dazzling sight causes vain terrors to be forgotten; the light of torches is reflected in a thousand ways from walls hung with stalactites as brilliant as diamonds; garlands festoons and elegant columns of alabaster are suspended from the damp vaults where porticoes and a thousand other more or less bizarre figures are formed. Over there is a stalagmite imitating a gladiator getting ready for combat; here an old woman crouching down; further away a brooding chicken, a vase, a font, etc., etc."

"I've heard much talk of those marvels," I replied, "and I'd be curious to see them."

"Nothing is easier. Follow me into the forest and, at the foot of that mountain raising its bald head above the clouds, I'll satisfy your curiosity for the last time."

We plunged into the wood in order to reach the foot of the mountain and I saw a further host of animals resting peacefully in the shade of the dense foliage; but, as almost all of them were familiar, I paid little attention to them.

"I was walking with my head down, in scholarly meditation, when a wild apple, hurled with force, struck me on the shoulder and reawakened my torpid attention. Surprised by that unexpected assault, I was looking around, without being able to discover where it had come from, when a second, launched in the same manner, came whistling past my ear, and led me to look up into a nearby tree.

"It's an ape!" I exclaimed. "That's an ape!"

"You're not mistaken."

"We're probably in Java or the Moluccas, for, if my memory serves me right, that species is only found there."

"Yes, in modern times, but in the geological epoch we're in, it lived in France, and it's in Provence that the naturalist Lartet found its fossil bones in 1837.[46]

"The gibbon, or wouwou," the demon added, "has a tranquil nature and rather mild mores, and it prefers fruits to any other nourishment. It always holds itself upright, even when it walks on all fours, because its arms are as long as its body and legs, which gives it a very bizarre appearance. It amuses itself in the reeds and climbs the tallest bamboo stems, swaying with its long arms in the manner of trapeze artists. It ordinarily attains four feet in height, lacks a tail and has slight calluses on its buttocks. Its face is flat and brown and the eyes are surrounded by a circle of gray hairs; it has canine teeth larger, proportionately, to those of a human; the ears are bare, black and rounded; the fur is wooly and soft, ash-gray in color. In sum, it would closely approximate human form if the excessive length of its arms did not render it deformed.

"Travelers recount that on the frontiers of China one sometimes encounters a frightful being named the féfé, which has human form, very long arms and a black hairy body, walking lightly and very rapidly. Woe betide the poor traveler who encounters one in the darkness of night! Like a sinister phantom, the féfé attaches itself to his footsteps, follows him silently; then, profiting from all its advantages, it seizes him from behind, enlaces him in its enormous arms, rags him into the depths of the rest and devours him pitilessly. If the féfé, cited

---

[46] This is a remarkably rapid reportage of Édouard Lartet's discovery of the first primate fossil found in Europe—actually in 1836, although it was only reported in 1837; he named it *Pliopithecus antiquuus*, and it was a crucial item of evidence in contradicting Cuvier's insistence on the fixity of species; a commission of enquiry was established by the Académie des Sciences, headed by Cuvier's former protégé and subsequent adversary Henri de Blainville, but Boitard obviously did not have to wait for its report before concluding that it was conclusive proof of transformism.

by Neuhof, is not an imaginary creature, it is perhaps only a gibbon whose story has been embroidered by credulity."[47]

After having observed the gibbon, which ceased to harass us as soon as it saw that we were not afraid of it, we continued to advance into the forest, and did not take long to find ourselves at the foot of the mountain, in a valley where a limpid stream ran.

I perceived, slipping through the foliage, a very extraordinary creature that I mistook at first for a man six feet tall, but I soon realized my error, for it had a body covered with fur and feet furnished with long digits like a hand. It was a chimpanzee, another species of orang, of which I have already given an account and a description in the *Musée des Familles* in 1836.

I followed it with my eyes and saw it enter a hut of foliage rather artistically constructed. Its female was sitting at the entrance of that picturesque habitation, tenderly occupied in caressing and nursing its infant.

"A few fossil bones of that animal will be found," the demon told me, "And people will not fail to mistake them for those of a human, because the geologist who will discover them will not have a skeleton of a chimpanzee with which to compare them rigorously. But if the work of the Englishman Tyson should ever fall into his hands he will be able to make that comparison and recognize his error. He will see that the chimpanzee had a femur proportionately thinner and longer than a human, a more curved vertebral column, smaller vertebrae with different apophyses, a narrower skull with a more receding brow, etc."

After having crossed the steam on the edge of which we found ourselves, we climbed the hill with a great deal of difficulty, for we were walking through a dense thicket.

"Where are we?" I asked.

---

[47] Buffon and Cuvier both identified the legendary fefe, or féfé, as a gibbon

"In the environs of Souvignargues, in the département of the Gard," the genius told me. He pointed to a hole in the rock. "And here's a cavern."[48]

We approached the opening, but the grotto was so deep and dark that, to begin with, I could not distinguish anything inside it.

"Let's go in," said the genius.

I confess that I hesitated, because I could hear the howling of hyenas in the vicinity, and the growling of bears. Some distance away, a rhinoceros and an aurochs were engaging in a furious combat. I thought that the cavern must be the lair of those dangerous animals, and I saw that the earth near the opening had indeed been recently flattened and trodden down.

"Are you afraid?" the demon asked.

"I fear encountering here animals even more redoubtable than the coati, the dog and he bear whose battle caused me so much emotion a little while ago," I replied.

However, the demon darted a glance at my so energetically ironic that I was ashamed of my weakness, and I went into the grotto with a determined tread. We advanced fifty aces in darkness, which thickened increasingly, and my foot collided several times with soft objects that I could not make out, and which almost caused me to fall.

"Let's stop," I said to the demon, sitting down on a projection. "I can't go any further until my eyes, dazzled by the bright light from which we've emerged, have become accustomed to the gloom."

Gradually, my pupils dilated, and I was able to perceive, vaguely at first, the objects that surrounded us. A hyena, with its skull split as if someone had struck it with an ax, was extended at our feet, and a few morsels of bar flesh, half-devoured, were lying on the ground here and there, exhaling a very unpleasant odor. I noticed a few bones that had been

---

[48] Presumably the grotto of Bézal, where animal bones dating from what would now be called the Pleistocene Era had been found in 1829.

gnawed by powerful jaws, for the marks of the teeth that had attacked them were still perceptible; but what astonished me most was a kind of bowl made of clay dried in the sun and not fired, very crudely made, and half full of the still-fuming blood of a hyena. The genius pointed out that its edges still bore the bloody traces of the lips that had drunk the disgusting liquid it contained. Beside the bowl I saw a fragment of flint, shaped in the approximate from of a trenchant ax, wedged in the end of a split stick, and secured quite firmly with strips of bearskin. The instrument vaguely resembled a Canadian tomahawk.

As I began to distinguish objects more easily, I sought to penetrate the depths of the lair with my gaze. First I discovered a kind of black mass, which I thought I saw move, which attracted my attention. Then I distinguished a bear-skin which seemed to me to be hiding an object extended on a thick bed of moss, grass and dry leaves.

Placing his finger over his mouth, the genius gave me a sign to remain silent and approach with precaution, which I did. Then he lifted up the bear-skin and revealed to my eyes the most singular and most horrible of all the animals that I had seen thus far. There were three of them, two large and one small, which I recognized as the young of the horrible species.

The male was lying on his side, sleeping almost in the attitude of a dog—which is to say, with his body curved in a circle. He might have had the stature of a medium-sized bear, and his entire body was similarly covered in smooth, brown, rather sparse hair. His forepaws terminated in a large flat lump of flesh divided into five fingers, much like the hand of an ape, but the fingers were thicker and more robust, and the palm of the hand was defended by a kind of sole of thick and callused leather. His body had almost the same form as that of a chimpanzee, but without the grace and lightness, for it was stout, thickset and sturdily muscled. In certain places it was devoid of hair, but it was difficult for me to describe the color of his skin, for it was covered with so much dirt and ordure that I could scarcely judge that it might be a dark coppery brown.

The animal's head was the most horrible thing of all. A long mane covered the cranium entirely and almost all the face, in such a way that one could only see, through that tangled wooly forest two enormous lips that terminated in an advanced and very large muzzle, which were themselves surrounded by a second reddish wooly mane, full of ordure, blood and little shreds of dried flesh. A little above those gross brownish-red lips, two oval holes appeared, which I recognized as nostrils, although they were not surmounted by any protuberance similar to a nose. An inch and a half above those holes, on either side of the face, two thick arches of stiff black hair framed two eyes that must, it appeared to me, although they were closed by sleep, be able to launch a ferocious glare. The rest of the face was covered by the hairs forming the mane.

I had the courage to bend down toward that extraordinary being in order to look at him more closely, but at that moment he clicked his teeth, grinding them against one another in such a frightful manner that I raised myself up again with a start. His sleep was not interrupted, however; mentally, I thanked Heaven for that.

The female was lying in almost the same attitude as the male, but a little hairless monster was hanging by all four paws on to her belly. Its skin was russet and livid, repulsively dirty, and I recognized it for her young. She only differed from her male by the paler brown of her mane, which only covered the cranium and not the face.

Those disgusting animals exhaled an odor so fetid, the result of their dirtiness, that I held my nose and asked the genius in a low voice what those extraordinary beasts could be.

At that question, the devil uttered a long burst of laughter, which woke them up. The female ran away on all fours, carrying her little one away, which clung on to her belly more forcefully; but the male uttered a kind of guttural and ferocious growl, darted a glittering glance at me, raised himself up on his hind legs, seized the flint tomahawk with his forepaws and, with a furious bound, launched himself toward me, raising the terrible weapon over my head.

At that moment I uttered a cry of terror, for I had just recognized the species of the monster...it was human.

The race of Cain had already penetrated into Gaul: a hideous and terrible race, of which the type can still be found in certain parts of New Holland.

JOURNEY TO THE SUN

Chapter I
An Old Friend

I had gone to my window in order to listen to the melancholy song of a nightingale that had built its nest in a neighboring garden. The night was superb and the vault of heaven was sparkling with a thousand twinkling fires. With both elbows on my window-sill and my chin in my hands, I was listening to the nightingale...but a harmony far more sublime gradually took possession of my soul; I fell into the delightful meditation with which you will be familiar, if you have ever traveled on a beautiful starry night. I ceased to hear the melodious bird that alone troubled the silence of my solitude, and my mind launched itself forth into the immensity of the skies. Sometimes, like Micromégas, I passed from one planet to another with a single stride; sometimes, like the romantic genii, I sat down on the radiant head of a comet, and even if I could not guide the stars like the sorcerer Melmoth, at least I could admire their celestial harmony.

Soon, my reverie became so profound that my soul, abandoning the Earth entirely, believed that it had found a mysterious guide who led it through the labyrinth of the infinite and explained to it the hundred thousand marvels that the heavens contained. That guide was the lame devil who had already shown me "Paris Before Humankind." What I heard him say—or, if you wish, what I thought I heard him say—was sometimes so extraordinary and bizarre that I would not dare repeat it as coming from me. Thus, in order to tell you what I have seen, it is absolutely necessary that I leave him the role for which he had taken responsibility, and, whether you take it as a fiction invented expressly to put me at ease, or you regard it as the brainchild of a slightly delirious imagination, it is necessary that you accept it, as I accepted it myself. In any case, although I guarantee the truth of everything that emerges from my mouth, it would be stretching a point to make the same engagement for what emerges from his, for everyone knows that demons, like all children of the imagination, are naturally inclined to utopias.

This is how our voyage commenced.

"What a marvelous spectacle!" I exclaimed. "How admirably that immense blue vault limits the horizon of our vast universe.

"Hee hee hee!" he said, laughing sardonically. "It seems that you've scarcely profited from the little lessons in logic that I've occasionally given you, for you've only made one remark to me and you've already uttered five stupidities. Firstly, what you see isn't a vault, but the immensity; secondly, that immensity isn't blue, but black, like everything that has no color, and it wouldn't appear like that to you if it weren't constantly inundated by the light of the sun; thirdly, your vault doesn't limit anything at all because space, like time, is infinite and boundless; fourthly, the horizon is on the earth, not in the sky, where there is none; and finally, the universe, comprising the imperceptible Earth that you inhabit, its little planets and its rather paltry sun is just a dot in infinity—less than a grain of sand in the ocean. Your statement is poetic, or at least you think so, but it's by arranging sonorous words like that, whose meaning is incomprehensible, or, what's worse, false, that one puts spokes in the wheel of science."

"I'll remember the lesson. As for the vault, I admit that if I make use of that expression, it's purely figurative, for I know perfectly well that the..."

"Say the segment of the sky; above all, be didactic."

"All right. I know very well that the firmament isn't a sold arch and that the stars aren't lanterns nailed to it; I know that space is infinite, but Monseigneur, to put your lesson to use immediately, I'll ask you what infinity is."

"Imagine that you have a bow in your hand, and that you shoot an arrow into the air, that that arrow has the ability to travel through space in a straight line without any deviation, and that it has been launched with sufficient force to travel a million leagues a minute."

"Well?"

"Well, after a billion years, that arrow would doubtless have covered a lot of ground, but it wouldn't be any closer to its target than when it left your bow, because infinity is boundless."

"I don't understand, even though I'm making my head ache following your arrow through space."

"Imitate the geometers: calculate; put figures one after another and penetrate yourself, like the stupid, with the idea that the figures prove something. And then, when you have a total formed by a row of numbers as long as the road from Paris to Rome, that total will still be nothing by comparison with the number of leagues your arrow will still have to travel in order to have spanned a tiny part of infinity."[49]

"Pardon me, Monseigneur, but I don't understand."

"I can well believe it, as I'm speaking in academic terms. Well, my dear chap, infinity is…nothing at all; now rack your

---

[49] Author's note: "A reasonable person never allows himself to be seduced by calculations. In fact, what results from the efforts of the greatest mathematicians? Often, definite conclusions derived from uncertain suppositions. For example, if one compares the calculations that prove the movement of the Earth with calculations that determine its shape, one finds on the one hand a complete evidence, which assumes nothing, and on the other, an evidence that leaves a cloud behind in which one can suppose anything one likes, because light never penetrates it. But the public believes blindly that everything is demonstrated because it is prejudiced, with good reason, in favor of the genius of inventors."

brains to imagine what that nothing is, and where its beginning and end can be found."

"Now I understand. Infinite space, eternal time, etc., etc., are all just abstractions to which we've fitted a name, a word, and it's that word that we utter in error, which makes us mistake the nothing for something, because we have the habit of representing things by words.

"I don't understand, either, why you tell me that the space of the heavens is black when I can see that it's blue; my eyes certainly aren't deceiving me: I see the sky blue, and I assume that the ether that fills space is that color.

"As for your ether, it's a stupidity that I advise you to renounce, for nothing proves that a particular fluid exists that fills space; its existence, if it has one, doesn't explain anything, not even the theory of waves of light, and it's very difficult to explain in itself—but what is very easy to demonstrate is that the ether isn't blue."[50]

---

[50] Author's note: "Encke, to explain how the long axis of the ellipse described by comets and their medium distance diminish progressively, found nothing better than to suppose a ether filling the regions through which those singular heavenly bodies travel, whose resistance, diminishing their velocity, also diminishes their centrifugal force and gives the sun more purchase on them to attract them. We shall show later that the etheric invention in question is at least useless, although it has been adopted without examination by the majority of astronomers."

As Boitard admits, he was going against the prevailing scientific consensus in refusing to believe that Johann Encke's observations of variations in the orbit of the comet named after him, whose return in 1822 he predicted in 1818, on the basis of his calculations, proved the existence of an "ether" capable of exerting friction upon it. On the other hand, his assertion that there is no void in space, on the grounds that light travels through it, look suspiciously like a endorsement of the notion

"You believe, then, in the void of space? It's a great question, which has agitated our astronomers a great deal."

"If there's a void in space it's at a distance so remote that the eye of an astronomer, armed with the most powerful telescope, has never been able to fathom it. The sky is full of light everywhere, at least everywhere that humans know; there is, therefore, no void, for light has body, and even a decomposable body. If a corner exists in space so distant from a sun that the sun's rays can't reach it, that corner is an intense and opaque black, a thousand times darker than the most profound terrestrial night, for light is composed of colors, and black in the absence of all the colors.

"If the sky appears to you to be blue, it's because you see it through a blue fluid, which tints with its color the objects that one sees through it, in the same way that green spectacle-lenses make objects appear green. That fluid is atmospheric air, and you can't doubt it when you look at a distant horizon. The mountain nearest to you appears green because there isn't enough air interposed between it and you for it to be tinted blue; one that is further away will appear bluish green, while the most distant of all, the one that limits your horizon, can seem entirely blue if it's far enough away for there to be a sufficient quantity of air between it and you."

"It would seem, according to what you say, that space is full of blue air, and it's doubtless the air in question that you'll make responsible for supporting the heavenly bodies to prevent them from falling. Make it spin and draw the heavenly bodies in its vortices, and there's Descartes resuscitated!"

"What you say there, my dear, is devoid of common sense, for I was only talking about the layer of atmospheric air. As for the heavenly bodies, why would they fall, when nothing in nature falls—not even the apple that, detaching itself from its tree, demonstrated to Newton the principle of attraction that other astronomers had previously suspected?"

of a "luminiferous ether," with which many contemporary scientists identified Encke's.

"What, then, is the attraction with which our scientists so easily construct the universe?"

"It's something very simple: it's a property of matter, like extent, impenetrability, etc. All bodies are mutually attracted to one another; those that contain more matter—which is to say, the largest or the densest—naturally draw those that contain less; it's the law of the strongest or the richest. The sun, for example, attracts the Earth and all the other heavenly bodies, not just because it's larger than any of them, but larger than all of them put together. A body that seems to you to be falling is nothing but a body drawn toward another body that is heavier than itself. You humans can that falling; now, as words don't cause any difficulty when their meaning is fixed, I see no inconvenience in continuing to make use of that expression, but only to replace the words "being attracted." We can even say that the attracted objects are "heavy," and "have weight," because we now know that weight is nothing other than the effect of attraction.

"Every molecule of matter attracts other molecules of matter. A body composed of a hundred molecules will attract a body composed of ten molecules with ten times as much force as it's attracted, because the square of ten is a hundred; the body composed of ten molecules will fall on to the other because it has less strength, and the speed of its fall will similarly be proportional to the number of its molecules, taking distance into consideration—for bodies are attracted more energetically the closer together they are.[51]

"Will that attraction explain to me why falling bodies constantly tend toward the center of the Earth?"

---

[51] Author's note: "Newton concluded from very thorny calculations these three consequences, which are one of the principal bases of astronomy: firstly, the force that solicits the planets is directed toward the center of the sun; secondly, that force is in inverse proportion to the square of the distance from their center to the center of the sun; and thirdly, that it is proportional to their mass."

"If you think about it a little, you'll see that the center of a globe is always the part that presents to an object the most numerous pencil of attractive rays, because the line that traverses the center of the globe is the one whose path encounters the greatest number of attractive molecules."

"I understand all that very well, and only two objections remain for me to put to you. How can attraction be proven, and why, if the heavenly bodies attract one another, don't they fall on to one another?"

"I won't tell you that attraction is proven to all evidence by the exact solution of various astronomical problems, because you're not knowledgeable enough to understand me, but I can give you more material proofs. When a ship is sailing under full sail it travels, I'll suppose, at six feet per second; now, if it takes a lead pellet a second to fall from the top of the mast to the deck, it follows that, the vessel advancing six feet during that second, the mast will draw away during the fall and the pellet will land six feet away from the mast. Well, my dear, nothing of the sort; the pellet is attracted by the mast and drawn by it; it obeys its attractive power and comes to land exactly as the foot of the mast, deviating from the vertical line.

"When a vessel in port is motionless on its anchor, take a drop of water and let it fall from the ceiling of your cabin to the floor, It is certain that in falling it will follow a straight line directed toward the center of the earth. Then mark on the ceiling the point from which it departed and on the floor the point where it fell. The anchor is raised, the sails are deployed and the vessel sails with the greatest rapidity; repeat our experiment then and let further drops of water fall from the same point on the ceiling. You might think that they wouldn't fall on the same point of the floor, because the vessel advances by a foot during the fall of each drop—well, you'd be wrong, for the vessel has become a power of attraction to which the drops of water are obedient; they deviate from the vertical line to follow its progress and fall at exactly the same point on the floor as if the vessel were immobile."[52]

"That very good, but why don't the planets fall into the sun?"

"This is the reason. When a body spins rapidly, the molecules composing it tend to draw away from the center of the body by virtue of a physical force called 'centrifugal force' by astronomers. You can verify that fact by a thousand experiments all as easy as one another. For example, place on a pivot or an axle a wheel, a round table or simply a plate. Spread water, sand or anything else on the late and rotate it with some rapidity. You'll immediately see the water or sand move to the circumference of the circle formed by the table or the plate, and then be thrown outside the circle to a greater or lesser distance, dependent on the greater or lesser velocity of rotation. That's how the performers in our public squares can place a glass full of water on a barrel hoops that they cause to turn rapidly in a vertical plane without spilling a drop, even though the glass is upside-down momentarily during each rotation of the hoop. Instead of falling, the liquid leans constantly on the bottom of the glass in order to draw away from the center of rotation, according to the law of centrifugal force. In any case, in order not to understand me, it would be necessary never to have seen a stone launched by a sling.[53]

"The planets can't, therefore, fall into the sun, because, launched in straight lines in space and not experiencing any friction in their course, their force of projection cannot be

---

[52] The correct explanation for this phenomenon, and the previous one, has to do with the lateral velocity imparted to the drop or the pellet at the moment of its release, not the attractive force of the ship or the mast. Even lame devils make silly mistakes.

[53] But to contradict him, it only requires one to be aware that the impulsion in either case comes not from a "centrifugal force" but from a tangential momentum—which, contrary to what the next paragraph alleges, is not the same thing.

eroded. Attracted by the sun, they rotate around it, but, the force of attraction being combated, firstly by the force of projection and them by centrifugal force—which is probably the same thing—an equilibrium is established that nothing can break, and which will last eternally, like all the properties of matter."

"That's all well and good, but it seems to me that if we were placed elsewhere than on Earth, we'd see things differently, and perhaps then the entire scientific scaffolding that you're trying to establish would collapse."

"Well, my dear, you're stubborn, but I'll try to convince you. Let's go."

Chapter II
In the Air

The demon took me by the arm and I felt myself gliding through the air with more rapidity than one of the meteors that one sometimes sees leaving a bright trail in the sky during a warm summer night. Sometimes the demon increased or diminished the celerity of our progress, in accordance with the greater or lesser interest offered by the various objects that the pointed out to me during our voyage.

It seemed to me at first that I was swimming in a thick blue-tinted fluid, and that I was heading toward the surface with some effort, like a diver in haste to get out of the water in order to breathe. I sensed, as I set off, that I must be plunged into that fluid at a great depth, for the weight of its mass seemed enormous to me, and pressed terribly on all parts of my body. While traversing it I verified what I had imagined several times in the depths of the ocean—which is to away that I passed through several rapid currents whose layers were superimposed and very variable in thickness; some were directed northwards, others southwards, and, in sum, in all directions. I asked the demon if he had chosen the depths of the sea for a departure-point, and whether we would soon reach the surface.

"My dear pupil," he replied, "We departed from the window of your study; we're not traversing water but simply the air of the atmosphere. Except that, before we left, I stripped you of the sentiment of habitude that continuous contact with the air has caused you to develop. You're therefore judging the fluid we're traversing like someone who is making contact with it for the first time—which is to say, without the prejudices born of habitude.

"In any case, don't be astonished if the air seems so heavy, for on the ground you support a column of it sixteen or seventeen leagues high, the weight of which is equivalent to a thirty-two foot column of water or a twenty-seven inch column of mercury. What you've mistaken for submarine currents are nothing but winds blowing from various points of the horizon, which are passing over one another.

"Air is extremely elastic, so the inferior layers—which is to say, those nearest the ground—are more compressed. Its elasticity plays a considerable role in the phenomena of animal life, and it's to its composition of seventy-nine parts nitrogen and twenty-one parts oxygen that all beings owe their respiration. It has the property of decomposing and refracting light, so it's to the air that we also owe dusk and dawn, gentle transitions that allow us to pass without shock from day to night and darkness to light. In its entirety, it forms what we can the atmosphere, and as I said, that atmosphere is no less than sixteen or seventeen leagues thick; it forms an immense limitless ocean that envelops the totality of the globe; in addition to air it contains, especially in its lower layers, greater or lesser quantities of water, hydrogen, electrical fluid, carbon dioxide, etc. It's sometimes a veritable chaos disrupted by storms, thunder, wind, hail, rain and all other weather phenomena."

Scarcely had the demon stopped speaking than we arrived on the surface of the atmospheric ocean; then it appeared to me to form a blue sea so transparent that I could scarcely perceive the enormous waves of its light and turbulent surface. When I looked into its depths, I perceived the earth forming a mountainous bed of a deep lapis blue.

I raised my eyes to the heavens, but how astonished I was! There was no longer a bright vault with all its azure glare, but an endless space, a dull and somber gray. The blue color had entirely disappeared, and I began to distinguish very clearly an enormous black cone that was marching with an extraordinary rapidity from west to east. At that moment we emerged from it, because it was nothing but the shadow projected into space by the terrestrial globe, and daylight had arrived for us. But what daylight! It bore no resemblance to that of the Earth., and the light departing from the Sun appeared me to be a white more dazzling than snow, without any other

133

colored tint. I understood that that was because no other body was reflecting the luminous rays, and in consequence, they were not decomposed.

I could no longer see the Moon, and no planet appeared in proximity; even the Earth was so far away that it only masked a tiny fraction of the sky. It appeared to me with an aspect so singular that I would certainly not have recognized it without the genius, who assured me that it really was my birthplace.

Imagine a mass rotating about is axis with a velocity of more than three-hundred and sixty-five leagues an hour. By virtue of another movement that impelled it from east to west, its course was even more astonishing, for its entire mass was traveling at seven leagues a second—which is to say, seventy times as fast as a cannonball. I had always heard it said that the Earth was round, but I saw that it was not at all. Not only could I see that it was flattened at the two poles, but swollen toward the equator, which, from where I was, gave it the form of an ellipse whose two axes were very close to the center, or, if you prefer, that of a very compact oval whose two points were on the equator.

I had also read in some book or other that the inhabitants of the Moon must see the Earth as we see the Moon, but twelve times as large, and I was able to verify the accuracy of that opinion. But the books added that the oceans and other seas would appear as large dark patches, while the continents would form bluish white patches. In that they were badly mistaken, for the terrestrial globe showed me a positively contrary aspect. The continents stood our darkly against a silvery white background furnished by the waters that enveloped the globe in all parts, and which reflected the light in the fashion of a polished body. At any rate, the land was designed in the middle of the seas exactly as on the kinds of maps that astronomers call global maps, and every part of the world passed before my eyes in a short time, as in a magic lantern.

We were still advancing through space; that immensity troubled me and I was afraid of my isolation. Just as I was beginning to become desolate, however, I perceived a bright body describing a curve in the sky and coming directly toward us. At first I could not tell what it might be, because it seemed to be much further away than it actually was, and if it had been round I would certainly have taken it for a heavenly body, but its irregular form remained similar to a lump of rock. Finally, when it was very close to me, it ceased to shine, became a reddish black, and appeared to me no larger than it really was: it was an oval block three or four feet long and about eighteen or twenty inches thick at its greatest width.

"What is that?" I asked the genius.

"It's a moon," he replied.

"How do you mean, a moon?"

"Yes, a moon—or, if you prefer, one of the satellites of the Earth."

"What! A moon two feet in diameter?"

"Why not? Size is irrelevant."

"Bah! Leave off; we only know one Moon on Earth, and I'm not departing from that."

"If you only believe in one Moon, that's because there's only one large enough for you to be able to perceive it; the others, although many of them are very close to you, are unknown to you because they escape your eyes by virtue of their small size. Personally, I know more than a thousand that are no larger than your thumb. When they experience a perturbation that pushes them into your atmosphere, the friction of the air wears away the force of their projection and they fall to Earth. Then you open your eyes and mouth and cry miracle, and believe that you're seeing stones thrown at you from the Moon. Then, to give yourself scientific airs, you call them meteorites, aeroliths, asteroliths, etc."

"Ha ha! I've got it now; I know what it is."

"Let's see."

"For a very long time, it's been said that stones fall from the sky, but skeptics refused to believe in such a phenomenon—which was, in any case, easier to deny than to explain. However, the event recurred so often before the eyes of learned people worthy of faith that it was necessary to believe it. From then on, scientists didn't take long to confirm it by numerous observations rigorously made. The phenomenon usually occurs in calm weather, or, rather, independently of any atmospheric circumstance. An igneous meteor, one of those named a bolide or fireball, suddenly ploughs through the air, and then bursts with a whistle or detonation as it falls to earth, and nothing is found in its place but a mineral mass—in a word, an aerolith.

"Almost all these stones are composed of the same chemical elements; they contain a great deal of silicon, iron, magnesium, sulfur, nickel, manganese and chromium; one also finds therein, at least in those that have fallen at Alais in Provence, a certain quantity of carbon.[54] Probably, substances susceptible to vaporize by virtue of a violent action of fire also enter into their composition, but inevitably evaporate by virtue of the prodigious heat that the friction caused the stones to experience when they traverse the atmosphere."

"You will notice," said the demon, interrupting me, "that these aeroliths cannot be formed on Earth, because nickel and iron are found therein in a metallic state that is not found in any terrestrial mineral aggregate. Continue."

"I'm just coming to the manner in which scientists have explained the phenomenon. The hypotheses advanced thus far to explain the singular phenomenon are limited to three. At first, it was thought that aeroliths were veritable meteors, which formed in the air by aggregation, like rain and hail, but their constitutive elements are not found in atmospheric air, although it has been analyzed at all the heights that humans can reach, and the elements of the air are always found to be the same all over the Earth.

What's more, nitrogen and oxygen, which are the principal components of the atmosphere, as you say, can't dissolve

[54] The first "carbonaceous chondrite" to be detected, which fell near Alais on 15 March 1806, was identified as such after chemical analysis by Jöns Jakob Berzelius, published in 1834.

the substances of an aerolith. Then again, if those elements existed in the air, it would be necessary to contend that their molecules are extremely disseminated there—so how could they come together rapidly enough suddenly to form a stone weighing several quintals, like those conserved at Ensisheim in Alsace, or three or four thousand stones of various sizes, like those launched by the L'Aigle meteor?[55]

Can one say that the stones are formed by chemical affinities? But the elements that compose them are only united by agglomeration, not combined. Can one advance that the aggregation has time to form, because the particles are sustained in the air for a long time between two clouds by an electrical effect, as Volta explains the formation of hail? But aeroliths most often fall when the sky is clear and offers not the slightest appearance of cloud.

"Then too, if all these causes were recognized, it would still remain to be explained how the so-called meteors describe a near-horizontal curve as they fall, and why that movement of horizontal translation sometimes has a velocity equal to that of the Earth circulating in its orbit."

"That's very good," said the demon.

"The author of *Mécanique céleste*, the celebrated Laplace, thinks that aeroliths are launched from the Moon by a volcano."[56]

"That idea seems rather droll to me."

"And yet it's the most plausible. In fact, if there are volcanoes on the Moon, which isn't proven, it's possible that they have enough force to launch a stone out of the atmosphere of

---

[55] The meteor shower whose debris fell near L'Aigle on 26 April 1806 also provoked a rapid reaction from the Académie des Sciences, who sent Jean-Baptiste Biot to investigate; his report was a crucial step in proving the extraterrestrial origin of meteorites, still highly controversial at the time.

[56] Pierre-Simon de Laplace published the five volumes of *Mécanique céleste* [Celestial Mechanics] between 1799 and 1825.

that body, and astronomers have estimated that force to be in the same proportion as that of certain terrestrial volcanoes.

"Once the aerolith has crossed the boundary that exists between the system of attraction of the Moon and that of the Earth, which can take place in any number of directions, it becomes, as you say, a satellite of the Earth, but a satellite that experiences enormous perturbations because of its small mass; those perturbations end up engaging it in the terrestrial atmosphere. That hypothesis doesn't explain the identity of composition of aeroliths, unless one supposes that all these miniature planets are of absolutely the same nature."

"What prevents that?"

"Where do they come from, then?"

"Oh, my dear, you're asking me an absurd question. They come from the same fabric as the others…and that's it!"

Chapter III
The Vehicle

I have forgotten to tell you that during this conversation, the genius and I were sitting on the aerolith and thus traveling as if on a flying dragon. Except that, in turning around the Earth, our miniature moon also had its own movement of axial rotation, so, with each of those diurnal revolutions, we had our head down and our feet in the air relative to the sun—but that position, however extraordinary it might appear to the pretty girls who are reading this, was not at all uncomfortable for me. I was like an inhabitant of New Holland who lives at our antipodes and with whom we Parisians are walking feet-to-feet without the slightest inconvenience to either of us.

It appears that shortly after the epoch of which I'm speaking, the moon that served us as a sofa experienced a perturbation that precipitated it on to the Earth, because I definitely recognized it in the natural history museum in Paris, where you can see it in the mineral hall, at the back of the left-hand gallery.

When I was well-rested and somewhat reassured, we departed at such a velocity that we soon arrived...you shall see where.

"I'm cold," I said to the demon.

"Well, I should think so," he replied, "for in the space we've just traversed, as in all of infinite space, the thermometer descends to fifty degrees below zero, never more and never less."

"I know; it's Fourier who said so.[57] Nevertheless, I'm cold.

---

[57] The mathematician and physicist Joseph Fourier (1758-1830) published his "Mémoire sur la température du globe terrestre et des espaces planétaires" [Essay on the Temperature of the Terrestrial Globe and Interplanetary Space] in 1827.

"That's perhaps because we're approaching the Sun, where we're about to descend in five minutes."

"You're joking, I think. If we were unfortunate enough merely to come within a few million leagues of the father of heat, we'd be roasted instantly. It's Newton who said that."

"Poor fool! Because a man is a genius, because he has torn the veil that covered one or two verities, does that mean that he's exempt from error, a diviner, a sorcerer? Newton is mistaken; you can judge for yourself."

On leaving the aerolith, I had initially seen the Sun a dazzling white, not orange, as we see it from Earth, and almost the same size. As we got closer, however, that size was augmented so considerably that it masked exactly half the sky from me. Its color remained a pure, dazzling white, but with immense areas that had a much brighter glare than the rest, and others that, by way of compensation, appeared to me at first to be dark blue, but which passed to lapis blue as we approached.

Those parts brighter than the others are what astronomers call faculae," the demon told me "and those you see blue-tinted are the spots."

I had always thought that the Sun was motionless in the center of the heavens, but I could see quite clearly by then that it was rotating on its axis like the Earth, not in twenty-four hours but in twenty-five days. I also saw that it had another movement, which was drawing it toward the part of the sky where the constellation Hercules is located. I asked the demon for some information, including the distance we then were from the Earth and the Sun.

"You know," he said, "that the Sun is thirty-four million leagues from the Earth. Now we're a million leagues from the Sun. Work it out."

"That heavenly body must be immense, for it appears to me to be covering half the sky at this distance, and we were only forty thousand leagues from the Earth when it already appeared to me to be only ten or eleven times bigger than the Moon."

"The Sun is thirty-two million leagues in diameter and almost a hundred million in circumference. It is, in consequences a hundred and eleven and half times larger than the Earth, in linear measurement; its volume is 1,384,472 times greater than that of the infinitesimal globe that you inhabit, and its density, or, if you prefer, its mass, compared to that of the Earth is in a ratio of 23,624 to one."

At that moment I experienced the greatest surprise, for I saw distinctly that what I had taken until then for blue patches were nothing but holes of some sort, which formed from time to time in a luminous atmosphere, through which I could distinctly perceive solid ground similar to ours; I even began to make out mountains and seas.

I naturally concluded that the sun was not, as I had previously thought, a body in combustion whose scoria, floating on the surface, formed spots, but a solid globe like the others; except that I saw that the globe was enveloped by two atmospheres, one exterior and entirely composed of light or luminous fluid, the other situated beneath the first and analogous to that of Earth—which is to say, composed of air. I cannot assure you that the air in question had nitrogen and oxygen exactly like ours for its elements, combined in the same proportion, because I did not have the opportunity to carry out an analysis, but what is certain is that it was very appropriate to the life of animals and plants, as you shall see in due course.

We approached the luminous atmosphere, and in spite of everything the demon said to reassure me, I shivered at the idea of plunging myself into an abyss of light, in which that fluid was so concentrated that it appeared to me to be a vast sea of undulating flames. I say "undulating" for want of a better way to render my thought, for it was more reminiscent of immense flakes of light, in rapid and continuous movement, mingling, separating and floating randomly, or as if driven tumultuously by an exceedingly violent wind. Imagine the terrestrial atmosphere covered by a host of clouds haring in all directions, leaving holes at intervals through which you can see a part of the sky: such were the clouds of luminous fluid, leaving holes through which the opaque disk of the sun was perceptible. There was, however, the difference that they were prodigious in size, and some of those flakes were no less than sixteen hundred leagues in diameter.[58]

I asked the genius what the nature of the luminous gas might be, but my question seemed to put him in a bad mood, and he replied, shrugging his shoulders, that it was the same as that of the miniature luminous atmospheres that form on Earth, which we call the aurora borealis, and that it was brighter because the gas was denser and more concentrated. I had to be content with that response.

We were still advancing, and soon found ourselves facing a hole through which we continued our route. I remembered then the opinion of one of our astronomers: Monsieur de Lalande supposes that eminences similar to mountains rise up from the nucleus of the Sun above a luminous ocean and offer the appearance of dark patches.[59] By reason of the conical form of those eminences, the layers of luminous fluid are less dense nearer to the summit, and consequently produce, by means of lesser illumination, the kind of dark ring that surrounds the patches, called the penumbra by scientists.

Two objections are fatal to that theory. Firstly, it would be necessary to suppose that the mountains move within the Sun, which would at least be singular, because the spots, even seen from Earth, constantly change position, sometimes in ten or twelve days, often in a matter of hours. In addition, the perfectly uniform tint of the penumbra and its clearly cut limits,

---

[58] Author's note: "Luminous rays emanating from an incandescent solid or liquid sphere enjoy the properties of polarization, while those escaping from an incandescent gas are deprived of them. It is the application of that principle to experiments made on the sun that leads to the opinion that we have advanced."

[59] Jérome Lalande first published this suggestion in 1795; it was widely quoted in astronomical texts of the early 19th century.

to the same degree on the outer side of the luminous surface and on the inner side of the dark spot, prove sufficiently that it is not produced by a degradation of the thickness of the luminous fluid.

I was soon informed with regard to the question, however, for when we had traversed the atmosphere of light, we saw beneath it a layer of clouds that overlapped around the edges of the spot through which we entered. Those clouds, illuminated from above, reflected toward the inhabitants of our little Earth a quantity of light much less vivid than the luminous atmosphere itself, and yet much brighter than the nucleus of the solar globe. That, as I was able to assure myself with my own eyes, is what forms the penumbra so embarrassing for the partisans of Monsieur de Lalande's opinion.

A very singular thing happened to me. In space, I had experienced a certain effect of cold, but supportable, although, as the genius had told me, the thermometer was indicating fifty degrees of frost—which is to say, at least twenty degrees lower than is commonly encountered at the glacial pole.

"You're cold," the genius had told me, because you're reduced entirely to your own heat; but you won't freeze, because your heat can't quit you by expanding into surrounding bodies, since, save for the light, you're in the void. You know that for a warm body to become cold, it's necessary for the caloric, which tends perpetually to equilibrate itself, to pass from the warm body into a cold body that is in contact with it. That law of the equilibrium of heat causes it to pass from one body to the other until the two bodies reach exactly the same temperature. But when a body is isolated in the void, as you were just now, it no longer loses the slightest fraction of its caloric."

"I understand that. But now that we're placed so close to the eternal source of heat, tell me why the cold appears to be increasing to the point that if I didn't blow on my fingers continually, I'd certainly get chilblains."

"That follows logically from what I told you. We're no longer in the void but in the second atmosphere of the Sun, analogous to that of Earth, as it's composed of a blue air, but much denser. That air is taking possession of your caloric, which wants to reach equilibrium with it, and that's why you'll soon be frozen if, by means of my demonic power, I don't invert the laws of nature for you.

Chapter IV
On the Sun

Scarcely had the demon finished speaking than we arrived on the surface of the Sun, a very lovely country, in truth, full of rarities that would be much appreciated by a collector of natural history, especially because of their so-called habitat, but in which taking a walk is rather difficult, because the smallest hillock is no less than twelve or fifteen leagues high—which is something of a hindrance to strollers seeking a point of view.[60]

As I was tried I wanted to sit down at first, but I found that I was overwhelmed by fatigue and lay down at full length on the sand. My head, my body and my limbs were all in contact with the ground, and yet I felt oppressed, heavier than I had ever been in my life. I tried to raise my hand to pass it over my eyes, but it seemed to remain attached to the ground in spite of me, and it was not without an unusual effort that I succeeded in raising my arm slightly, which I immediately allowed to fall back. I was very frightened; I thought I was ill, faint, and ready to die. The demon read my alarm in my expression.

"Calm down," he said. "It's nothing—except that your weight has increased, and you're not accustomed to carrying anything as heavy as your body is on the Sun."

"What! My weight has increased?"

"Certainly. How much did you weigh on the day you stood on the scale in the Champs-Élysées?"

"Exactly a hundred and fifty pounds."

"Well, here you weight, also exactly, four thousand and fifty pounds. That slight difference is enough to render your movements a trifle ponderous"

---

[60] Author's note: "The highest mountains on Earth are scarcely more than a league in perpendicular elevation."

In spite of my weight of four thousand pounds, surprise caused me to start like a roe deer.

"That can't be!" I exclaimed.

"And yet it is. Besides which, nothing is simpler. You know that the weight of a body is only the result of attraction. On Earth, you were attracted in such a manner as to be in balance with a hundred and fifty pounds. Now, as the attraction of the Sun is 23,624 times greater than the attraction of the Earth, you're also attracted 23,624 times more than you were; but as the force of attraction is at the center of the Sun, and diminishes in proportion to distance from the center, making the relevant deduction, bodies here weight twenty-seven times as much as on Earth. Now, a hundred and fifty multiplied by twenty-seven is four thousand and fifty.

"That variation in weight shouldn't astonish you, for it occurs even on the Earth. A body weighs less on a high mountain than at sea level, although the difference is too slight to be noticeable. It's quite appreciable if one weighs the same body at the equator, which is swollen and hence more distant from the center, than at the pole, which is compressed, and the difference is a hundred and ninety-fourth. So, a body that weighs a hundred and ninety-three pounds at the equator weighs a hundred and ninety-four if it's transported to one of the poles. One can ascertain that fact by making use of a spring dynamometer, a kind of balance that has no need of a comparative weight.

"Furthermore," he added, touching me with the tip if his crutch, "in order that you don't remain stuck to the ground like a limpet, I'll set nature aside again in your favor and liberate you from the law of attraction."

He had no sooner touched me that I got up, feeling fine and light, promising myself to seize every opportunity to take advantage of my journey to the Sun and bring back all the observations I could make.

The prejudices of childhood are so deep-rooted that even evidence cannot always cure us of them, and the proof is that with regard to the Sun, I could not rid myself of the idea of an ardent furnace. In that regard, I had read such singular calculations published on Earth that there was good reason to tremble in my position. For example, Monsieur Pouillet, by means of an ingenious crystal toy, had found that the luminous atmosphere of the Sun must rise to twelve hundred degrees of heat, and you will notice that that is seven or eight times more than is require to melt any metal, and to volatilize them, as well as diamond, the least fusible of known substances.[61] Herschel had done even better than that; he had determined that the heat of the Sun was three thousand times greater than that of the Earth.

I could not get over my surprise, therefore, on finding a very comfortable temperature, warm at first rather than cool, in truth, but which, thanks to a cloud that soon came to intercept the sight of the sky, passed an instant later to a mild freshness. I understood then that there was some hidden mystery there, beyond my intelligence, and addressed myself to the genius in search of information.

"It will be easy for me," he said, "to enlighten you briefly on this matter, which seems to interest you so much. Heat doesn't come from the Sun."

"That's a joke. If I were to repeat that on Earth, scientists would make fun of me."

"It's true. One of the chemical properties of complete light—solar light, if you prefer—is to develop the caloric that exists in an inert state in bodies, and not to give it to them, for nothing can be given anything that it doesn't have. Light, as you know, can be decomposed into violet, blue, green, yellow,

---

[61] Claude Pouillet (1790-1868) developed his pyrheliometer in 1837 and published his *Mémoire sur la chaleur solaire* [Essay on Solar Heat] in 1838, shortly before the serialization of Boitard's story began. His calculation (eighteen hundred degrees Centigrade) was mistaken, but was not corrected until 1879.

orange and red rays, etc.[62] Now, it appears that it's to the red ray and its components that it owes the property of stimulating, or revealing, so to speak, caloric, which is the principle of the heat that is only the effect of its development."

"So, according to you, caloric isn't hot?"

"That seems to me to be demonstrated. Take two pieces of iron, as cold as you like; rub them together and they'll warm up, all the more so if you rub them more rapidly and more forcefully. Certainly, you're not giving them heat; you're only developing the caloric they contain. Throw cold water on to quicklime and heat is given off. A thousand other bodies give rise to heat, and even fire, by combining chemically. To know that, it's only necessary to have struck a match on the side of a box.

"You can see that all those effects are independent of rays of sunlight or heat coming from that globe. The last fact is proven even by evidence from geological discoveries; in digging wells or descending into the depth of mines, it's found that heat increases by one degree for every ninety feet of depth. If heat came from the sun, and the Earth didn't have its own heat, the phenomenon would occur in the inverse direction, and there would be more heat as one got closer to the surface that the solar rays strike.

"Besides which, you've doubtless noticed how the cold intensifies as you climb a high mountain. In one of the hottest

---

[62] Author's note: "Light is decomposed by causing it to pass through a crystal prism, when the rays present themselves in the order we have just established. If each of these rays is passed through another prism, it no longer decomposes, from which one concludes that they are simple. The original beam of light can be recomposed by receiving all the rays dispersed by the first prism on a lens; having reunited them into a single beam at its focal point, the lens reproduces the white image that is painted on a piece of cardboard when it receives a ray of sunlight directly through a hole in a chamber into which no other light can penetrate."

countries in the world, Peru, if you go up to the Quito plateau, fourteen hundred toises above sea level, you'll see that the thermometer, in any season of the year, never gets above five degrees. As you continue upwards the winter becomes more rigorous, and eventually, reaching a height of two thousand four hundred toises, you no longer find anything but eternal ice and a temperature as cold as that in the polar regions. And yet you're bathing in an immense quantity of rays departing from a Sun perpendicularly overhead.

"If those rays brought heat with them, you'd be burning, as in the torrid zone of Africa. Nothing of the sort, however, because, the matter composing the atmosphere of those high mountains being very sparse and enclosing very little caloric, the light can only develop what the matter contains—which is to say, very little.

"The natural state of bodies is always to be in combination with a greater of lesser quantity of caloric, of which they are never completely deprived, for if that happened, they'd become harder than diamond. It's the caloric interposed between their molecules that, in separating them, gives them their softness, ductility and elasticity. That's what, by virtue of its quantity, causes them to pass, first into the fluid state and then, increasing further, into a gaseous state. Without caloric, water and all other liquids would be nothing but rocks, icicles harder than iron. It insinuates itself with extreme facility between the molecules of all known substances, but they, in their turn, let it escape with the same facility. That's why they pass so easily from hot to cold.

"Have you never thought about the implausibility—the absurdity, I might say—that there is in believing that an entity can always give without ever receiving, like always taking money out of a purse without ever putting any in? Well, the Sun would be in exactly the same position; for thousands of years it would burn without ever being consumed; for thousands of centuries it would send forth enough caloric to fill the universe and wouldn't be exhausted!

"Then again, poor imperceptible ant, in your demented pride, you arrange the universe as if it had only been made for you; you shrink the grandeur of creation to your scale. For if heat came from the sun, as you imagine, there would only be one habitable globe, I don't say only for humans, but for all its animals, plants and organic matter, and one that is one million three hundred and twenty-eight thousand times less voluminous than the Sun, fourteen thousand seven hundred times less voluminous than Jupiter, eight hundred and eighty-seven times less than Saturn, seventy-seven times less than Uranus, and more than a million times less than the millions of stars that fill infinite space.

"Your imperceptible Earth would be the only one inhabited, while all the other worlds would be burned or frozen! The planets would be deserts a thousand times more sterile than the burning sands of Africa and the icy plains of the poles; all the heavenly bodies, whatever their number, their immense size and importance, would only have been created for the pleasure of your eyes—or, rather, for the pleasure of astronomers who, by means of their telescopes, discover thousands of them that you have never seen. Isn't that the ultimate in human pride and misery?"

"Monseigneur Devil, I confess that your tirade is very fine, but it doesn't explain to me how it's possible to live, for instance, on Saturn, where it must be, in view of its distance from the Sun, eighty times colder than Paris, whether heat comes from the Sun or only light, for after all, the later must also act in proportion to distance, and in that case, its action would be eighty times weaker."

"What you say there is true, but one thing you're not taking into account is that Saturn also contains eighty times more caloric than the Earth, which compensates in such a fashion that the development of heat is almost the same."

"That's good; but on Mercury, for example, it will be seven times hotter than Senegal, and there are certainly no lions or elephants that could resist that."

"Not at all, my dear—except that there is seven times less caloric in Mercury, which compensates for the sevenfold increase in light. I won't tell you that the proportion between light and caloric is always measured in such a manner that the heat is exactly the same as on Earth, but it can vary considerably—by ninety degrees, for example—without hindering vegetal and animal organization.

"You'll find examples of that on Earth, for you'll encounter blue foxes and white bears near the pole in thirty degrees of cold, and elephants, lions and negroes on the equator, in sixty degrees of heat, which makes a difference of ninety degrees Réaumur, the same that exists between ice and boiling water. So, if the organic matter of the Earth can experience without inconvenience a variation in temperature of ninety degrees, it's necessary to be very limited to be unable to imagine it modified in such a manner that it could experience without inconvenience a greater scale of variation."

"That's very well argued, but who can affirm it?"

"Anyone who judges the wisdom of creation in that which is as yet unknown by the wisdom of creation in that which is known. It seems to me that that's logical."

"I agree."

"If you want to see an example of that wisdom for yourself, raise your eyes to the sky of the place where we are, and you'll realize that, although there is only one goal in nature, there are many ways of attaining it. Look at those thick clouds floating incessantly between the luminous atmosphere of the sun and its respirable atmosphere; they're like a great veil intercepting the intensity of the light, and only allowing as much as they require to reach the eyes of the inhabitants of the sun. Those clouds are incessantly renewed by vapors rising from the seas, lakes and rivers, and they sometimes fall as fine rain to refresh the verdure of the woods and meadows."

"On our Earth. it's the sun's rays that vaporize the waters and disseminate them in the atmosphere; I don't see how that phenomenon can operate here if the clouds are always interposed between the luminous atmosphere and the globe."

"My dear, if you had been a little less dazed by your arrival here, you would have seen at that moment that the place where we are was inundated with light, that the heat here was much greater than it is at present, although quite supportable, and that in consequence, the water of that pond you see there must have been rising as vapor to form clouds. This is why: the luminous atmosphere offered a large lacuna, forming the spot or hole by means of which we entered; now, the light of the sides of that hole came to strike the ground, albeit softened by the penumbra we've mentioned; the result was a development of caloric, heat, vaporization and all the ensuing meteorological phenomena."

"But then, as the lacunae of the luminous atmosphere succeed one another very rapidly, there must be very disagreeable alternations of heat and cold, dryness and humidity, rain and fine weather, much more rapid than on Earth."

"The difference is perhaps not as great as you think, but in any case, it's necessary in this land, where there's no alternation of seasons, or of day and night. I assume that you're enough of a naturalist to know that it's the alternation of heat and cold that is the cause of the movement of matter—something easy enough to imagine, especially in organic bodies.

"One could perhaps define life by means of two words: contraction and dilatation; contraction when the molecules of a body draw closer together because the intercalary caloric between them is escaping; dilatation when caloric is introduced into a body and separating the molecules in order to make room for itself. Those two phenomena are entirely due to the alternatives we're talking about.

"Fix the temperature of a region at whatever thermometric degree you wish, but invariably, animal and vegetal activity will be suddenly stopped; of a country rich in verdure, replete with life and movement, you will have made a sterile and silent desert. That's why the planets—the Earth, for example—which have days and nights as they rotate on their axis and present different regions by turns to the sun, which have seasons by virtue of tilting annually on their axis, are covered with living beings, and why their poles, which don't experience those alternatives, are deserts devoid of verdure."

"I suppose, then, that the sun must be inhabited over its entire surface, for it can't have any icy poles."

"On the latter point you're mistaken, for its brilliant atmosphere only extends about thirty degrees to either side of its equator, with the result that the world's poles are as cold and almost as dark as ours."

"All of that is singular, but very interesting."

"Since it interests you, I'll initiate you further into the secrets of nature. You'd risk making a grave error if you judged what happens here by your senses, because I've abstracted you from the effects of attraction and heat; I'm therefore going to show you the truth, and I what I've told you weren't true, the eternal wisdom that can't fail would have lacked foresight, and the Sun, along with the majority of the other celestial globes, would be uninhabitable.

"The atmosphere of the sun, being considerably more extensive and heavier than that of Earth, charges the beings that live on the ground with an enormous burden. In addition, the force of attraction being in proportion to the density of the Sun, it results that the bodies that inhabit it are attracted toward its center—or, which is the same thing, weigh—as I've already said, twenty-seven times as much as they would weigh on Earth.

"Now, you'll understand that if nothing counterbalanced that frightful force, the beings would be crushed, or, rather, matter could not be organized, for want of being strong enough to sustain the eternal struggle between life and death; and if it were organized in spite of that, the living bodies would be twenty-seven times denser, and, in consequence, harder, than they are on Earth, which isn't supposable."

"Could you speak to me a little more clearly, Monseigneur?"

"I'll try. The force that enables living matter to release itself from physical laws and chemical affinities is called 'vital force' by scientists, but if they spoke more frankly they would have called it 'the force unknown to us.' It's the force that fights for life while chemical affinities and physical laws fight for death."

"I understand now."

"Well, that vital force finds is principle in caloric, the alternatives of that fluid and its quantity calculated in a fashion to maintain the equilibrium of the struggle; that's what renders the matter of the sun appropriate to struggle against attraction and death."

"That's not as clear."

"If bodies, on the Sun, in order to obey attraction, were twenty-seven times denser—which is to say, if the molecules composing them had a force of cohesion—the force that brings them together and causes them to adhere to one another—twenty-seven times greater, they would also contain twenty-seven times as much caloric in a latent state, without developing a sensible heat. Now, when light comes to act on that sum of caloric, it follows that its effect will be twenty-seven times as great, without that heat being able to liquefy, melt or vaporize the animals, plants etc; in that fashion, equilibrium would be as perfect as on Earth, and, all things being equal, the machine would work as well as ne could wish."

"Pardon me, but it seems to me that you've confounded the force of cohesion, which is a chemical phenomenon resulting from affinity, with attraction, which is a physical phenomenon, etc."

"And I tell you that you're babbling, and don't know what you're saying. Astronomical attraction, molecular attraction and the force of cohesion are exactly the same thing, although you've separated them methodically in your books, and the same cause that augments the density of a globe also augments in the same proportion the density of the bodies on that globe; if the bodies of that globe didn't have a density proportional to it, their molecules would obey its attraction and disseminate, which would inevitably give rise to chaos."

What I could see most clearly in all of that was that the capricious demon easily got into a bad mood, and for that reason, I called a halt to my questions. As I had rested sufficiently, I got up and started walking toward a green meadow that I perceived in the distance, and the demon followed me without saying a word.

Chapter V
An Encounter

The Sun is a very pretty place! Magnificent lakes, scarcely two or three thousand leagues across, with waters as limpid as the purest crystal, and an immense quantity of fish, all very colorful; little hills five or six leagues high, covered in forests in which one can see a host of animals running, jumping and bounding, very extraordinary with regard to species, but all having a considerable analogy with the animals of Earth, because they are composed of the same elements; streams fifteen or twenty times as wide as the Seine, rolling their silvery waves through a rich countryside or precipitating from rock to rock, forming little waterfalls five or six thousand meters high! I've heard mention of Niagara Falls as a marvel, and I've seen the fountains of Saint-Cloud and Versailles playing several times, but I confess that the Sun's cascades are something more grandiose—to make use of the expression of a traveling novelist.

On emerging from an arbor composed of fruit-trees whose name I didn't know, all of which bore with a great deal of grace a quantity of strange and delightfully-perfumed fruits, I suddenly found myself in the midst of perfectly cultivated fields. There were almost the same vegetables as among us, but their grains were prodigiously developed in proportion to their foliage. For instance, the plants analogous to our cereals were scarcely larger than our rye, wheat, rice, corn, etc., but their ears were a foot long, and I plucked a few grains as large as walnuts. That was, I learned subsequently, the result of savant cultivation dating back fifty or sixty thousand years.

I suddenly made a reflection, and ear gripped me. I had read Voltaire's *Micromégas*, and *Gulliver's Travels*, all equally amusing, not to mention Cyrano de Bergerac's excursions to the Moon, and I said to myself: *If the people of Jupiter and Saturn are several hundred toises tall, how big must the giants of the Sun be? If I find myself in the path of one of them, he will certainly crush me underfoot without seeing me.*

With that, walking with greater precaution, I began looking to the left and he right, raising my eyes to the sky, or at least to the altitude of Mont Blanc, fearing to see at any moment, in the vicinity of the clouds, the frightful head of an enormous giant. The result of that was that, no longer looking ahead of me, I bumped rudely into something that was in my path.

That something was nothing other than a little woman about three feet tall, who, knocked down by the impact, rolled on the grass uttering lamentable cries. Her howling attracted her father and her husband, and I thought I was about to have trouble on my hands, but I was unworried by that once I had cast a simple glance over the newcomers.

Imagine two individuals about four feet tall, with short and very thin legs, large feet devoid of toes, but armored with a single nail, very hard and very thick garnishing the extremity of the instep, almost like a small hoof. As for their hands, that was a very different matter; they had six long, strong fingers much like ours.

What astonished me most about those singular creatures was their head; it would have caused a Parisian phrenologist to fall into raptures. I estimate that it alone must have had a full third of the total weight of the curious individuals, for it was almost as big as a pumpkin. What rendered it even stranger is that it consisted almost entirely of cranium, and the face only occupied a small portion of it. As for the rest, I can't give a clearer idea of the people of the sun than by comparing them to certain large-headed caricatures by Dantan.[63]

---

[63] The sculptor Jean-Pierre Dantan (1800-1869) became more famous by virtue of his parodic busts of famous people than his elder brother Antoine-Laurent, who was a serious sculptor. This notion of future human evolution, favoring the development of the brain over that of the body, was to become standardized, especially after it was echoed in H. G. Wells' depic-

After having picked up his wife and made sure that she was not injured, the husband approached me and started singing a pretty musical phrase, the words of which I did not understand. On seeing him come toward me I adopted a defensive pose, thinking that he was about to attack me, but his little ballad, in a minor key and a very soft *gracioso*, immediately persuaded me that he had no hostile intention.

Demons only laugh when cats are on fire, says the proverb, so the accident that had just occurred had made mine smile broadly. He touched me with the tip of his crutch, and I immediately understood the language of the inhabitant of the Sun.

"Poor Savage from the Earth," sang the Solarian, extending his hand to me amicably, "I'm very sorry for you and I'd like to be able to console you for the accident that has just occurred to my wife, but I'm a simple man devoid of eloquence; I only posses five hundred and seventy sciences in depth, and only speak or sing two hundred living languages and twenty-four dead ones; I've only written eight hundred tragedies, ten thousand dramas, as many operas, six epic poems and one good epigram. Forgive my ignorance, therefore, and the simplicity of a rustic, if I can't improvise a melody sweet enough to restore calm to your soul."

Astonishment caused me to fall from my height in listening to that ballad, and, turning toward the demon I asked him whether there were little houses in the region and whether hazard had not brought us into the vicinity of a lunatic asylum. What surprised me even more was the father, who, in spite of his white beard, his venerable air and his quavering voice, started twittering in his turn:

"Young savage," he sang, in a major key and an *allegro* tempo, "I read astonishment on your face, and as I like strangers, even when, like you, they have little brain, I shall

---

tion of "The Man of the Year Million," but Boitard was the first person to apply the relevant argument to the hypothetical question.

take pleasure in satisfying your curiosity. First of all, I see by the stirring of your soul, painted in your features, that you want to know why we sing as we speak instead of dragging out our words in the same tone and the same tempo, with an insipid monotony. Once, we were barbarians, as people doubtless still are in your homeland, and spoke in tedious prose like you. But today, thanks to the progress of our organism and our intelligence, each of us has become a naturally excellent composer, and we no longer speak except in song, which renders speech more expressive and gives the faculty of rendering thoughts and sentiments energetically. However, things weren't going as well until, finally, after fifty-three centuries of strife and dissension, a sage had the idea of establishing schools of morality."

"Bah!" I exclaimed. "What good did that do you? Far better to have a good penal code."

"It served to teach people that individual happiness can only result from general happiness," replied the old man. "The consequences of that fecund principle were deduced; the Solarians understood that, in order to be happy, they each had to contribute, by individual virtues, to form the sheaf of public morality; from then on, laws, governments and everything that follows therefrom become unnecessary; there is no more need of punishment when there is no one to punish; there is no more need of protection when there are no longer any oppressors."

"What! You don't have any legal code, police, administration or public treasury?"

"All of that serves no purpose, for the Solarians, all being virtuous, have no need to be maintained; we emerged from barbarism a long time ago."

"You told me that you read my soul and divined my thought; that phenomenon of penetration is fortunately impossible in my homeland, even for the greatest sorcerers. Do you have more senses than the humans of my species—seven or eight, perhaps? The Earthly scholars of the eighteenth century thought that the inhabitants of other planets might have senses that we lack, and in consequence, perceptions and thoughts whose nature we cannot imagine."

"Matter," the Solarian replied, "has received from God general properties that characterize it: width, depth, impenetrability, etc. Those properties are the same everywhere, and the consequences that flow from them are the same, for the same causes always produce the same effects; it follows that everywhere that there is matter, it is organized in the same way, and the beings that it forms, emerging from the same mold, also have the same general properties. As the beings of the most advanced period, and hence the most perfect, the Solarians have five senses resulting from all the possible organic combinations."

"You speak as if you know all those combinations."

"I know, at least, their possible results on humans and everything that exists. The body can only enter into relationship with them by contact; that law is without exception; the senses, therefore, whose property is uniquely to put us in rapport with exterior bodies, are merely modifications of touch. Nothing is easier than to calculate those modifications. Matter can only exist in three states: solid, or hard; liquid, or soft; fluid, or gaseous. In the first case, it is coarse touch that puts it in rapport with us. In the second, it acts by the division of molecules on taste; reduced to vapor but a greater molecular division, it acts on the sense of smell; in the gaseous state, its elasticity lends itself to hearing and sight because of its undulations. You see, therefore, that all of its possible combinations are appreciable through one of the five senses; if it were otherwise...."

I saw that the old man was about to commence a metaphysical—which is to say, boring—dissertation and hastened to cut him off.

"Do you know," I asked him, "how your globe came to be populated?"

"Like all the rest. A long time ago—a very long time, perhaps two or three million years—the Sun underwent a revolution: a general upheaval that destroyed everything that existed, animals and plants. Our scientists are not in complete agreement regarding the nature of that catastrophe; some call it Phutonian and claim that it occurred by fire; others say that it was a cataclysm or universal deluge. What is certain is that there had already been an infinite number of similar revolutions before the one of which I speak, and that there will be a great number of others, succeeding one another at long intervals, in millions of future centuries.

"After that catastrophe, matter, which can only be modified and never destroyed, recommenced its organization in obedience to its chemical and physical properties. You can imagine that the first modifications of its organization were very simple. Mildews, mushrooms, mosses and lichens were the first plants; infusorial animalcules, zoophytes and shelled mollusks were the first animals; imperfect plants, or cryptogams, and then those whose seeds only contain one cotyledon, followed thereafter. Plants with two cotyledons ornament verdure with their beautiful flowers, equipped with sex organs—which is to say, pistils and stamens—did not appear until long afterwards.

"It is thus that nature has followed the rational progress from the simple to the composite. It has been the same for the animals; after the oysters came, successively, the cephalodods, which have no well known respiration; then the crustaceans, which respire by means of gills; then fish, which respire in the same manner but whose blood is red; then the reptiles, the first to have lungs and aerial respiration, but with cold blood; and the birds and mammals, whose blood warms in more complex lungs. Among the mammals, those which lived on herbs and seeds appeared first; then came the carnivores, which only nourished themselves on prey; then the quadrumanes, which are both frugivores and carnivores, and finally, Solarian humans, who are omnivores.

"But the first Solarians differed very little from apes. Having become the foremost, they multiplied greatly, because they had the faculty of nourishing themselves on anything, and because they were vigorous, agile, adroit and intelligent.

When I say intelligent, that's compared to the other animals and not the Solarians of today. I judge that, not only because history has conserved memories of barbarity for us, but more positively still by virtue of the skulls and other human fossil bones that are found buried in the depths of the ground, and which belong to the first inhabitants of this globe.

"On the mere inspection of an entire skeleton, one cannot deny that the physical must have dominated the mental considerably; their heads were small, like yours—I beg your pardon for the comparison—and an enormous face took up three quarters of it, in such a manner that little space remained or the brain. Since then, the habit of mental exercise has perfected the brain of Solarians, to the point that it has achieved the gracious development that you can judge by my son-in-law, my daughter and myself."

Yes, indeed, I thought, silently, *those heads are as graceful as a pumpkin on a skittle-pin.*

"That development is the necessary consequence of the usage that is made habitually of any organ. The enormous stature, the height of six feet, and the long, sturdy, muscular legs of the first inhabitants of the Sun rendered them more appropriate to dispute a prey than conduct a mental discussion. They had broad shoulders, like a beast of burden, and feet equipped with five ridiculous and useless digits. They fought one another like tigers, calumniated one another like demons, committed all sorts of crimes and cowardly actions, had laws and governments that were often impotent to contain them; in sum, as you can see, they differed very little from brutes. But the Sun was then only in its sixth geological period."

Exactly the period that the Earth is presently in, I thought. *But I'll refrain carefully from telling him that.*

"The rapid multiplication of the species led to the need to live in large-scale society, then to a commencement of industry, and that to intelligence—or, if you prefer, the knowledge of the truth, so far as it is permitted for humans to know it. Then the mental, quite naturally reacting upon the physical, forced the latter to fashion the dignity of the human species in a more rational manner. The Solarian, with time, no longer resembled an ox for stature, an ape for form and a cat for character, and became what he is today, in the fiftieth geological epoch: the most intelligent and most beautiful of creatures."

"With these words, the little old man drew himself up to his height of three feet, tapped the ground with his foot-hoof, tried to lift up his enormous pumpkin-like head, and seemed very satisfied with himself.

"I'd be obliged to you," I said to him, "if you'd care to tell me why you have six fingers on each hand, when you don't have any digits on your feet."

"When a gardener makes a bed of roses," he replied, "he throws away the young plants that produce simple and paltry flowers in order to cultivate and care for those that produce the most complete and most beautiful flowers. Our sages have done the same for our species, and their principal concern has always been the perfection of the human race by means of marriages between selected individuals."

"As you do for your dogs, horses and pigs," the demon said to me, interrupting.

The old man continued: "Far from cutting off a sixth supernumerary digit that a child bore by hazard—let that word pass for the sake of brevity—they took greater care of him, and when the child was an adult, he was only able to marry a young woman with the same title of nobility. That finger, at first inert, improved over time; a noble caste resulted that was so superior to the other Solarians in the perfection of touch and the finesse of the thoughts resulting therefrom that they multiplied greatly. It ended up naturally invading the globe and confounding in its bosom, by means of alliances, the ignoble race of five-fingered humans.[64]

---

[64] Thus far, the Solarian's argument is strikingly similar of the line of argument set out by Darwin in *The Origin of Species*, but the next paragraph lets it down, by virtue of its erroneous

"You know that if one cuts the tails off all the fogs in a family of pointers, after eight or ten generations, the pups of those dogs are naturally born tailless; that is the natural law of the modifications of organic matter. Thus, young camels are born with bare and blood-tinged knees like their parents, even though they have never knelt down under a heavy burden; thus, the races of domestic animals have been modified, to the point that less difference is found today between a bear and a lion than between a pug as big as a fist, a round head and a short, thickset body, and a tall greyhound with a pointed nose and a light tail. Well, when we began to become civilized, we got rid of useless digits by means of amputations repeated for seven or eight generations, and a hard and solid corn, produced by friction during walking, formed us a very solid natural shoe, comfortable and very pretty."

"It seems to me that you ought to be walkers as good as English horses; doubtless you like traveling a great deal?"

"No, for we know that happiness is perhaps only found in the fatherland and in the family; so we only quit them when it's absolutely necessary. In that case, we travel, but our feet are useless to us for that."

"I understand—you go on horseback, in a carriage, a locomotive or a steamboat, for you appear to me to be advanced in the arts."

"My dear savage, I can see that you think us still barbaric, for you suppose that we use extremely ridiculous means of transport, such as we had a hundred thousand years ago—which is to say, at the commencement of our civilization. We travel through the air, by means of balloons with wings or fins, or by flying in the fashion of swallows."

"What! You know how to steer balloons and fly with wings?"

"In my turn, I'm astonished by your surprise at such a simple thing. You must be very profoundly ignorant not to

conviction regarding the inheritance of acquired characteristics.

comprehend a problem of mechanics whose solution you have before your eyes every time that you see a fish swim or a bird fly."

"I can see," I said to him, admiringly, "that if you only have five senses, like us, at least you've obtained much greater advantage from them. If you're only a simple inhabitant of the countryside, as your son-in-law says, what are the members of your Academy of Medicine? They must know what quartan fever and cholera are, and only ever kill one in twenty of their patients."

"They don't kill any, for the reason that we have no academies here, nor sick people, nor physicians. After the study of morality, that of the human organism is the most important, so there is not one of our ten year old children who does not know the human organism and its physiology well enough to preserve himself from disease and heal his injuries."

"You appear to me to be extraordinary people, who know everything!" I exclaimed, with a redoubling of admiration. "As I have a very pronounced liking for astronomy, I'll renounce Monsieur Arago's course if you'd care to tell me what you know about it."[65]

"Astronomy?" said the old man. "What's that?"

"I mean the science that treats the movements, distances, the size, the physical constitution, the eclipses and all the other phenomena of heavenly or celestial bodies."

"I don't know what you mean by heavenly or celestial bodies. I only know the atmosphere composed of air, the clouds above and the luminous fluid above the clouds; I never heard mention of any other things."

"What! Through the holes in your atmosphere and by means of your telescopes, you've never seen the Moon, the Earth, Saturn, Jupiter, or at least Mercury and Venus, which are so close to you?"

_____

[65] The great scientist François Arago (1786-1853) gave annual public lecture courses at the Paris Observatoire from 1812-1845, which were very popular.

"I'm absolutely ignorant of what you mean."

In the beginning I had mistaken my Solarians for lunatics, and at that moment the old man turned the tables on me. He turned to the demon and asked him, with a pitying expression, whether I was subject to fits of dementia.

The demon smiled and said: "However much science a man has, he can only know what falls under his senses; as it impossible for heavenly bodies to be seen when one lives on the Sun, it's impossible for the Solarians to have any idea of them. For them, astronomy could never be anything but a poetic utopia, if they had been able to divine it."

"It seems strange to me," I said to the genius, "that the inhabitants of the center of the universe cannot see what surrounds them, while one can see from the Earth, at a much greater distance, much smaller globes that do not have any light of their own."

"It is because the sun is luminous that the other heavenly bodies remain veiled to them...I'll explain it to you," he added, addressing the words directly to me. "When you were on Earth, you've heard it said that the stars are visible in daylight from the bottom of a well."

"Yes, of course I've heard it said, and furthermore, it's what I believed; but I had myself lowered into a muddy well, from which I couldn't see anything at all."

"If you couldn't see anything, it's because the rays of sunlight, reflected by the atmosphere, form a luminous curtain that prevents the stars from being perceived, their light being too weak in comparison. Your credulity, therefore, made you do something foolish, as often happens."

"But why did the luminous curtain of the atmosphere prevent me from seeing the stars from the bottom of a well, whereas one can see them perfectly well in broad daylight with a telescope."

"This is why: it's sufficient for one light to be sixty times weaker than another for our eye not to be able to perceive it in the presence of the other. Now, the rays of the sun furnish

166

sixty times more light to our atmosphere than it receives from the brightest stars."

"That seems unlikely to me."

"You can assure yourself of it by a very simple experiment. Place an opaque body between two lighted candles; it will necessarily cast two shadows. Without changing the location of the opaque body, pick up one of the candles and move it away. As you take it further, you'll see the shadow fade away, and when the candle is sixty times further away from the opaque body than the candle that hadn't changed position, the shadow will be imperceptible."

"In that case, I don't understand why one can see the stars with a telescope.

"Because the shadow becomes visible if the illuminating or illuminated body is in motion, as you can assure yourself by agitating the candle you have drawn away. Now, the telescope, in considerably augmenting the size of objects, augmenting the velocity of their movement in the same proportion, and it's for that reason that their light becomes apparent in those instruments."

"It's annoying that we can't perceive any heavenly bodies from here, for I could have given this old man a lesson in astronomy all the easier to comprehend because we're placed at the center of our system."

"If that's all that's needed to satisfy you both, I can enable you to give your lesson before continuing our voyage to the planets."

With those words he pulled out of his haversack three pretty pairs of glasses similar to those one uses at a play, and gave us one each, saying that they had the magical property of enabling the sight to penetrate a luminous atmosphere, and that of magnifying objects and diminishing distances as much as the big telescope in the Paris Observatory. In fact, we had no sooner raised them to our eyes than we discovered perfectly the starry vault of the heavens, as we would have been able to do on Earth—which was very useful to me, in the rest of my astronomical voyage, especially when I was on the ring of

Saturn and on an extinct volcano on the Moon, as the reader will see in due course.

So, we saw…what I shall recount another time.

Chapter VI
The Planets

You doubtless remember that you left me on a mountain on the Sun in the company of the lame devil and a Solarian with a big head. We raised to our eyes the opera-glasses that the genius had given us and we saw...precisely the same things that we would have seen from the Earth on a beautiful starry night—which is to say, heavenly bodies and constellations. I recognized the latter at the first glance, but it was not the same for the planets, which, seen from the Sun, appeared to be placed in an order quite different from that seen from Earth. I shall enable you to understand that.

Firstly, it's necessary for you to know that our astronomers count two superior planets, Mercury and Venus, one intermediate planet, which is the Earth, and eight inferior planets, to wit Mars, Vesta, Juno, Ceres, Pallas, Jupiter, Saturn and Uranus, in addition to the moons of several of those worlds.[66] They call Mercury and Venus "superior planets" because they are located between the Sun and the Earth; they give the name "inferior" to the others because they are further away from the Sun than our little terrestrial globe. All those planets and moons, counting the Sun, compose our "planetary system," but that system, compared to the others that populate immense space, is almost nothing: a plaything; a drop of water in the sea.

It is as well to tell you that I am repeating there, word for word, the astronomy lesson that I gave my Solarian. Now, when he heard me speak so disdainfully of a system whose

---

[66] Most astronomers refer to Venus and Mercury as "inferior planets" and the rest as "superior," reckoning the Sun as a base rather than an apex. Boitard changes his mind about the propriety of his inversion later in the text and falls into line with the majority.

center he inhabited in his quality as a citizen of the Sun—or Middle Kingdom, as the Chinese say—he opened his little eyes and mouth wide and exclaimed: "Oh! Oh!"

His speech was short, but I found it very logical, and I replied: "Yes, Monsieur, a drop of water in the sea, less than half a drop in the Ocean, almost nothing. Look at the thousands of stars that decorate the celestial vault with their scintillating light, look at the numerous groups that they form in the immensity of the skies, those constellations to which the ancients and moderns have given such ridiculous names: the Great Bear, the Oxherd, Hevelius' Sextant, the Fly, the Giraffe, etc, etc., etc.; look at the Milky Way, the nebulae formed by stars heaped up, so to speak, on top of one another."

"I'm looking at all that with admiration," said the Solarian, "but what does it have to do with your drop of water and your Ocean?"

"It's because each of those stars, each little shining dot that you perceive in the sky, no matter how tiny it might be, is a Sun larger than ours; because each of those suns has its planets rotating around it; because each planet has its satellites or moon that illuminate it during the night; and because the inhabitants of the majority of those planets and moons are absolutely ignorant of the existence of your Sun, because its smallness and its distance hide it from their sight."

"Ah! ah!" said the Solarian.

I found that reasoning as judicious as the first.

He said: "But Monsieur Terraquean, I can't see any difference between what you say are planets and what you call stars, forming constellations. Do you expect me to rely on your word?"

"No, certainly not, on your own eyes. Firstly, you will see that the planets, although bright, only enjoy a borrowed gleam, which they owe to the reflection of the Sun's rays, so they do not scintillate, as it's said. The stars, on the contrary, have their own light; like our Sun, their atmosphere is independently luminous; so they are said to scintillate—which is to say that their light is tremulous. Go on, look."

"But I can't see any difference in the scintillation."

"Eh? What are you saying? Let's see…well, in truth, I can no longer see any difference either! That's singular! My professors at college told me that, though. No matter; we have a surer means. Notice that among the millions of stars that the ancients mistook for lamps suspended from a crystal vault, which is very picturesque, there are only eleven that move rapidly from west to east, while all the others are motionless and remain in the same position, or very nearly, relative to one another. The eleven that move are the planets; the others are the fixed stars, the suns."

"But what is our Sun, then—for it seems to me that it isn't moving, at least by comparison with the planets."

"Of course; it's simply a fixed star like the other suns."

"I'd like to know the history of fixed stars, their distance and their physical constitution."

"So would I," I said.

"Me too," said the demon."

And there was a moment of silence, which I finally broke, in order not to compromise my professorial dignity.

"You know," I said, "how one measures an inaccessible distance, and, in consequence, what astronomers do to measure the distance between the Earth and the Moon, the Sun, etc. One of the most elementary propositions of geometry is that the angle subtended by an object varies in inverse proportion to the distance of that object from the observing eye. On the other hand, trigonometry determines the relationship that exists between the dimensions of an object, its distance, and the angle it subtends. Thus, an object that subtends an angle of one degree is at a distance equal to 57.38 times its dimensions; if the angle is one minute, it, 3,438 times its dimensions, and 206,000 if the angle subtended is one second."[67]

---

[67] Author's note: "It results from this that, knowing the diameter of the Earth, if one knew the angle it subtends with the stars, one would also know the distance of those stars. To operate in any other circumstance, one takes a known size as a

"I'm not very good at mathematics," said the demon. "Can't you arrive at the results without going via those methods."

"All right. When one measures the distance of a planet, one takes the terrestrial radius or diameter as a base; now, as that diameter is known to be three thousand leagues, it's easy to measure the angle it forms with the planet, an angle known as the parallax. It's easy, as I say, to deduce the distance of the planet rigorously. But when it's a matter of a star, that base of three thousand leagues, which appears enormous, is so tiny compared to the distance of the star, that it doesn't open an appreciable angle. How, then, can a larger base be found? Messieurs Hook, Bradley and Flamsteed had the ingenious idea of finding one of seventy million leagues. This is how..."

Before continuing my astronomy lesson, I picked up a stick and traced a figure that I shall describe to you. "Suppose," I continued, that I want to measure the distance between the Earth and a planet. I take for a base the diameter of the globe, three thousand leagues, or even the half-diameter. The visual lines between the two points on the planet form an appreciable acute angle with the base, which I can easily measure with a protractor. Knowing the length of the base and how my two visual lines are inclined to it to form the two acute angles, nothing is easier than to calculate the distance at which the visual lines must meet to form the triangle, and that distance is precisely that of the heavenly body.

"The astronomers that I cited just now, seeing that the length of the Earth's diameter was insufficient to serve as the base when it was a matter of measuring the distance of a star,

---

base and measures the angles formed at its extremities by the visual lines that depart from the object whose distance is to be measured. Those angles measured, their sum is subtracted from 180 degrees, which is the measure of half a circle, and the remainder gives the angle sought, by reason of the mathematical proposition that the three angles of a triangle are always equal to two right angles."

had the idea of taking for a base the diameter of the great circle known as the ecliptic, which the Earth travels in a year in circling around the Sun. At the spring equinox, the Earth being at certain point of the ecliptic, the three astronomers, equipped with their instruments, draw a visual line from the Earth to a star in the constellation Draco. At the autumn equinox, the Earth, having traveled half its course, is on the other side of the Sun, and our astronomers draw another visual line from the Earth to the same star in Draco. They have, therefore, for the base of their triangle, the diameter of the ecliptic, and that diameter is nothing less than seventy million leagues.

"But alas, when it's a matter of measuring the angles formed by the inclination of the visual lines, it's found that the lines are so inclined to the base that they don't form an appreciable acute angle, even with the most perfect instruments—which is to say that the lines rise perpendicularly, as if they were parallel, and, in consequence, will never meet to form a triangle. If the visual lines had been inclined by only one second, the distance of that star in Draco would be calculable, and that distance cannot be less than 5,000,000,000,000 leagues."

"You're frightening me," said the Solarian, "and my mind can scarcely follow you to such prodigious distances."

"Wait, wait, my dear; I still have to make one little calculation. The star in Draco about which I'm talking is one of the largest and closest to us, but our astronomers discover by simple sight seven different magnitudes, all very appreciable, and the smallest must be seven times further away than the largest—from which it follows that their distance must be at least 35,000,000,000,000 leagues. But we're not there yet, because..."

"That's very good, my dear," said the demon, with a hint of ill-humor as he passed his crutch over the sand where I had traced my geometrical figures. "I've already said that I don't like mathematical demonstrations. If you want to please me revert to your ordinary chatter and leave the boring geometry there."

"It results from that immense distance that, seen with our best telescopes, those which magnify the most, the stars have exactly the same appearance as when seen by the naked eye: they're luminous points, and that's all. If they appear to us to be fixed, it's because their distance prevents their movement being apparent to us, for it's certain that they do have, as our Sun does, orbits that they travel periodically in a given time. In certain constellations, and especially in nebulae like the Milky Way, they appear to us to be heaped one atop another, and yet their distance from one another cannot be less than 5,000,000,0000,000 leagues.

"Each of those suns, as I told you, has its own system, its planets that circle around it, and to which it sends heat and light, exactly as the Earth receives it from our Sun. Those planets are probably inhabited, like ours; if I knew their density and heir volume, I could deduce therefrom the matter that composes them and its properties; from that I could easily conclude whether the inhabitants have or have not any analogy with those of Earth."

"You mentioned nebulae," said the Solarian, "and the Milky Way. What is that?"

"If you lived on Earth, on a fine night, you would not fail to remark parts of the sky illuminated by a white light forming patches of various sizes, named nebulae, and even a belt that embraces an entire circumference of the sky, and is called the Milky Way. Those patches and that wide zone are only accumulations of stars, which can be distinguished quite clearly with a telescope, and it's the light they emit that gives those parts of the sky the white tint that the ancients attributed to an overflow of Juno's milk.

"The Milky Way is not uniformly extended in a straight line or equally luminous everywhere, because the stars forming it are not placed symmetrically and different areas have more or fewer. For example, one night, Herschel directed at a nebula a telescope whose field of view or opening only embraced fifteen degrees of the sky. He saw 116,000 stars pass through in a quarter of an hour, and on another occasion,

174

258,000 in forty minutes. That might give you a glimpse of the extent that that occupies the visible space of the sky, for if Herschel had left his eye at the telescope for an entire revolution of the celestial sphere—which is to say, twenty-four hours instead of forty minutes—he would have seen 9,288,000 pass.

"Now, assuming that they are only 5,000,000,000,000 leagues apart, which is the least distance possible, the astronomer's eye would have traveled in space an extent of...of...wait; as I'm unfamiliar with the words I'll give you the extent in numbers: 46,440,000,000,000,000,000 leagues; and as I said, that extent is nothing by comparison with space, but it's enormous by comparison with our little planetary system, which is only 1,324,000,000 leagues in diameter."

All your figures don't say very much to the mind when they surpass a certain familiar number," said the Solarian. "Couldn't you help me to understand the enormity of the distances, as far as possible, by a simpler means?"

"I can easily do that. A cannonball crossing the space that separates us from the Sun, if it conserved the velocity with which it emerged from the muzzle, traveling at 633 leagues per hour, would take about six years to arrive at the Sun. Light travels much more rapidly, because it crosses that space in eight minutes, at 70,000 leagues per second. Now, to arrive at the nearest star at the same velocity, it would take more than three years, and at least twenty-one years to arrive at a star of the seventh magnitude. That's not all; astronomers, by means of powerful telescopes, have recently discovered a series of new stars that cannot be distinguished, like the latter, by simple sight, and which, according to Herschel, continue decreasing until the sixteenth magnitude.

"'So,' the astronomer says, 'in the innumerable host of telescopic stars, there must be some whose light has taken at least a thousand years to reach us, and when we observe them, and take note of their changes, it is their history of a thousand years ago that we are reading and writing.'

"If the Sun were suddenly extinguished, that would be perceived on Earth eight minutes later; if a seventh-magnitude star were suddenly extinguished, we would only perceive it on Earth twenty-one years later; and if a star of the sixteenth magnitude were to be extinguished now, we would only perceive it after a thousand years."

The Solarian passed his hands over his brow, shook his huge head and said: "Stop, I beg you, talking to me about an immensity that surpasses the limits of my intelligence and crushes my imagination."

"So be it. The ancient astronomers, in order to be able to distinguish each fixed star easily, had the idea of classifying them in distinct groups, or constellations, and as I said, they gave those groups the most bizarre names of people, monsters, animals, etc., the shapes of which they traces on their celestial maps, although the arrangement of the stars often has not the slightest analogy with those ridiculous objects. Furthermore, the moderns have not failed to outbid the ancients in that regard.[68]

"Before going any further, and since we're talking about the synonymy of astronomers, I ought to remind you that the 'fixed' stars are not fixed, as one can be assured by comparing the most ancient observations with those of today. It is true that their movement is so slow that it takes many years, and even centuries, to be perceptible, at least with regard to positional change; that is because of their distance, which renders negligible for us a space traveled that might be vast compared to the orbits that our planets follow.

"However, by means of the changes that take place in the intensity of the light of certain stars, among those called 'variable,' it is easy enough to deduce the time of their revolution. For instance, one of the most remarkable is placed in Cetus and bears the designation Omicron;[69] its period is 334 days.

---

[68] The original article includes a long footnote at this point giving a complete list of constellations, with their common French names and the number of visible stars in each.

[69] Author's note: "Astronomers give the stars in constellations the names of Greek letters in order to recognize them."

'The star conserves its maximum brightness,' Herschel says, 'for about a fortnight, and sometimes appears then as a beautiful star of the second magnitude; it then decreases for about three months until it becomes completely invisible for approximately five months; then its brightness increases for the remaining three months of its period.'

"I conclude therefrom that during half of its course it is moving away from us, and that it is approaching during the other half, that it describes an ellipse, one of whose summits is orientated in our direction, and that during the fortnight that it appears bright to us its travels the curve formed by that summit. The constellations of Perseus, Cepheus, Lyra, Antinous. Hercules, Serpentis, Hydra and Sagittarius each offer us a star analogous to that one; Cygnus and Leo each present two."

"I'd like to believe," said the Solarian, that that is a demonstration and that the stars are moving through space, but it doesn't prove that, like my Sun, they have planets rotating around them."

"I'll try to establish that. Algol is a star in Perseus that appears to be a star of the second magnitude for sixty-two hours; then its brightness suddenly decreases, and in the space of two and a half hours it is reduced to the fourth magnitude; it then starts increasing again, to resume its habitual brightness in three and a half hours, the full extent of its period being approximately two days, twenty hours and forty-eight minutes. Goodricke, who was the first to observe the phenomenon,[70] thought with reason that an opaque body, consequently a planet, is circling the star and comes periodically to interpose itself between it and us."

"Is it necessary to conclude that there are, in visible space, as many planetary systems similar to ours as there are stars?"

"Not at all. Those planetary systems don't all resemble ours, because there are some that have two suns, and we only have one."

---

[70] In 1782.

"Two suns! That seems singular to me."

"However, it is demonstrated today by twenty-one years of observations made by William Herschel between 1778 and 1803, and observations that his son has continued to the present day. It results therefrom that between thirty and forty have been found of these systems with two suns rotating around one another, accomplishing their revolutions in various lengths of time, one in 1200 years, others in 628 years, 80 years, 43 years, etc.; but what is most extraordinary for those who do not know the law of complementary colors is that the two suns are never the same hue; if one is red, the other is green; if one is yellow, the other is blue. The inhabitants of planets illuminated by them must, in consequence, have red days and green days alternating with white, tallow or blue days and obscure nights. Truly, if all that had not been mathematically proven, I would think that I were traveling in an enchanted land to which a beautiful dream had taken me."

I was at that point when we saw arriving and rising over our immense horizon a very large globe that was advancing toward us with such rapidity that one could easily follow it with the eye; it was moving in space while rotating about its axis, just like a ball launched by a vigorous player of skittles. Its color was pale white, like the Moon when one perceives it during the day.

I confess frankly that I did not recognize it, because I had never seen anything similar from Earth. In my disappointment, I turned toward the genius, who smiled at my embarrassment, and then said: "What you see is Mercury, the planet closest to the Sun, and it's because you're looking at it from this globe—which is to say, from approximately three times closer than from Earth—that you see it nearly three times as large; it also appears to you to be traveling more rapidly for the same reason, and also because it's velocity really is more rapid than that of any other planet, which it owes to its greater proximity to the Sun. If its glare is less bright, it's because you're placed at the source of the light it receives.

"Mercury is 13,361,000 leagues from the Sun and its diameter in 1,200 leagues, or two-fifths of that of the Earth. Its days are 24 hours 5 minutes 2 seconds, and its years 87 days, 23 hours 15 minutes 44 seconds—which is to say that it turns on its axis in a little more than 24 hours and completes the ellipse that it describes around the sun in nearly 88 days, which, given its distance from the star, means that it its traveling at forty thousand leagues an hour as it moves along its orbit.

Chapter VII
The Planetary System

"Let us pass on to the most beautiful of the planets, which has been named Venus because of its brightness, and which has also been called the Shepherd's Star, because it sometimes shows itself in the morning and sometimes in the evening, at the time when pastors are bringing forth or taking home their flocks. Its mean distance from the Sun is 25 million leagues; its size is slightly less than that of the Earth, for it is some 2,800 leagues in diameter; the velocity at which it travels in its orbit around the Sun is less than that of Mercury and more considerable than that of Earth, for it advances at 29 thousand leagues per hour. Its days are 23 hours 21 minutes 19 seconds and its year is 224 days 16 hours 49 minutes. The orbits described by Mercury and Venus are enclosed within that of the Earth. Let us now pass on..."

"Pardon me, Monseigneur," I said to the demon, "but it seems to me that you're abridging singularly, and if you go at that pace, we'll soon be at the far end of the world."

"My intention," he said, "is to pass in review for you the entire planetary system, in order that you can get a clear and precise idea of it to begin with; then, as I'm going to take you to all those worlds, you'll have time to study them in detail. However, I can extend myself a little on the one you perceive as a little, rather bright star, around which another bright dot is turning, which seems to be touching it. You'll deduce that it's a matter of the Earth and the Moon."

"Permit me, Monseigneur: I see all those planets round and bright over their entire surface, like full moons, and yet on Earth, I've often seen Venus and the Moon present themselves to my eyes as silvery crescents. Why is that?"

"Because from Earth your eyes embrace both a part of those bodies turned toward the Sun and struck by its rays, and another part in shadow, turning its back to the sun, to make use of a vulgar expression; whereas from here, being placed at the center or source of those rays, they travel the same lines through space as your sight and necessarily fall on the same points."

"One more question. Mercury is smaller than Venus, and Venus smaller than the Earth, and yet I see the Earth much smaller than Venus, and Venus much smaller than Mercury..."

That's because objects, in accordance with the laws of optics, appear to us to diminish in size in proportion to their distance from the viewpoint from which one is looking at them. Astronomers have taken advantage of that fact and deduced useful consequences therefrom in order to determine the movement of certain heavenly bodies by means of their apparent size, increasing or decreasing, compared to their actual size. But let's get back to the Earth.

"You doubtless know that it's nine thousand leagues around, which gives it a diameter of nearly three thousand leagues; but as it is not precisely round, bulging slightly toward the equator and being slightly flattened around the poles, the diameter is not exactly the same everywhere. For example, a line passing through the Earth from one pole to the other passing through the center of the globe, would be 2,800 leagues of 2,280 toises each; the same line passing through the equator would be 2,870 leagues, and would, in consequence, be ten leagues longer. The flattening at each pole is thus nearly five leagues, or, if you want more precision, 10,600 toises. If the line passed through France at the forty-fifth degree of latitude—through Lyon, for example—it would be 2,864 leagues."

"I knew that the Earth is flattened at the poles, and I even know why."

"Bah! Tell us that."

"It's because when our globe was in fusion, the liquid matter, by virtue of the effect of the centrifugal force resulting from the rotation, must have flowed away from the poles and accumulated toward the equator."

"Ha ha! It's my turn now to take lessons," said the genius, smiling. "Are you going to tell me how it came about that the globe was in fusion?"

"Nothing is easier. Launched into space by the Sun, of which the matter composing the Earth is merely the froth..."

"Now you're going to say silly things again. Remember that at this moment we're on a mountain on the Sun, not in a furnace."

"My God! I was thinking about that. That's true. How can it be that some of our astronomers simultaneously admit two contradictory facts: to wit, firstly that our globe was once incandescent, and still is in its interior; and secondly that the Sun isn't. Come on, let's seek the explanation elsewhere...ah! I have it. In the beginning, the Earth was encountered by a comet that set it on fire, and..."

"One moment. Comets are incapable of setting anything on fire; they have little or no heat of their own, and are not even luminous, as is proved by the phenomenon of polarization."

"However, it's necessary that one or other of these causes liquefied the globe."

"Why is it necessary to liquefy the globe to explain the flattening of the poles? Are not water and the matter that it holds in solution, the air and the molecules of matter that it carries, and the light bodies that are constantly forming or organizing on the Earth's surface obedient to the mechanical laws of rotation as well as pebbles in fusion? Are they more firmly attached to the nucleus of the Earth than any other matter in fusion? Could they not have drawn away from the poles just as easily as molten lead?

"In addition, my dear, there's another little difficulty. Let's admit that the Earth in fusion was launched from the Sun—you don't suppose, I hope, that it was spherical in form, that it was detached from the furnace with its globular form?"

"Certainly not. It owes that form to its movement of rotation."

"If its rotation was able to impose the form of a ball upon it, the laws of mechanics must not have been the same then as they are now, because, supposing the material to be liquid, it would have taken the form of a flat disk, not a sphere. Not at all: it has taken the form of a globe; then, when that sphere was well rounded, mechanical law changed in order to deform the ball and remake a disk by flattening it at the poles. You can see that it's not possible."

"I don't say that it first took the form of a perfect sphere, but that of a flattened globe."

"But then there would have been two laws of mechanics diametrically contrary and operating simultaneously, one to make the formless splinter a sphere and the other to make it a disk."

"I confess that that's very embarrassing; I hadn't thought of it. Are you, who know so many things, going to tell me how the Earth, as well as Saturn and other planets, are flattened at their pole if they've never been in fusion?"

"My dear, if anyone asks you that you can reply that you don't know, and you'll be sure of not being mistaken—all the more so because, if you go on to give other mechanical reasons, you might be put into embarrassment by being asking why other planets that have, like the Earth, a rotational movement, are nevertheless not flattened but perfectly spherical; why Ceres and Pallas, which also rotate, are neither flattened not spherical but irregular in form, etc., etc. And if you say that it's because those planets have never been in fusion, you'll be asked what necessity there is for the Earth ever to have been molten, when that necessity doesn't exist for the others."

"Well, let's not talk about the flattening of the poles any longer, but leave me my little theory of the liquefaction of the globe, for it's almost proven by a host of geological experiments. By means of thermometers placed in the depths of artesian wells, mines, subterranean caves and other profundities, it has been found that the Earth's heat increases by one degree per ninety feet as one descends into its entrails, and after work

done with as much talent as care, one of our scientists has published the contention that the augmentation is one degree for
forty-six feet. According to him, the entire mass of the globe,
with the exception of a crust that is no more than twenty
leagues thick, is composed of molten lava, entirely similar to
that which springs from volcanoes, and he considers the latter
as the ventilators, or rather as the safety-valves, of our globe."

"That hypothesis is certainly ingenious, but let's see
whether it can stand up to criticism. Let's first occupy ourselves with the facts that serve to establish it. Geologists have
studied what they call the mineral crust of the Earth, and in
accordance with the phenomena that they have observed there,
they've deduced the general phenomena of the globe. You
realize that it has been concluded on the basis of probabilities,
and that they've been obliged to establish for that a kind of
statistics of chance.

"But the mineral crust observed or supposed to be known
is, so far as I know, no more than 1,700 feet in depth below
the surface of the Ocean; at least, what is certain is that no
thermometric experiments have been carried out below that
depth. 1,700 feet, neglecting fractions, are 283 toises; now, in
proportion to the radius of the Earth, 283 toises is one in
11,531. It is, therefore, on a rather slight knowledge of one
eleven-and-a-half-thousandth of the thickness of the Earth that
geologists claim to judge the totality of the globe. It's as if I
wanted to judge the interior of a ball nearly fifty feet in diameter by a fraction of an inch of the thickness of its surface.
You'd tell me what people say to fools, that it's necessary not
to judge a tree by its bark, especially when that bark is exceedingly thin. If we were prepared to believe these gentlemen,
there would be boiling water only 8,212 feet beneath Paris—
which is to say, a little more than a quarter of a league beneath
the ground on which we tread so tranquilly.

"And that, however, is what they call facts and observations. If these observation were even identical everywhere…but they aren't. That increase in heat, fixed at one
degree per 46 feet by one, is fixed at one degree per 24 or 37

feet by another, one degree per 56 feet or one degree per 90 feet by the majority. That is because the increase in heat is not submissive to the same law all over the Earth, because experiments have proven that it can be two or three times as great in one place than another. They ought, it seems to me, to have compared the figures to find their average, and concluded quite naturally that such variable heat cannot have come from a common source.

"Thus, the facts invoked to produce the incandescence of the interior of the globe prove nothing, for the reason that it is not sufficient to know one eleven-and-a-half-thousandth of a composite body to know the totality of the body and determine the species of phenomena associated with it.

"Now let's reason differently. At a hundred degrees on the centigrade thermometer, water boils and evaporates. No refractory substances are known, including diamond, that do not melt or volatilize at a temperature that never surpasses three or four hundred degrees—let's say five hundred to accord a generous margin. It follows that any body heated to five hundred degrees and above, whatever its nature might be, will have passed from the solid state to the liquid, or vaporous, or that of gas, and sometimes all three, according to its nature. In a gaseous state, it will occupy a greater volume as it experiences more heat, and its volume can then be several times greater than when the substance was in the solid state. That posited, let's see what follows.

"Admitting, like the scientist of whom we spoke just now, that the internal heat of the Earth increases at an average of one degree per 46 feet, that of the center of the globe ought to rise to the prodigious temperature of 252,580 degrees. Now, even if the Earth were made of diamond, it would not be liquefied, but in a gaseous state, and that gas would be so rarefied that, in a mass equal to that of the atmospheric air, it would occupy perhaps a thousand times more volume. Even supposing that the force of expansion doesn't make our poor globe explode like a shell, it would follow that the entire Earth, not including its solid crust, would be composed of less

185

matter than perhaps Mont Blanc or the Puy-de-Dôme, and then, compared to its volume, it would be a thousand times lighter than a feather of the lightest down, for the caloric that would form the immense part of its mass is imponderable."

"But nothing proves that the heat increases with the same intensity all the way to the center of the globe," I said to the demon.

"For the phenomenon to occur as I describe it," he replied, "there's no need for it to do so. It would be sufficient for it to increase in that progressive proportion until a depth of five leagues, at the most.[71] Now, far from the Earth being as light as a feather, it's five times heavier than water, heavier than lead. How can you enable me to understand that at an equal volume, a gas can be as heavy, or even heavier, than the substance that furnished it by expansion?"

"I confess that the proposition is not sustainable. Well, I'll grant you that the interior of the globe is in a solid state, but at least you'll agree with me that in the beginning it was in a state of fusion."

"Not at all. Since that dilates substances, on cooling they must shrink and lose volume. However, it's certain that the Earth, more than three thousand years ago, was exactly the same size as it is today; thus, it has not been subject to cooling."

"How can you know that?"

"I know it by virtue of ancient astronomical observations, and I'll demonstrate it to you, although I don't believe you're intelligent enough to understand the demonstration perfectly at present. This is it. If the volume of the Earth had varied by the effect of dilatation or contraction, the motion of the Moon would also have varied; now, that hasn't happened,

---

[71] Author's note: "The geologists who have exaggerated the subterranean heat least make it increase one degree per thirty meters. On that basis, it would rise to five hundred degrees at a depth of only 45,000 feet, or between three and four leagues."

for the duration of the sidereal day is exactly the same today as in the most remote times, and we have several thousand years of observations that prove it."

"What is the historic time of which you speak by comparison with the number of centuries that might have elapsed since the Earth began to cool?"

"Those historic times, those four thousand years that elapsed between the first astronomical observations made in ancient Egypt and our own day are more than sufficient for us to establish calculations with mathematical exactitude. Buffon, the author of the "système de l'incandescence du globe,"[72] has calculated the time that it would require for a ball of the size and hardness of the Earth to lose its heat progressively until cooling completely, and it results from those experiments that four thousand years would be sufficient for it to lose more than a third, which would have a prodigious influence on the size of the globe. Now, the observations I've cited prove that its size hasn't diminished. You can understand, my dear, that the earth acts on the Moon by reason of its mass, its volume and its distance; if it had diminished in volume, the distance would have increased; the three combined causes would have acted in other proportions, from which continual perturbations in the revolutions of the Moon would have resulted throughout the period of cooling, and those kinds of perpetual oscillations would still exist today. However, since the time of the Egyptians, since the first eclipse mentioned in history, the motion of that heavenly body has not been seen to accelerate or show down for a minute, or a single second.

---

[72] This is not actually the title of an essay but merely the way in which Buffon refers back to the theory by which he calculated that the planets would take to cool after their emission from the sun, as tabulated in *Les Époques de la nature* (1779). Boitard's argument is specious because it is the mass of the Earth, not its volume, that determines the gravitational attraction between the two bodies, and the distance between their centers of gravity.

"But let's leave the discussion there and return to the movement of your little terrestrial globe. You see it advancing with less rapidity than the superior planets because, being further away from the sun than them, it is attracted to it with less force; its distance from the star is about 35 million leagues, and it rotates around it with a speed of 24,720 leagues per hour; its complete revolution, or, if you prefer, its year, is 365 days 5 hours 48 minutes 49 seconds.

"The orbit that the Earth describes in traveling around the Sun isn't circular but slightly elliptical, like those of all the planets. In addition to that rotational movement it has others, from which result the succession of days, nights and seasons. It rotates on its axis in twenty-four hours and turns each of its sides toward the Sun, one after another, during that space of time. The result of that is that the side facing the sun is illuminated for twelve hours and the other is in darkness for the same length of time, along the line that faces the Sun constantly, which is known as the equator.

"But the Earth has another movement, which is a kind of oscillation operating from south to north and north to south, in such a manner that it does not present its equator perpendicularly to the Sun all the time. For six months, that oscillation carries us northwards toward a point that traces another line named the Tropic of Cancer, and the days diminish for us,[73] but the same reason causes them to increase for the part of the

---

[73] This passage is confusing, partly it is not clear what is meant by the "us" to whom the sentence refers twice. If, when the Earth's axial tilt is such that the Sun appears to be above the Tropic of Cancer rather than the equator, that is the winter solstice, the hypothetical viewpoint in question must be in the southern hemisphere. The demon's next speech, however, inverts the pattern and places "us" in the northern hemisphere. The idea that the Earth "oscillates" is also confusing; later in the text Boitard repents of having said that and blames it on a printer's error supposedly omitting the word "apparent" before "oscillation."

globe placed beyond the equator; for that part, summer comes when it is winter for us. When the Earth presents the Tropic of Cancer perpendicularly to the Sun, at appears to stop momentarily in its motion; that stopping-point is what is called the winter solstice. Then its oscillation recommences in the opposite direction for six months, until it pauses again at another line known as the Tropic of Capricorn; during that second motion, we drawn nearer to the south again and the days augment at the expense of the nights. When the time is reached when the sun turns back again, that is the summer solstice."

"That's rather difficult to understand," I said to the genius.

"Nothing is easier," he replied, shrugging his shoulders. Then, with the tip of his crutch, he traced a figure on the sand and said: "Let's suppose that A is the Sun and B is the Earth. It's obvious that the Sun is perpendicular to the line that we call the equator. We, who are above the equator and those who are below it receive the sun's rays slightly obliquely, and we're in spring, the others in autumn, while the people inhabiting the line will be in the middle of summer and enjoy equal days and nights.

"Now let's suppose that, by virtue of its oscillation, the axis of the Earth or, if you prefer, its poles, are inclined. The sun's rays, instead of striking the equator perpendicularly, strike the Tropic of Cancer. We, who are here, will have the longest and warmest days of the year, because we'll be closer to the Sun, and those who are in the south, the Hottentots, for example, will be in the shortest and coolest days. We'll have summer and they'll have winter.

"Let's pass on to another position. The oscillation of the Earth has continued, not only have the poles resumed their upright position but they are inclined in the opposite direction. Then the sun's rays strike the Tropic of Capricorn perpendicularly, and the Hottentots, being closer to the Sun, will have the longest and warmest days, while we, in the north, are in winter and have the shortest days of the year.

"But it's for the inhabitants of the poles, in particular, that the oscillation produces a singular effect. For six months those at the north pole remain plunged in darkness, and in the meantime, those at the south pole has a six-month day; it's true that the day in question is always a trifle somber, but also, the six-month night is never very dark, even without the aurorae that often illuminate them.

"The Earth has other combined movements, but very slight, with much less important for the inhabitants. I won't talk about them.

"Relative to the position we occupy now on the Sun, the planet that presents itself to your eyes after the Earth is Mars, 52,613 leagues distant from us. The ellipse that its orbit forms in combination with that of the Earth renders the distance between the two planets very variable. Its days are 24 hours 31 minutes 42 seconds, its year 686 days 23 hour, 30 minutes 42 seconds and a slight fraction. Its orbital velocity is 19,740 leagues per hour and its diameter 1,560 leagues.

I'll show you Vesta, Juno, Ceres and Pallas at the same time, in order to demonstrate one of the most singular facts in astronomy. The ancients only knew eight 'planets,' to wit, the Sun, Mercury, Venus, the Earth—which they didn't count in the number of the planets in antiquity because they regarded it as the center of the universe and were unaware of its globular form—Mars, the Moon—which is no longer a planet for us but a satellite of the Earth—Jupiter and Saturn. Recently, Vesta Juno, Ceres, Pallas and Uranus have been discovered, and this is how.

"There exists between the distances of the planets known in antiquity, in relation to one another, an extraordinary numerical relationship. If one takes the following numbers: 0 for Mercury; 3 for Venus; twice three, or 6, for Earth; twice six, or 12, for Mars; leave a gap for twice twelve, or 24; but twice twenty-four, or 48, for Jupiter, and twice forty-eight, or 96, for Saturn, one has the series 0, 3, 6, 12, gap, 48, 96.

"Now, if one adds the number four to each of these figures, one obtains 4, 7, 10, 16, gap, 52, 100—and those last quantities express the order of distances between the planets and the Sun.

"Kepler, struck by that astonishing relationship, was bold enough to suggest that a planet ought to exist to fill the gap at 24 or 28, and that if it were possible to discover further planets more distant that those known, they would be found in the relationship of twice ninety-six, or 192, plus four, etc.

"Now, this is what is marvelous. On 1 January 1801, Piazzi discovered Ceres, which exactly filled the gap by furnishing the number 24 + 4. A short time later, Herschel discovered Uranus, the comparative distance of which is twice ninety-six, of 192, plus 4. The result is that today, in accordance with Kepler's prediction, we have the complete series of numbers."

"It seems to me, Monseigneur, that there's a slight difficulty in the symmetrical relationship of the distances of the planets. I can clearly see the gap that you've identified between 12 and 48, or between Mars and Jupiter; you've filled it with Ceres, which couldn't be done better, but what do you make of Vesta, Juno and Pallas, which are also located between Mars and Jupiter?"

"Aha! It's here that the stick prods you. But we'll get out of it by begging you humbly to believe that Ceres, Vesta, Pallas and Juno are only fragments of a single planet that, one day, without our knowing why, blew up like a bomb and launched four shards into space, which formed four planets."

"The Devil probably blocked its volcanoes, its safety-valves as Monsieur Something-or-Other said, and *bang*—like a firework. Fortunate are the believers, for the kingdom of the heavens belongs to them! But Monseigneur, tell me sincerely, do you believe what you've just told us?"

"Tee hee! That depends. The chances of probability are in favor. For example, it's proven, I think, that Kepler's calculation is false if there have always been four planets between Mars and Jupiter; therefore there was only one. It's proven, it's said, that all planets ought to be globular, but these aren't; therefore they're arguments of a spherical planet. It's proven, so far as we know, that the orbits of planets don't intersect, but these do; therefore they're four fragments departed from the same point, which they pass through at each revolution. If they every encounter one another they'll stick together, and there'll only be one planet again between Mars and Jupiter.

"I'll also remark in favor of this opinion that the four new planets, as if they had received a force of impulsion different from all the others, have orbits that deviate considerably from the zodiac, or the path of the other planets.

"Juno, discovered by Harding on 1 September 1803, is about 92 million leagues from the Sun; it's 475 leagues in diameter and its year is 4 years 128 days.

"Ceres comes next, its diameter is only 50 leagues, with makes it a tiny miniature Earth; it's 95 million leagues from the Sun and its years is four and a half years long.

"Pallas presents itself next, and it was Olbers who first discovered it, on 28 March 1802. As small as the previous one, as its diameter is only fifty leagues, its distance from the Sun is 96 million leagues and its year is four years 7 months and 11 days; it has an extremely elongated elliptical orbit.

"The least distant of the four, Vesta, is 81 million leagues from the Sun and was discovered by Olbers on 29 March 1807. Its year is 3 years 66 days and 4 hours. It's so small that its disk is hardly perceptible, so it's thought to be 25 leagues in diameter at the most.

"Those four planets are only visible with a telescope, and it's doubtless for that reason that they were discovered so late. Furthermore, it's quite probable that others will be discovered among the stars composing the constellations, for it will take a long time for all of the latter to be studied in that regard; there might be some that have been regarded as fixed but which have a planetary motion.

"Now here's Jupiter and its four moons; it's the largest of the planets and, after Venus, the brightest. Its diameter is 33,000 leagues, from which it results that it's fourteen hundred and seventy times as large as the Earth; the speed of its rotation on its axis is extremely rapid, for its days are only 9 hours 56 minutes long; its distance from the Sun is 179,575,000 leagues, and the rapidity of its velocity 10,650 leagues an hour, which gives it a year of 11 years 317 days.

"Saturn, with its seven moons and its singular ring, presents itself beyond Jupiter; its nebulous appearance, dull and leaden, is perceptible with the naked eye. Its days are 10 hours 50 minutes; its year is 29 years 5 months 14 days; it's 329 million leagues from the Sun; its diameter is 26,000 leagues, and it travels 7,920 leagues pr jour in its orbit.

"Here's Uranus, the latest planet known and not for long, for it was discovered by Herschel on 13 March 1781. Its distance from the Sun is no less than 662 million leagues, and its diameter is 12,000 leagues; its year is 84 years and its velocity 5,580 leagues per hour. That's almost all that astronomers know about it at present."

"How large our universe is!" I exclaimed, enthusiastically, when the demon had finished speaking.

"How small and paltry all those planets are," said the Solarian, shaking his huge head. "The world I inhabit, which you call the Sun, appeared to me until today to be rather mediocre in extent, but I didn't know how many globes there are that are scarcely a six-hundredth the size of mine. Truly, if I didn't have before my eyes one of the inhabitants of the Earth, that imperceptible dost lost in space, I could never have believed that there were living beings enclosed forever in those tiny morsels of mineral matter dispersed around the Sun. Tell me, Monsieur Earthman, don't you find it very cramped on your little miniature world? I'd be very curious to pay it a short visit if I could."

"That can be so easily arranged," said the demon, "that we can leave this very instant."

Chapter VIII
Mercury

"Monseigneur," I said, "you made me travel on an aerolith in coming here; couldn't you procure the comfort of a small comet on the way back?"

"Presumably, my dear, you don't know what a comet is, or you wouldn't make such a request."

"Comets? But nothing is simpler!"

"Let's see."

"They're heavenly bodies whose extraordinary aspect, rapid and seemingly irregular movement, the long tail that has been compared to tresses—especially those of Berenice—and unexpected appearance and disappearance, has caused astonishment and admiration to humans in all times, or superstitious fear. Even today, when we have ceased regarding their movements as irregular, their special nature and the role they play in the economy of our system are as unknown as ever. A comet is ordinarily composed of a more or less luminous central point that is called the nucleus; luminous trails and tails, and a nebulosity that surrounds the nucleus, to which the name of hair is given. That nebulosity and the nucleus, taken together, form the head of the comet. Often, however, the bodies have neither a tail, nor hair, nor nebulosity, and simply consist of a more or less luminous dot with the appearance of a star, It is sufficient, in the eyes of astronomers, for a body to be a comet, if it is 'animated by a proper movement and to describe an ellipse of such eccentricity that it ceases to be visible during a part of its rotation.'"

"Your definition, my dear, does not appear to me to be worth very much, for in sum, what tells you that these bodies with neither tails not hair, which describe very eccentric ellipses, are not planets? What tells you that a greater or lesser degree of eccentricity can change the specific nature of a body and bring about a systematic change, when you haven't even determined the degree of eccentricity, except approximately?"

"Pardon me," said the Solarian, "but I don't understand exactly what you mean by ellipse, eccentricity, etc."

"This is what it is," I hastened to say. "An ellipse is nothing other than what sketchers call an oval, and the more elongated the oval is, the more eccentric the ellipse is." I drew one for him. "The two points are called the focal points of the eclipse. The long line is the major axis, of which the two extremities form the summits of the ellipse where they encounter the curve. The distances between the focal points and the summits are called the focal distances. The mid-point between the two focal points is the center of the ellipse, and a line drawn through it at a right-angle to the major axis is the minor axis. The interval between the center and one of the focal points is the eccentricity, and the more eccentricity the ellipse has the further it is from the form of a circle. If I transport one of the focal points, by means of an abstraction that calculation permits me to make, to an infinite distance, my prodigiously elongated ellipse becomes a parabola.

"I'll come back to comets. The Sun always occupies one of the focal points of the ellipse described by the comet, and the summit nearer to that focal point is named the perihelion. The opposite summit is called the aphelion. The distance between the comet and the sun when it passes the former summit is known as the perihelion distance. From the Earth, one can scarcely perceive comets except when they are at their perihelion, or in its vicinity.

"In ancient times these bodies were mistaken for meteors that formed in the atmosphere, or at least no one knew that they followed a regular course. Ancient astronomers did not think they were subject to the laws regulating the other heavenly bodies, and thought that he wandered from system to system through the immensity of space. Since Kepler's discoveries, however, the identity of their movement with the laws of gravitation has been recognized, and it has been possible to submit them to calculation like other bodies whenever they have been observable for long enough. The curves they describe have been determined and it has been ascertained that they move in extremely elongated ellipses.

"The number of comets observed between antiquity and the present day is very large, since it goes back several centuries, but many more are being discovered as the days go by, thanks to the perfection of the telescope, and it can be estimated without exaggeration that several thousand exist. 'Sometimes,' says Herschel, 'these bodies are only visible for a few days; at other times they can be seen for several months; some move with extreme slowness, others with extraordinary speed; it frequently happens that the same comet offers examples of the two cases in different parts of its course.'

"The comet of 1472 described a celestial arc of 120 degrees in one day, which is two thirds of the sky. The movement of some is direct—from west to east—that of others retrograde, from east to west; others have a tortuous and quite irregular course. They are not confined, like the planets, to certain regions of the sky, but travel indifferently in all directions. The variations of their apparent dimensions are no les remarkable than their velocity. Sometimes they appear first as faint nebulae endowed with a very slow movement; by degrees their movement accelerates; they become larger and project their appendage behind them, which, in those cases, always increases in size and brightness until they approach the Sun and are lost in its radiance. Some time later they reappear on the other side, drawing away from the Sun at a velocity that is rapid at first but gradually diminishes.

"It is only after having passed the Sun that they shine with their full splendor and their tails attain the final term of their development, so the action of the sun must be regarded as the cause of that extraordinary emanation. As they draw further away from the Sun their movement slows, the tails dissipate or are absorbed by the heads, which diminish in brightness continuously themselves and end up disappearing, never to return, at least in the majority of cases. A comet that describes an elliptical orbit, however elongated its axis might be, must have visited the sun before and must, unless it experiences some perturbation, approach it again at the end of a determined period; but if it describes a hyperbolic orbit, once it has drawn away from its perihelion, it will never return to the sphere in which we can observe it; it must visit other systems or be lost in the immensity of space.

"A few comets, but small in number, describing ellipses, can be considered as belonging to our solar system. One of the most remarkable is Halley's Comet, thus named because of Edmond Halley, who calculated its course or parabolic elements, as astronomers put it, in 1682. The analogy of the results he obtained with those obtained by Kepler for a comet observed in 1607 inspired him with the idea that it might be the same one; he inferred that its period of revolution must be 76 years, and that it was identical with one that appeared in 1531 and was observed by Apian. In consequence, he dared to predict its reappearance for the end of the year 1758 or the beginning of 1759. But there was a question of whether the attraction of the large planets might influence the orbit of the comet.

"Clairaut attempted the difficult calculation and found that its return to perihelion would be delayed by 100 days by the attraction of Saturn and at least 518 by that of Jupiter, which fixed the return between the middle of April and the middle of March 1759. In fact, the comet reappeared at its perihelion on 12 March of that year. Messieurs Damoiseau and Pontécoulant calculated its next return to perihelion; the former fixed it at 4 November 1835 and the latter at 13 November the same year. That difference of calculation was doubtless due in large part to the fact that Damoiseau and Pontécoulant had not adopted the same masses for the perturbatory planets. At any rate, the comet appeared and was observed from Rome on 5 August 1835; it reached its perihelion on 16 November and disappeared after having been observed for the last time from Vienna by Littrow on 27 January 1836. Isn't that precision admirable?

197

"But if Halley's Comet was the first whose orbit was calculated, several others have been calculated since, including the 'short period' comet observed in 1805, whose revolution is three and a half years; the 'six year' comet, which takes that time to travel its orbit and was observed for the first time in 1772. With regard to the latter comet, I must tell you a little story. One of our astronomers, who died a few years ago, had predicted that the comet would pass so close to the Earth in 1805 that it would crash into or set fire to our poor Europe, and on the basis of that prediction, all the believers had a nervous tremor that obliged them to decamp as soon as possible to America, to await the terrible catastrophe there, ready to wear mourning for their fatherland. The comet passed by at the time indicated by the astronomer, but two millions leagues away from us, in an extremely innocent fashion. Then the Parisians recovered their gaiety and set about writing vaudevilles about the comet."

"Before we depart," said the Solarian, addressing himself to me, "could we not have a brief recapitulation of what you have said about the mass and dimensions of the planets, and render those things as sensible as possible by means of a vulgar comparison?"

"Vulgar to the point of triviality, and it's Herschel who will make it for you. This is what he says:

"'Imagine a field or a flat meadow and place a two foot globe there to represent the Sun. Then Mercury would be represented by a mustard-seed have for its orbit 164 feet in diameter; Venus a pea on a 284-foor circle; and the Earth another pea on a 430-foot circle. Mars would be a large pinhead on a 654-foot circle; Juno, Ceres, Vesta and Pallas grains of sand in orbits between 1,000 and 2,000 feet; Jupiter an orange on a circle of 2,200 feet; Saturn a small orange on a circle of 4,000 feet, or very nearly a third of a league. Uranus would be a large cherry on a circle of 8,200 feet, or three-quarters of a league. If one wanted to imitate the planets in their orbits Mercury would describe a length equal to its diameter in 41 seconds, Venus in 4 minutes four seconds, the Earth in 7 minutes, Mars in 4 minutes 48 seconds, Jupiter in 2 hours 56 minutes, Saturn in 3 hours 18 minutes and Uranus in 2 hours 16 minutes."

I had scarcely finished when the demon, seizing both the Solarian and me, each by one ear, lifted us up from the summit of the mountain, and hurled us into space with a velocity that no expression can render. In less than a minute we had traversed the two atmospheres of the Sun and the empty gray space that separated us from the planet nearest to us—which is to say, Mercury.

When we were still a certain distance away, the genius, sniggering in a very sly manner, observed to me that it was exactly like a game of skittles.

"Presumably," he added, "this one has never been in fusion, although it's three times closer to the Sun than the Earth; its poles aren't flattened, and yet it rotates on its axis with the same speed, for its days are twenty-four hours long."

I pretended not to hear the sarcasm, and we penetrated into Mercury's atmosphere, which I found slightly denser than Earth's, although the difference was not as great as I believed to be the opinion of our astronomers. But what surprised me more was to find a very moderate temperature, although Newton had calculated that Mercury receives seven times as much heat from the Sun as the Earth does.

"That comes," the genius told me, "from the fact, as I've already revealed to you several times, that the Sun doesn't send heat, but the light that gives rise to it by acting upon caloric. Although Mercury receives seven times more light, it contains seven times less caloric, from which a compensation results, and the temperature here is similar to Earth."

We set foot on the ground in a vast plain covered in a kind of grain or grass that I took at first for Indian bamboo, for the plants were at least twelve or fifteen feet high. We sat down on a clump of coarse hard moss in order to rest from the rapidity of our journey, and I made a few reflections analogous to those I had made on arriving on the Sun.

I was very simple, I said to myself, *to believe in Micromégas and monstrous giants. There are certainly no giants in the universe and I'm one of the most beautiful humans in creation*—I darted a glance at the little Solarian—*and I shall probably only see pygmies on the globe we're on now, for, Mercury only being two-fifths as large as the Earth, it's evident that the people who inhabit it...*

A horrible noise resounded in our ears and was repeated by echoes, like claps of thunder. And yet, it was not thunder, but a terrible voice, compared with which the bellowing of a bull or the roaring of the lions of the Sahara would only have seemed sight murmurs.

I got up, very frightened, and was looking around when I suddenly perceived a frightful being bounding along some distance away. It was at least eight feet tall and, in general, resembled a man—but seen in detail, it was an extraordinary monster. Its body was long and thin, covered with hair; its feet were flat, very long, equipped with five fingers capable of seizing objects, absolutely like those of an ape; its head was very small, much more so proportionally than that of a human, prolonged in front by a kind of prominent muzzle split by a mouth, or rather a maw, which extended on either side all the way to the ears. Its large and robust hands were armed with flat but very strong fingernails terminating in sharp points.

On perceiving us, the monster uttered another cry as terrifying as the first and started bounding in our direction. It was already extending its hairy arm toward me, and I was already regarding myself as doomed, devoured and digested when the genius extended his crutch toward the furious animal, touched it, and suddenly appeased its anger. Then it considered us very attentively for a moment; it approached, if not meekly, at least with curiosity; then it sat down tranquilly beside me and stated making grimaces that would have made me laugh if they had not frightened me.

When I had recovered from my alarm sufficiently, I asked the demon what the singular beast might be.

"Look at it carefully," he said. "You know it because it has its analogue on Earth."

Indeed, after having examined it very attentively, I remembered Cuvier's characteristic description in *Règne animal* volume I,[74] page three: "Arms long; brow receding markedly; small, compressed skull; pyramidal face, black, as well the hands; brown body."

"I've got it!" I cried. "It's a pongo."[75]

"Not at all," said the demon. "It's a human."

"What! A human? Pongos are human on Mercury?"

"Why not? Aren't humans only distinguished from animals by the superiority of their intelligence? Well, on Mercury, this one is also the most intelligent of living beings. In any case, I'll give you a specimen of the accuracy of his reasoning by enabling you to chat with him."

The demon made a sign, and the Solarian and I found ourselves informed of the language of pongos. This is the conversation that resulted.

"Monsieur Ape," I said to him, with all the politeness that his long teeth and sharp fingernails merited, "why were you angry with me when you caught sight of me? Have I, by chance, offended you without meaning to? Is it because I'm on your property?"

---

[74] Originally published in 1817, although the reference is probably to Volume I of the revised edition of 1829.

[75] The term "pongo" was invented by the Comte de Buffon in his *Histoire naturelle* to describe larger great apes like the orangutan and the gorilla (which he confused) from the smaller jocko (the chimpanzee). In the original version of the specific volume indicated, Cuvier classified the pongo as a kind of baboon, but changed his mind later and decided that the pongo was an orangutan, so that is what volume I of the 1829 edition alleges, and Boitard seems to agree. It is worth mentioning that in the interplanetary journey in Restif's *Les Posthumes* the inhabitants of Venus look like orangutans, although they are intellectually more advanced than humans.

"I wasn't angry," he replied. "I simply wanted to eat you because I'm hungry. As for property, I don't know what it is."

That, I said to myself, privately, *advertises an excessively young civilization, it's a long way from this pongo to a Parisian lawyer.*

"What! You were about to commit such a great injustice, Monseigneur!"

"There's no injustice, since I'm the stronger. Isn't the most general natural law that the stronger eat the weaker?"

"I agree with that up to a point, but I don't believe that humans have been created expressly to furnish nourishment to pongos."

"All beings weaker than me have been created to serve as aliments for my female, my children and myself."

"That's a frightful egotism!"

"And yet," the Solarian replied to me, "it's the egotism that is the primal cause of society. Humans, in coming together, only abandoned a part of it to ensure protection, in order to enjoy the rest peacefully. I wouldn't be astonished if the pongos soon united in the body of a nation."

"They've already begun," said the demon, "for they live in families, they build huts, and they come together in numbers in order to attack elephants; they dress their wounds with macerated leaves; and finally, which is much more characteristic, they make war on one another.

"Besides which," he continued, "Mercury hasn't always been inhabited by pongos. Once—which is to say, three hundred thousand years ago—it was populated by humans absolutely similar to those of the Sun; but those humans, by virtue of cultivating their intelligence, finished up attaining all the mental perfection of which they were capable, and *esprit* killed them."[76]

"Have they gone back to spirits in this land?"

---

[76] The word *esprit* has several meanings in French; I have left it untranslated because the narrator takes the wrong inference, thinking that the demon means "spirit" rather than "intellect."

"You misunderstand me; I'll explain myself better. On Mercury and the Sun, the mental perfectibility of humankind has a limit fixed by their material nature; as the intellect gains, the physique loses, in regular and invariable proportions. The brain develops at the expense of the body, which atrophies for want of exercise; the head becomes enormous, the legs thin and unsteady; the chest shrinks the vertebral column weakens and becomes curved; all the faculties weaken to the point that the species no longer conserves anything but unhealthy runts exhausted in advance. Finally, the race gradually diminishes and ends up being completely annihilated.

"Such has been, on Mercury, the revolution that has destroyed the human species; such will be the one that will destroy it on the Sun. But matter is modified and does not die; it conserves its properties eternally, from which it results that the Solarian and the Mercurian are reborn from their ashes like the phoenix. After having passed through the circle of all the modifications, globes return to what might be called the primal zoological periods. Animals become organized; their organization improves, or, rather, is complicated, by the march of the centuries, and soon, here's the pongo who has come to replace the humans of Mercury who once inhabited these now-deserted countries. The pongo will be improved, and..."[77]

Another strange noise was heard. It was a kind of resounding melody, like that of a great cathedral organ, which interrupted the genius by drowning out his voice. That extremely loud music had something rather pleasant about it, and yet it proceeded chromatically by semitones and even quarter-tones, which rendered it rather bizarre to an ear accustomed to our diatonic music. I was about to ask what instrument could make such a noise when I perceived a warbler as large as a

---

[77] This scenario of degeneration and replacement was subsequently echoed in an Earthly context in Edmond Haraucourt's "Le Gorilloïd" (1904; tr. as "The Gorilloid" in *Illusions of Immortality*, Black Coat Press, ISBN 978-1-61227-075-3.).

thumb, which was nevertheless making that resounding concert all by itself.

"There's a little animal with an extremely loud voice," I said.

"Not at all; it's a warbler analogous to the chirping warbler that you know, and its voice only seems loud because it's resonating in an atmosphere more compact than that of the Earth."

Scarcely had the genius pronounced those words than the little bird flew away, and in spite of its exceedingly small wings, I was astonished to see it cleave through the air with a rapidity compared to which the flight of a swallow is merely slow. But I understood very well that that was the effect of two causes: firstly, the density of the air, which offered a more facile point of support than the light air of my native land would have done; and secondly, Mercury having a much smaller mass than the Earth, it also has a lesser force of attraction.

That idea immediately made me try an experiment. Although naturally not much of a dancer, it has sometimes happened, when fashion permitted one to do something other than walk while dancing, to perform an entrechat *quatre*, without ever being able to elevate myself as far as a *six*. In order to make my experiment I leapt up, and was delighted with myself when I found that I could easily surpass a *six* and even a *huit*. Delighted to find that eminent merit in myself, I continued to leap and prance with a lightness that would have made a dancer at the Opéra envious.

The Solarian looked at me in amazement, shaking his huge head. The demon laughed and held his sides, and the pongo, carried away by his instinct of imitation, started capering, turning somersaults and making perilous leaps—from which the inhabitant of the Sun concluded that he already had a tendency to advanced civilization.

We both certainly developed a good deal of grace; but in spite of the vivacity we put into it, I found a slowness in our movements that would not have permitted us a *galop* or a

204

sauteuse; in spite of all our efforts we were always in the slow measure of a minuet. That was because bodies that fall on Mercury only travel at a dozen feet per second, while they travel sixteen on Earth. When executing an entrechat we remained the air a quarter longer than one does at the Opéra, which does not permit a very lively dance.

Finally, weary of dancing, I was about to sit down when the demon told us that we were about to quit Mercury in order to go to Venus.

"Because," he added, "Everything interesting that you might see here, you'll find again there."

The pongo wanted to go back to his woods, but the genius told him, touching him with his crutch, that he was to come with us, and immediately, all four of us departed through space.

I scarcely had time to see one high mountain on Mercury, probably the one that, by extending its shadow toward one of the edges of its disk, causes it to appear indented when seen from Earth, a particularity that has allowed our astronomers to calculate the various revolutions of the planet.

Chapter IX
A Comet

It had not been a minute since we departed from Mercury when we perceived a comet that the demon had mentioned to us. What struck me most forcibly was its tail, which was no less than forty million leagues long.[78] As we got closer, the comet seemed less bright to me, and when we were very close—which is to say, within twenty or thirty thousand leagues, it did not appear to me to be any more so than the light vaporous mists high in our atmosphere that are silvered by the sunlight. I could no longer doubt then that those singular bodies do not have a luminosity, even a phosphorescence, of their own.

I had immediately perceived, or thought I had perceived, an opaque nucleus placed in the middle of the comet's head; but on getting closer, that nucleus became transparent, and I did not take long to assure myself by the sight of my own eyes that it was simply composed of a gas slightly less dilated that the one that formed its atmosphere. It had considerable analogies with the dry fogs that have sometimes astonished Earthly naturalists so much.

Eventually, we entered its atmosphere—or, if you prefer, its hair; it was composed of a gas so rare and diaphanous that it appeared to me to be a thousand times lighter than the air we breathe on Earth. The only thing that enabled me to recognize the atmosphere was the light of the sky, which

---

[78] Author's note: "Comets have been seen, such as those of 1769 and 1615, with tales so long that their heads reached the zenith—the point of the sky directly above the observer's head—while their tails were still touching the horizon. It was estimated that the tail of the comet of 1680 was more than 41,000,000 leagues in length."

ceased to be a dull gray, as in space,[79] because the phenomenon of refraction occurred in the gas in the same manner as in
ordinary air, and for that reason the sky began to appear indigo
blue, but of a very pale hue.

I also observed something that seemed to me to be very
singular, although I had already heard mention of it from astronomers, which is that, before arriving at the nucleus, we
had to traverse three similar atmospheres, which entirely surrounded it, and which were separated from one another by
immense intervals, empty and, in consequence, dull gray, because the sun did not find any matter there to refract it.[80]

---

[79] Author's note: "Mademoiselle d'Angeville, whose courageous excursion on Mont Blanc has been reported in the
newspapers, has been kind enough to send me an interesting
note in which she says: 'The sky became an infinitely deeper
blue the higher I went, like watered-down indigo. That dark
blue is the general hue of the sky seen from enclosed locations
such as a garden, but at those high altitudes that deep shade
only existed above me head, and always faded toward the
horizon.' Everyone, especially painters, knows that the color
indigo is merely a mixture of blue and black."
Henriette d'Angeville (1794-1871) climbed to the summit of
Mont Blanc on 4 September 1838, the first woman to do so on
her own feet (her only predecessor had been carried part way
by her guides).
[80] Author's note: "'In comets that have a nucleus, the parts of
the hair neighboring that nucleus are ordinarily rare, diaphanous and not very luminous; but at a certain distance from the
nucleus, the nebulosity suddenly brightens, in such a way as to
form a luminous ring around the comet. One sometimes sees
two and as many as three of these concentric rings, separated
by dark intervals. One understands, moreover, that what appears to be a circular ring in projection, must in reality be a
spherical envelope.' (*Leçons d'astronomie*, p, 203.) The ring
of the comet of 1811 was 10,000 leagues across; it was 12,000

As we got closer to the nucleus I saw it become paler, and then take on a transparency such that on approaching it, it no longer seemed to be anything but an enormous globe of crystal. Finally, when we arrived there, I was able to assure myself that it was not composed of solid matter, but a mixture of different gases, the density of which was nearly equal to that of the air forming the terrestrial atmosphere. We traversed that bubble of air, which might have been five or six thousand leagues in diameter, and I remarked very clearly that its density augmented as we approached its center. Having arrived there, I was not a little astonished to encounter a small solid globe, a quarter of a league in diameter at the most, resembling a little miniature Earth, although it had no vegetation, and consequently no animals.

We rested there for a few moments, and while the Pongo gamboled and the Solarian slept, I questioned the genius, who replied to me:

"For the astronomers of your homeland, comets are a great subject of astonishment, doubt and even polemic. Some assert that they have no solid nucleus and are entirely gaseous; others argue that they are globes analogous to those of other planets, but less dense, and neither understand the role they play in nature. I shall reveal al that to you. These bodies are nothing other than the elements of the matter that have formed the globes. Originally, these elements were floating at random in infinite space, occasionally forming enormous clusters of gas, similar to light clouds of prodigious extent. I say "clusters of gas" because there was no solid matter then; there was absolutely what ancient peoples have named chaos, for all those gases were mixed, without any order, and that was because no center of gravity existed yet, and in consequence no weight

---

leagues distant from the nucleus. The comets of 1807 and 1799 also had rings 12,000 and 8,000 leagues across."

François Arago's oft-reprinted *Leçons d'astronomie* was first published in 1837.

determined toward a point, but a thousand feeble and confused attractions, canceling one another out in their effects.

"When I talk about the origin of things, I'm not claiming that the entire universe was nothing but chaos, but only that minimal fraction of matter that you call your solar or planetary system. Throughout eternity there have been chaotic regions in infinite space ready to give birth to new systems; systems still young and full of energy and life; and old systems more or less exhausted; and finally, systems returning to the chaos from which they had emerged, and which, in the course of millions of centuries, will reproduce new worlds. That rotation of life and death, incessantly succeeding one another, of youth and decrepitude, of composition and decomposition, is a general law of nature, which regulates the entire universe as well as your petty globe, your domain and your family.

"Every cluster of gaseous matter was then, as it is today, a comet, a kind of nest in which a globe would be born, as you shall see. When two gases capable of forming solid matter by their combination encounter one another in certain proportions, they are compounded and condensed; that forms a nucleus; that nucleus, even if it is only the size of a fist, has become a center of attraction, and new solid matter falls on to it as it is formed by chemical combinations, gradually increasing the size of the nascent globe at the expense of its gaseous atmosphere. The result of that is quite simply that comets become planets, and the Earth that has seen you born is nothing other than that.[81]

"That is why comets exist today in the primitive state of gaseous clusters, in which astronomers cannot detect any solid

---

[81] This cosmogony echoes Restif's in seeing comets as the precursors of planets, but in Restif's, comets are the living offspring of the sun, whose orbits decrease as they cool down and which become planets when they die—a notion from which Boitard feels compelled to dissent. Restif's cosmogony also makes much of the notion of cometary impacts with planets and disastrous near misses, which Boitard similarly rejects.

nucleus; they have so little density that their attraction is almost non-existent; thus, one has been observed that passed between the satellites of Jupiter without causing the slightest perturbation in their march, so little action did it have upon them even though its volume was vast compared to theirs. That is why other comets have been observed that have a solid nucleus, but very small, or sometime the size of one of our larger planets; they are nascent worlds. Finally, that is also why others exist that consist entirely of a nucleus without a tail or hair, because the tail and hair, in solidifying, have formed a globe similar to that of the planets; they are newborn worlds.

"That explains why the orbits of comets are more or less irregular. You can see that, their density varying continuously compared to their volume, continual perturbations result therefrom. Those bodies must, therefore, commence by wandering randomly in the heavens, and then regulate their movement gradually as they acquire solidity, finally ending up by settling around a sun that they encounter in space once they have become veritable planets. You understand now why astronomers have observed comets that lose some of their brightness and size every time they make further appearances in our system; why there are some whose periodicity cannot be calculated; why some show themselves only to disappear forever thereafter, etc., etc.[82]

"Once it was believed that the appearance of a comet had a certain influence on the course of the seasons, but, thermometric experiments having proved that they have no effect on

---

[82] Author's note: "Aristotle mentions the tail of the comet of 371 B.C., which occupied a third of the celestial hemisphere, or sixty degrees. That of the year 1618 had, it's said, a wake 164 degrees in length. The comet of 1680 had a seventy-degree tail. That of 1770 travelled its orbit in five and a half years, and after having been escorted in the heavens by Jupiter it disappeared completely."

temperature, that prejudice has vanished to give way to others, of which the principal ones are these.

"People have wondered whether it is possible for a comet to collide with the Earth, and, if so, what would happen as a result. It is certain that these bodies traverse our solar system, that in their course they cross the orbits of the planets, including the Earth. Rigorously speaking, it is therefore possible that one of them might encounter our globe, but if one submits the fact to the calculation of probabilities, one finds that that there is only one chance for and two hundred and eighty-one million against, which ought to be reassuring for cowards. In any case, listen to what would result from that impact, according to our astronomers:

"'Its effects would be frightful. If the Earth were struck in such a manner that its orbital motion were canceled out, everything that is not stuck to its surface, such as animals, waters, etc., would depart at a velocity of seven leagues per second. If the impact only slowed down its motion of rotation, the seas would be hurled from their basins, the equator and poles would be exchanged, etc.'

"And if I quote you the words of the author of *La Mécanique céleste*, there is even worse: 'If the axis and movement of rotation were changed,' he says, 'the seas abandoning their former positions to precipitate toward the new equator, a large proportion of humans and animals drowned in the universal deluge or destroyed by the violent shock imparted to the terrestrial globe, entire species annihilated, all the movement of human industry overturned: such would be the disasters that the impact of a comet would produce.'

"One can see then why the Ocean has covered high mountains, on which it has left incontestable evidence of its sojourn; one can see how the animals and plants of the south have been able to exist in the climes of the north, where their remains and imprints can be found; finally, one can explain the novelty of the mental world, whose monuments scarcely go back beyond five thousand years."

"You're frightening me! What! It's possible that such a catastrophe might be repeated?"

"Don't worry. All that is merely the innocent romance of a geometer weary of posing figures and who, in order to relax, abandons his imagination to utopias without foundation. I could prove to you mathematically by the invariability if the terrestrial latitudes that the Earth rotates around a principal axis, not a momentary one, as it would be if it had received an impact that had displaced the axis in question, but you're not enough of a geometer to understand me.

"Then again, I don't believe that there's the possibility of an impact, even if the Earth and the comet have a direction necessary for it. If the mass of the comet were smaller than that of the Earth, when the errant body arrived within the power of attraction of our globe, far from falling on it, the force of its trajectory in combination with its gravitation would result in its rotating around the Earth and becoming one of its satellites. The Moon, Saturn's ring and all the planetary satellites had the same origin. But if, on the contrary, the mass of the comet was more considerable than that of the Earth, it is the latter that would become the satellite of the comet, and it would be drawn through space by it into new skies."

"What you're telling me there is scarcely more reassuring. Hurled away with a speed of seven leagues a second or frozen in space are not much better than one another."

"What tells you that you'd freeze? Hasn't Fourier proven that the intensity of cold in space can't descend below fifty thermometric degrees?"

"Believe me, that would be quite enough to freeze me to the marrow of my bones; I can no longer take off my furry slippers and my cotton bonnet when the temperature drops to zero."

"You'd get accustomed to it. White bears play on the ice-floes of the North Sea at a temperature of 32 degrees below zero, while the giraffe is tranquil and enjoys all the pleasures of life on the equator at 45 degrees of heat; Lapps kill the bears of the floes and negroes hunt giraffes on the equator, and that's a difference of 77 degrees. Now, with better-furred slippers and a woolen bonnet, I don't see why a difference of 50 degrees should kill you, all the more so as, if the winters were cold, your summers would probably be hot, because you'd pass terribly close to the sun.

"But all that won't happen, for the matter of comets is so rarefied, so distended, if I might use that expression, that its force of attraction is almost negligible compared to that of a solid globe, so none is known that has satellites. It's for the same reason that they easily escape, in whole or in part, the attraction of other bodies."

"You say 'in part'; is that because you believe, as many people do, that the dry fogs of 1783 and 1831 were matter detached from the tail of a comet?"[83]

"No, and for two incontrovertible reasons. The first is that in 1783 and 1831, those fogs only masked the sky in certain parts of the Earth—which did not, however, prevent astronomical observations from taking their normal course, and we are assured that no comet was manifest in our system. Cer-

---

[83] Author's note: "The fog of 1783 lasted for a month; it began almost on the same day at places very distant from one another. It extended from North Africa to Sweden; it also occupied a large part of North America, but it did not extend over the sea. It rose up above the highest mountains. The wind did not appear to be its vehicle, and the most abundant rains and strongest winds could not dissipate it. It spread a disagreeable odor, was very dry, did not affect the hygrometer and possessed a phosphorescent property. (*Leçons d'astronomie.*) The fog of 1831 had a great analogy with that one."

The "great dry fog" of 1783 is now thought to have been caused by a volcanic eruption in Iceland. Arago, contradicting the theory that the 1783 fog was caused by a comet, pointed out both the possible volcanic origin of the 1783 fog and its analogy with the 1831 fog, but he latter remains stubbornly unexplained.

tainly, if we had plunged into its tail, we would have seen its head.

"Secondly, those fogs did not extend over the sea, or, at least not beyond forty or fifty miles from the coasts; which proves, it seems to me, that it's necessary to seek the causes in some phenomenon that was occurring on or in the land of our continents and not in the sky or even in the atmosphere; for then, occupying Europe from North Africa to Sweden and extending over a part of North America, it would necessarily have covered the portion of the Ocean that separates Europe and America.

"However, supposing that an encounter between a comet and the Earth could have taken place, what would happen? Nothing. Our globe would pass through it like Franconi's horse through a paper hoop;[84] perhaps, in traversing it, it would draw away with it a small portion of gaseous matter, and that would be the whole extent of it."

We were at that point in our conversation when the Solarian woke up and the Pongo ceased gamboling. Then we abandoned the comet and departed for Venus, where we did not take long to arrive.

During the trajectory, I had remarked that Venus, like Mercury, has phases similar to those of the Moon, and I was able to perceive that because we had not traveled in a straight line in departing from the Sun; otherwise, evidently, I would always have seen Venus full—which is to say that the part I perceived would have been constantly illuminated by the sun's rays, coming from the same direction as me. The planet seemed to me to be brighter that the others because it has an atmosphere that is proportionately more extensive.

---

[84] The two sons of the famous equestrian Antonio Franconi (1738-1836) founded the Cirque Olympique in Paris in 1806, and renewed the project twice more in 1817 and 1827 after forced closures.

Chapter X
Venus

Venus is slightly smaller than the Earth, its diameter only being 97% of ours, which is to say, approximately 2,800 leagues. Its years and days are also shorter, the former being only 224 days, 16 hours, 41 minutes 27 seconds, and the days 23 hours 21 minutes. Its form is spherical and its surface is dotted with high mountains whose projected shadows make the horns of its crescent seem truncated when seen from Earth. It is a very pretty land, and not very hot, although it is only twenty-five million leagues from the sun and, as the genius told me, its caloric is almost as abundant as that of the Earth. That is because its atmosphere is always covered with aqueous vapors that rise from the surface of the seas and form a cloudy veil that intercepts the direct light of the sun's rays.

We descended on to a lovely lawn carpeted with delicate grass and lichens, at the entrance to a forest and on the edge of an azure sea. I noticed that the ocean had no tides, for its shores were grassy and florid all the way to the water's edge. I made that observation to the genius, who told me that on all the planets that have no moons or satellites, the oceans cannot offer the phenomenon of a flux and reflux. I understood the accuracy of that reflection, because I knew that on Earth our tides are only due to the combined attractions of the Moon and the Sun.

Another singularity that struck me no less when the demon acquainted me with it is that Venus, instead of having four seasons every year, like Earth, has eight. He explained the cause to me,[85] but in spite of that, I was no less surprised to

---

[85] Author's note: "Its axis has an orbital inclination of 75 degrees, and the north pole of that axis inclines toward the twentieth degree of Aquarius, departing from Earth's Cancer. Consequently, the northern region of Venus has summer in the

see seasons of 28 days each bringing no modification to the beautiful vegetation, which I found in general quite similar to that of the Earth. I attributed the cause to the fact that its 28-day winters and summers are neither cold enough or hot enough to suspend vegetation, and I understood from then on that on that fortunate planet, the temperature, varying very little, must offer an eternal spring.

Thus, I found the land constantly ornamented by verdure and flowers, the trees always laden with nascent and ripe fruit, the plains populated by animals frolicking gaily in green pastures, and the forests inhabited by a multitude of birds with bright plumage and melodious voices.

While the Solarian and I conversed about the beauty of nature, Pongo had slipped into the forest in pursuit of a few timid animals. Suddenly, we heard him utter cries of distress, and we did not hesitate to race into the wood to bring him aid. It was just in time, for we found him at odds with two or three Venusians, who, armed with sticks and stones, would easily have put an end to him. The genius interposed his all-powerful crutch, and order was instantly restored.

The Venusians were biped animals like Kaffirs and Pongos, but they differed from both by rather clear-cut characteristics. Their height did not surpass five feet six or seven inches and their reddish-brown bodies were entirely covered with tawny hair tending to blond. Their muzzles were more prominent than that of Kaffirs, to less than that of Pongos; they lacked thighs and calves, like the inhabitants of some Australian islands; their feet were very long, like the feet of the islanders of some islands of New Zealand, and—a very remarkable thing—the big toe was opposable to the other digits, as

_____

signs when we have winter, and winter in those when we have summer. As the greatest declination of the Sun on each side of its equator extends to 75 degrees, its tropics are fifteen degrees from its poles and its polar circles as far from the equator. It therefore has two summers and two winters at its equator in each if its annual revolutions among some savages of South America. In sum, I cannot give you a more accurate idea than a certain figure of a human fossil that I have described elsewhere. Bearskins hung from their shoulders and they had sticks in their hands, or rather clubs, which appeared to have been appropriately shaped with trenchant stones.

"Here," said the demon, "are the monarchs of nature on Venus; there are no other beings as yet more perfect than these rough sketches of humankind."

"Are they civilized?" I asked.

"Only humans are capable of civilization, because they need to live in society, and society leads to civilization. The Venusians have strength, courage and agility, they only live in mild climes; their bodies are covered with a thick hairy coat that protects them from the vagaries of the weather; they easily find an abundant nourishment; why should they become civilized? On the equator of Venus they will always remain the same, but as the race multiplies, it will be obliged to extend toward the poles, and then new climates will force them to acquire new habits; their intelligence will develop, their nature will be modified, and they will be forced to live in numerous society. In any case, you're going to hear the conversation between this one and Pongo.

Indeed, I remarked the two apes, who were still making threatening gestures at one another in spite of the magical power of the crutch. I say the two apes, because only one of the Venusians remained.

"Brigand," said the latter, in a language that closely resembled the clucking of a turkey, "Why are you attacking me in my own territory when I haven't done you any harm?"

"Because I've just learned what property is; it pleases me; it's a good idea. I too wanted to have a hut of foliage like yours and a club to kill other animals. Not knowing how to make such things myself, I thought it simple enough to take them; I would have eaten you afterwards."

"What! So you don't have any idea of justice and injustice?"

"I don't know what that is."

"You're a barbarian, a brute devoid of intelligence, and if I'd been allowed to do it, I'd have made you my slave, which would have taught you justice."

"That," said the genius, "is the beginning of all civilizations. As soon as there is yours and mine, one gradually sees the birth of morality and vice, violence and weakness, and then everything that follows of abominable crimes and heroic virtues."

"Monseigneur Demon, permit me to observe that until now, you have always shown me humans and apes, which is inevitably becoming a trifle monotonous. Are all globes populated in the same manner?"

"I believe I've already told you that, matter being the same everywhere, it obeys the same laws of organization, and that the same causes produce similar effects."

"Pardon me, but if you hadn't told me that matter is identical everywhere, how could I have learned it?"

"By reflection. You know the volume, the mass and the density—or, if you prefer it, the weight—of planets; you know the laws of gravitation, to which everything is absolutely obedient in the same manner as our globe; you know about caloric, the great motor of everything in the universe that has movement; you know about light, which inundates the worlds, its effects, its refraction, all phenomena acting on the planets exactly as on your world, and many other effects that reveal causes similar to those active in your homeland. Reason, logic and analogy oblige you, therefore, to conclude that matter on other worlds has the same properties as on Earth. If you thought otherwise, you would fall into hypotheses that are not based on any fact, and you would be whistled by the scientists of Paris, who no longer want to know anything but facts, until they know what they might do with them."

"That's odd! I expected to see humans with wings, oxen with sails, pigs with ruffs and a thousand other marvels. Not at all—it's almost the same as back home."

"If the marvelous is absolutely necessary to amuse you, I can show you some, albeit of another genre. Let's go."

He made a sign to the Venusian, who immediately ceased arguing with Pongo and marched ahead of us.

We arrived after a quarter of an hour at the entrance to a charming valley, opening on to a vast plain covered with rich pastureland. A magnificent river was parading its limpid waters there, flowing through verdant hills ornamental by the most cheerful vegetation. I noticed in particular that palm trees of several kinds, pines and yews were dominant in the forests by virtue of their number and gigantic stature. The Venusian, whom we knew to be named Kojas-Morou, made us turn right and follow the banks of a steam for a while, along a belt of rocks that formed a kind of amphitheater. In order to enjoy the magnificent view that was deployed around us, we climbed up on to a little plateau covered with fine grass and moss, and, gripped by admiration, we sat down there.

The sun was beginning to rise over the horizon, and I was only slightly surprised to see that it was twice as large as if I had been looking at it from Earth; I easily explained that phenomenon to myself by reflecting that I was seeing it at much closer range. What I did not understand so easily, however, was the color of the sky, which appeared to me to be a lapis blue a thousand times brighter than all the blues I had seen employed in Paris by Destouches, one of the most gracious of genre painters,[86] and yet I could not say that it was as deep as the indigo skies of Monsieur   . That color was so singular that the demon perceived my astonishment.

"That hue," he told me, "results from a very simple effect. Doubtless you know that air is blue and colors with the same tint the objects one sees through it. The coloration has more intensity as the layer of air interposed between an object and your eye becomes thicker. Now, the atmosphere of Venus being much more considerable than that of Earth, you can

---

[86] Paul-Émile Destouches (1794-1874).

understand that the sky, when it is uncovered and cloudless—which is rare here—must appear much bluer."

At that moment the demon interrupted himself, made me a sign, and with an ironic wink of the eye indicated the Solarian to me, who was yawning as if to dislocate his jaw. By virtue of a sympathy as commonplace as it is inexplicable, Pongo and Kojas had joined in unison, and I felt an inflation beneath my own ears, announcing that the contagion was about to reach me. I shook my head sharply to repel the charm, and I asked the sage Solarian if he was uncomfortable.

He reflected momentarily before replying, and then, with a great deal of gravity, said: "Alas my dear, living on love and clear water, that's the great question with which sages, philosophers and legislators ought to occupy themselves uniquely and incessantly, for it's the term of human perfection, the *nec plus ultra* of civilization, the maximum of the happiness reserved by Providence for our humankind."

I was amazed, and thought the old man was lapsing into delirium, but he continued:

"When I say love, you understand that I'm talking about the holy love that Heaven has placed in the heart of the honest man for everything that is good, for everything beneficial; the amour that makes the heart of the artist ardent for the beautiful, that of the soldier for glory, that of the citizen for the fatherland, that of the pious man for the author of creation, that of the judge for justice, the philanthropist for...."

"Etc., etc., etc,..." I said.

"Exactly," he replied, and continued: "By means of mutual education and ignorant brethren ne can resolve the first part of the question, but alas, alas, what of the clear water, my friend, what of the clear water? There's the nub of the difficulty. How to replace the beefsteak and plum pudding by clear water! And yet, without that, the diner will kill everything; it's him who..."

At this point the Solarian started yawning extravagantly, and was unable to resume his discourse until five minutes later.

"Yes," he added, "there's no morality, virtue and innocence without clear water." (Further yawns.) "Since we left
the Sun, nothing else has entered my stomach, and judge, my
dear, the perversity of human nature, judge how far away humans still are from perfection, since my stomach is in full in-
surrection against the principles that I've preached for so
many years. Alas, I sense, blushing with shame, that a slice of
mastodon on the grill would give me more pleasure at this
moment than a glass of water, even if it came from the classi-
cal spring of Hippocrene."

"Well then," interjected the demon, "while waiting for
humans to be able to live on love and clear water, I'll send
Pongo and Kojas out hunting, and, given the virtue of my
crutch, we'll be very unlucky if we don't savor a plate of venison, as Walter Scott says thirty-one times in a single octavo
volume."

Scarcely had he spoken than Kojas-Morou put two fingers in his mouth and uttered a shrill whistle. At that signal,
more than two hundred Venusians hidden in the rocks showed
themselves, armed with clubs, bows and spears. Kojas, their
prince, and Pongo set themselves at their head, and they all ran
into the plain, while nevertheless observing the most profound
silence.

I noticed that many of them were guiding animals on
leashes, which I took at first for hunting dogs, for they were
perfectly trained to flush out, pursue, seize and kill game.
When I looked at them at closer range, however, I realized that
they were not dogs but very strong and courageous hares,
whose natural ferocity the Venusians had tamed completely.
They closely resembled the hares of Meudon forest near Paris,
with the difference that they surpassed the stature of the largest mastiffs and their mouths were armed with two rows of
formidable teeth.

The Venusians dispersed into the plain in various small
groups, which took up positions in the most favorable spots to
wait for the game, while others beat the bushes with the
bloodhound-hares.

Suddenly, a timid animal emerged from a bush and fled with the rapidity of an arrow; it was a dog of large size. The hares were unleashed, and set out in pursuit of it, filling the air with their howls. The poor dog evaded the formidable pack for some time, making a thousand zigzag turns, and passing over its own trail to put off its intrepid enemies, but fatality rendered all its tricks futile, for an arrow whistling through the air put an end to its life and its miseries. The furious hares fell upon the innocent denizen of the grassland furiously, and would have torn it to pieces if the hunters had not immediately snatched it away from their brutal ferocity.

Kojas, proud of the success of his hunt, came to deposit the tribute at our feet. Pongo skinned the prey very neatly, we cooked it over hot embers, and I had my first meal since my departure from Earth. If any of my readers coming back from Algeria remembers having witnessed a ceremonial feast among the Arabs, he will know that a cutlet of roasted dog is the best thing that one can eat in Algeria, as on Venus. The Solarian, especially, did honor to our "venison," and it was only after swallowing half of it that he resumed his discussion of love and clear water.

In spite of the beautiful things that he had to say, we stopped listening, because Kojas-Morou, delighted to do us the honors, gave the signal for the hunt to be resumed. We then saw the packs of hares give way to packs of intrepid and well-trained mice, which chased and forced several wild cats. Grouse and hooded quails, bearing little bells on their feet, were launched into the air in pursuit of cowardly falcons, of which they took possession without difficulty.

I rubbed my eyes, pinched my arms and shook my head—in sum, all the gestures of a man who, attacked by a nightmare, tries to wake himself up, on seeing hares, mice and grouse hunting dogs, cats and falcons. I thought I was asleep and dreaming, so extraordinary and contrary to nature did it seem.

The demon read what was passing through my mind.

"Poor gawker," he said, shrugging his shoulders.

"One moment, Monseigneur! I live in Paris, it's true, but I haven't always, and your expression appears to me to be entirely unwarranted."

"My poor friend," he said, "you're a man and an inhabitant of Earth, so you're a gawker, since gawking in the essence of human nature; for your part, your astonishment proves it. Because there are dogs that hunt hares in your homeland, you imagine that it must be the same everywhere."

"Monseigneur, I'm very sorry to have to tell you, but you're not cut from the cloth of which great naturalists are made, if you don't sense the power of analogy. Nowadays we judge everything by analogy, and that's why France is swarming with great men, from the porter's lodge to the highest attic! Analogy is the rule of everything, governs everything and is never mistaken; it's the sibyl of legislators! See how it leads infallibly to the truth—here's an example. One finds in the earth a fossil skull, a scapula and a phalanx, all monstrous, and quickly, quickly, let's seek analogies and we'll know what the strange fossil is.

"'It has a trunk,' says one scientist, 'analogy proves that it was an elephant.'

"'No,' says another, 'look at the strength that the muscles of its neck must have. It was a whale.'

"'You're wrong,' replies the third, 'those long teeth prove that it was walrus.'

"As for me, who is speaking, I arrive with a phalanx of the front foot, and I prove beyond doubt that it was a mole eighteen or twenty feet long, without a tail, and I sustain that the *Dinotherium giganteum* is nothing other than the ancestor of the moles, which..."

I did not have time to finish, for the demon, the Solarian and even the Pongo were holding their sides and laughing. That shocked me singularly, and I fell silent abruptly.

"My poor friend," said the demon, "it's precisely because you can only judge, in the feebleness of your human intelligence, by analogy, that your so-called science is merely a heap of poverties in the midst of which three or four verities are buried, like diamonds lost in the mud. When you know the slightest wisp of matter, when you have recognized all the laws that give it its properties, when you understand yourself, when you know, you'll have no need of analogies that lead you astray more often than they enlighten you. You'll know that the dinotherium was neither an elephant, not a walrus, nor a whale, nor a mole, but a dinotherium. You'll also understand that hares could hunt hounds in the woods of Meudon, because you'll know that matter can be organized in those of millions of billions of ways, with analogies completely different from those you know, and then..."

"And then...?"

"And then you'll be more knowledgeable than me, and there'll no longer be only one being in the universe who...but let's go," said the demon, making a grimace as if one of the bones of our venison had got stuck in his throat.

The Solarian immediately offered him a glass of clear water; but the only response he received was a sinister and thunderous glare.

We left, and traveled through space, taking the inhabitant of Venus with us.

Chapter XI
Mars and Beyond

"It's singular," I said, as we hurtled through the heavens, "that I can't see any sign anywhere of the ether invented by Encke in favor of comets."

"Well, I can certainly believe that you can't see it," the genius replied, "since it doesn't exist. You can imagine that if that ether existed, and had an effect on the movement of comets, it would also have an effect on that of planets. Now, however slight you suppose that action to be, it would eventually obliterate the force of projection that sustains heavenly bodies in the void; the resistance they encounter would reduce their velocity, centrifugal force would diminish, and end up no longer existing, and all the heavenly bodies would collapse on to one another."

In the course of our journey we passed quite close to the Earth and the Moon, but as we were going to come back to them in the last place, the demon would not permit me to descend momentarily in order to freshen up. We therefore continued on our route without stopping, and did not take long to enter into the atmosphere of Mars, the first of the superior plants departing from the Sun, from which it is 52 million 613 thousand leagues away. Its days are almost the same length as ours—24 hours, 31 minutes 22 seconds, to be precise—but its year is almost twice as long as ours, since it is 686 days 23 hours 30 minutes 42 seconds.

Mars is a pretty little globe no more than 1,500 leagues in diameter, where the temperature is almost the same as that on earth, although generally a little colder. Its poles are much flatter than ours, because its diameter in the direction of their axis is only 1400 leagues, which gives each of them a flattening of fifty leagues.[87] The landscape is intercut by plains, valleys and hills, but there are no high mountains, and the soil is everywhere an ocher red similar to the terrains of red sandstone that we know on Earth, but of a more vivid hue.

The atmosphere there is quite similar to that of Earth, neither higher nor thicker, whatever a few astronomers might say who have established their assertion on facts that are more than dubious; but the flattening of the poles is the cause of their being covered every year by a quantity of ice much more considerable than those of Earth, which occasions, when the wind blows directly from the north or the south, sudden transitions of temperature that often ruin vines and melons.

Since the terrestrial globe has its icy polar regions and mountains covered in ice and snow, which only melt partially when they are alternately exposed to the sun, I was not astonished that the same causes produce the same effects on Mars. I assured myself that the resplendent polar patches that are observed there from Earth are due to the sharp reflection that light experiences in those icy regions, and that the diminution of those patches, when they are exposed to the sun's rays, is an effect of the influence of that star. For instance, the patch at the southern pole was extremely large in 1781, as it ought to have been, since that pole was emerging from a twelve-month night, and had been deprived on sunlight throughout that time; it was smaller when observed in 1783, and gradually diminished after 20 May until the middle of September, when it seemed to become stationary.

In that epoch, the south pole had enjoyed eight months of summer, during which it had constantly experienced the influence of solar radiation, although it is true that in the end, that radiation was so oblique that it could not offer any considerable benefit. On the other hand, the north pole, which had fallen into a profound obscurity after twelve months of exposure to

---

[87] Author's note: "The Earth's poles are only flattened by five leagues—which is to say, nineteen times less than those of Mars."

the sun, appeared less considerable, though doubtless augmented in volume. It was not visible in 1783, given the position of the axis, which did not permit us to see hat pole. At any rate, as the planet's axis is inclined to its orbit by 61 degrees 33 minutes, the variations of the seasons there are scarcely sensible, and the temperature is almost the same in all latitudes.

On that globe, I felt a marvelous lightness, and could easily jump to a height of nine feet, while on Earth I could scarcely raise myself by three. The genius told me that whereas I weighed 150 pounds on Earth and 4,050 on the Sun, by virtue of the same law of attraction, I only weighed 50 pounds here.

"Now," he added, "the muscular strength having nevertheless remained the same, it's obvious that, jumping to a height of three feet in Paris, the same thrust ought to raise you nine here."

We had come down at the base of a hill covered with palm trees, banana trees and large number of aromatic bushes, among which I recognized a cinnamon. Pongo, who had decidedly taken on the perilous role of scout, climbed the hill momentarily, followed by our savage Venusian; we heard him call out to us with a cry containing ore admiration than fear or anger, and we saw the Venusian making signals. We headed toward them, and they showed us a village some distance away, which a clump of trees had masked from our views until then.

The village only consisted of huts similar to beehives, but we noticed doors and windows therein, and other traces of nascent architecture. There were streets of a sort, well enough aligned, and a square shaded by pandanus trees and acacias. As we drew nearer, we heard the shrill sound of a musical instrument that had some analogy with a bagpipe, and a swarm of young children emerged from the habitations, singing, in order to come and dance in the shade of mimosas.

"There are some funny beasts," opined Pongo.

"There are some fine slaves," said the Venusian.

"There are some pretty negresses," I said in my turn.

"There, finally, are some humans," murmured the Solarian.

The demon contented himself with shrugging his shoulders, with a pitying expression, on hearing our exclamations.

I shall not give you a description of the inhabitants of Mars, because you have doubtless seen their identical analogues on Earth; they resembled, closely enough to be mistaken for him, negroes of the Congo, with the single difference that their hair, instead of being curly and wooly, was long and flowing.

The demon, addressing himself to the Solarian, asked him with a snigger how he recognized those brutes, going naked and eating raw flesh, as human. "They have huts," he added, "but beavers have better ones, or at least more comfortable; they live in society, but ants, bees and elephants live in society; their language consists of a vocabulary of fifty words, like that of some Australasian islanders, but a well-trained dog understands sixty; their skin isn't covered with hair, but Turkish dogs and frogs have no hair; they walk on two feet, but so do cockerels; they have bearded chins, but billy-goats have them too."

Without being disconcerted, the Solarian contented himself with pointing to something with his finger; it was a venerable old man kneeling before a piece of crudely sculpted wood representing a frightful monster. On perceiving us he stood up and came toward us to offer us hospitality.

"What were you doing over there?" asked the inhabitant of the Sun.

"Worshiping God," replied the old man.

The demon went pale; then a whirlwind suddenly lifted us up, and in the blink of an eye were found ourselves transported to Juno, ninety-two million leagues from the Sun. The Marsian had remained with us.

There, nothing was similar to what we had seen elsewhere; it was no longer a globe that we were in but a formless mineral mass rolling through space, like one of those enormous fragments of mountain that Briareus with the hundred arms hurled into the skies against the gods. Immense fissures vomited forth rivers of boiling lava; thick black smoke poisoned the atmosphere; and a profound silence saddened the soul, announcing that those bare and sterile rocks were still under the empire of death. Not a single sprig of verdure on which to rest the eyes, not one bird flying in the air, not one insect sliding through undergrowth: immobility and death everywhere; that was all.

The form of the planet was entirely angular, without any symmetry, from which it resulted that a vertical plumb-line sometimes varied a great deal over distances that were sometimes very short, for want of having a fixed center of gravity like the center of a sphere. The force of attraction is very weak there, and a body on Juno scarcely weighs more than a twentieth of what it weighs of Earth. We were assured of that fact by a small accident that had no other consequence than cheering us up momentarily and making us forget the frightful bleakness of the landscape that surrounded us—a landscape that reminded me of what the Earth must have been like in the geological epoch that we call the Plutonian.

Our Solarian philosopher, rejoicing in finding himself fifty times lighter than on the Sun, his fatherland, wanted to play the young man, and without waiting for me to hold out a hand to him, he braced himself to jump a fissure in the rock eighteen inches wide; but as he did it without reflection, he put all the muscular strength into it that he would have done on the Sun, and instead of leaping a foot and a half, he suddenly departed into the air like a shuttlecock launched by a racket.

Pongo, who had taken quite a shine to the old man, though that he was flying; he launched himself after him, grabbed him by the beard thirty or forty feet up in the air and, after they had both turned five or six somersaults in mid-air, they fell back as slowly as if they had a parachute, and landed on their feet, thanks to a perilous leap that the ape very appropriately caused our philosopher to make, who was coming down head first.

That little incident cheered the demon up, and he became as lively and talkative as usual.

At that moment we saw the Sun. small and pale, which was about to set behind a rock. The spectacle was saddening us when the genius said: "The planet we're on accomplished its annual revolution in 4 years 28 days, but its diurnal revolution is much less, comparatively, for it accomplishes it in 24 hours.[88] As it's only a hundred and fifty leagues around and, thanks to the lightness of which the savant Solarian has just given proof, we'll be able to walk six leagues in an hour, we can easily go around the world in the space of one of its diurnal revolutions and, by that means follow, the sun, or the daylight, for as long as we want to, by heading westwards—which is to say, in the inverse direction to the planet's rotation."

We all applauded this proposal, and we immediately set forth, walking with long strides. As we went, I asked the genius a few questions.

"Do you think," I said, "that Juno also has a winter and a summer."

"Certainly, since its axis is inclined relative to its orbit."

"Ha ha! I understand. Its axis oscillates, like that of the Earth."

"Who told you that the Earth's axis oscillates?"

"You did, Monseigneur."

"You haven't understood me, for the oscillation about which I talked to you is, as I told you, only apparent,[89] and furthermore, it results positively from the fixity of the Earth's axis. I'll explain that to you by drawing a diagram that will render the matter a little clearer.

---

[88] Author's note: "This is a pure supposition, for no one has yet been able to ascertain the diurnal revolution of Juno."

[89] Author's note: "In the preceding article, an omission by the printer of the single word 'apparent' when I talked about a third movement of the Earth, consisting of the apparent oscillation of the Earth's axis, obliges me to return to the subject in order not to cast my readers into a bad error."

"If this is the orbit of the Earth, seen not perpendicularly but at slight angle, or, if you prefer, the circle that the Earth describes in its annual revolution around the Sun, the axis of the Earth being fixed—which is to say, always conserving the same inclination—is drawn parallel to itself through the various points on the circumference. The rotation of the globe on its axis doesn't change its inclination to the plane of the orbit.

"Now, if the Earth is at this point on 21 March, at the spring equinox, it will have moved through ninety degrees, a quarter of its orbit, by 21 June, the summer solstice. As the position of its axis hasn't changed, you can see that one pole is illuminated while the other is in shadow.

"Let's slide our globe around a further ninety degrees; here it is at the autumnal equinox on 21 September. Let's continue to slide it around its orbit for another ninety degrees, and on 21 December, the winter solstice, as its axis has not been disturbed and has conserved the same inclination, you can see that the pole previously illuminated is now in shadow, and vice versa. Thus, there is daylight for six months at the south pole in this half of the orbit, and daylight at the north pole during the other six months. Seen from the Sun, where we are placed, the axis of the Earth has experienced, for us, during its annual route, an apparent and purely optical oscillating movement resulting, as I told you, from its fixity."

While talking and making strides of forty or fifty feet, we arrived at the summit of the formless rock that hid the Sun from us. What surprised me most was not seeing the star move ahead of us without leaving us behind, like the star of the Magi, but finding myself on the edge of a bottomless precipice, almost as perpendicular as a wall, at the bottom of which I could see the sky beneath my feet as well as above my head and before me, without interruption. That resulted simply from the face that Juno, instead of being spherical, formed a gross triangle, and we had reached one of its points. We all stopped, seized by fear.

"You're not going on?" said the genius. And we saw him lean his body forward and gravely descend that almost vertical slope in a position only slightly inclined to the plane of the slope.

We did likewise, and far from falling, as I would have expected, I found myself perfectly upright, although in the same attitude as the genius. That caused me to realize that the center of attraction of a non-spherical planet is not determined like that of a round globe.

We perceived from there three other planets rolling in space in orbits not parallel to the celestial equator, which is a phenomenon with no other example. In their rapid courses they seemed to be coming directly toward us, which inevitably alarmed me.

"That one," the genius told me, "is Ceres; it's only three million leagues from the one we're on; it's exactly the same size and just as irregular in form.[90] Herschel has seen clearly from the Earth that it has an atmosphere, because he has found that it has the appearance of a nebulous star, surrounded by mists that often change thickness and location. Furthermore, my dear friend, all planets have an atmosphere, more or less dense, as you've experienced thus far, and astronomers can deduce that verity from the following simple reasoning.

"Every kind of matter has a density and a specific weight appropriate to it; the heaviest species is necessarily placed at the center of gravity and the lightest at the circumference of a globular mass. Now, in order for a planet to have no atmosphere, it would be necessary that among all the simple or compound substances it contains, there would be not one fluid or gaseous, for if there were even one, that one would come to its circumference and form an atmospheric envelope; it would therefore be necessary for there to be in that planet neither fire nor caloric, for flame supposes the existence of hydrogen and combustion that of oxygen, and caloric has the necessary ef-

_____

[90] Author's note: "I am giving here the proportions of the four little planets according to the opinions of Herschel. Schroeter believes that Juno and Ceres are each 475 leagues in diameter, and Pallas 700."

fect of reducing the hardest substances to a gaseous state. It would thus be necessary to suppose that the substance of planets is very different from what we know, and that it has neither the physical nor the chemical properties of it, from which the other mechanical laws necessarily follow.

"Now, if that matter obeyed other mechanical laws, everything that our learned individuals know about the mass, density and volume of heavenly bodies would be pure supposition; it would only be by chance that they had discovered and predicted the times of eclipses, the orbits of bodies, comets, etc., etc.—in sum, all astronomical science, all the laws of motion discovered by Newton, Kepler and others would be nothing but romances more favored by hazard than the predictions of Nostradamus and Thomas Moulth."[91]

"It's said, however that the Moon..."

"You can make me your observation when we're on the Moon; for the moment, let's occupy ourselves with the place where we are. Look, there's Pallas rolling in the sky four million leagues away from us, and which is very recognizable by its white glare; it has the same dimensions and is just as irregular as the other two.

"Further away you can see Vesta, which, even from here and with the excellent glasses that I've given you, only appears as a luminous dot, of which you can distinguish the disk any more that astronomers place of the Earth. That's because that miniature globe is no more than 25 leagues in diameter, and a good greyhound, capable of covering 37 leagues in a day; one could easily go around it in 48 hours; it's 11 million leagues from us—which is to say, 81 million leagues from the Sun, for it's much closer to it than Juno, Ceres and Pallas.

"I won't take you to those little globes, because you'd only see there, very nearly, what you see here. But to demon-

---

[91] Thomas Moulth is named in *Petit manuel du devin et du sorcier* [The Diviner and Sorcerer's Pocket Handbook] (1854) by his grandson Nathaniel as a "celebrated astrologer" but his fame has all but vanished from human ken.

strate to you that they might be nothing more than shards of a world that once circulated between Mars and Jupiter, I'll represent by four circles the orbits that they travel, and you'll remark that those orbits all intersect at a single point, and that they all return to pass that point, which is in conformity with that the laws of mechanics require, supposing that it's at that point that the explosion of the large planet occurred. Now let's go, and leave the world of spirits there."

"The world of spirits!" I cried, with admiration. "What, Monseigneur—is there really a world of spirits?"

"Certainly, and that world is Pallas."

"In the name of your omnipotence, Seigneur Demon, don't let me pass so close to the world of spirits without showing me a few of them. Since my childhood, I've been devoured by the desire to see spirits, but alas, alas, I've been everywhere, in salons, in theater foyers, in literary societies, etc., etc., and I've never found a spirit or genius—except you, of course and a few of your friends scattered in France…and without wishing to offend Your Highness, they're all rather poor devils."

"My dear, a genius is something that doesn't leap to the eyes of everyone, and perhaps you've rubbed shoulders with more than one in the courtyard of the Institut without recognizing him. It's therefore necessary for you to take these spectacles, and you'll see."

He placed large spectacles on my nose, similar to those of the singer of *La Belle Bourbonnaise*,[92] and we headed toward Pallas. I thought we were going to descend on the solid part of the planet, but I was mistaken; we remained at the entrance to its atmosphere, suspended between its ground and its sky, balancing gracefully in mid-air, like kites retained by a string.

---

[92] Two comedies with that title were published in 1839; the one featuring a character wearing enormous spectacles was by Théophile Dumersan.

At first I could only see a light mist, offering an immense, slightly undulating surface, like that of a vast ocean during a flat calm. The surface was neither a veritable fog, nor water, but that of the gaseous mass forming the atmosphere of Pallas. Soft sounds, faint but strange, soon came to strike my ears; it was like a light evening breeze gently agitating foliage, or the distant sound of a stream murmuring in a meadow. I distinguished a sweet melody, however; I even thought I recognized a few bars of airs by Rossini and soft voices modulating them in a strange language. I replaced the spectacles over my eyes and turned my head toward the place from which the melancholy harmony seemed to be coming.

Imagine my astonishment! I saw living beings of a form so singular that my imagination could scarcely grasp them, even with the aid of my eyes. They were a thousand times more transparent than the purest rock crystal, a thousand times lighter than an autumn leaf carried away by a gust of wind; they were gliding over the surface of the atmosphere like the luminous meteors that excite, on a summer evening, the fear or admiration of travelers. Their eyes were shining with a pale gleam that would not have been able to compete with that of a firefly. I saw long robes of silvery vapor floating around their limpid bodies, the undulating creases of which designed their airborne forms. Their hair descended to their knees and resembled, in its undulations, flames devoid of light or color.[93]

I could distinguish perfectly beings that had the greatest analogy with women, but of a truly celestial beauty, for nothing in them recalled the unfortunate infirmities of human nature. The men had more characterized faces, but, if it had not been for the melancholy inscribed in their features, they would have resembled angels perfectly.

All of them were holding in their hands a lyre of a less diaphanous substance, coarser than their bodies, apparently

---

[93] In the world of the spirits featured in Restif's *Les Posthumes* the souls of the Earthly dead walk on the surface of our atmosphere in a similar fashion.

made from compressed air. They were singing, and although I d dot understand their words, their mysterious music penetrated my heart; their melancholy voices caused my heart to comprehend, and I shed tears.

"They're angels singing the praises of the Lord," I said to the genius.

"No, no," he replied. "They're creatures afflicted by the imperfections of their species who are singing their dolor. 'Why,' they're saying, 'has nature composed us of a substance so coarse, so heavy? Why has she enveloped our intelligence in a rind of matter as impure as the air that we tread with our feet? Alas, we're condemned by destiny to crawl heavily above the clouds, and our eyes alone can elevate our souls toward the heavens.' In sum, my dear, they're lamenting only being formed of the dust of the air, and only being deformed and material creatures."

"What! Material creatures? And yet, without these magical spectacles, I couldn't even perceive the location they occupy."

"That doesn't prevent them from being material, like you. There's only one difference, which is that there's no possible combination between light and their substance."

"May I become a spirit if I understand a single word of what you just said."

"That's because your science is still in default. Listen to me: first, it's necessary for you to know that light isn't luminous in order to conceive of the physical constitution of the Pallasians."

"That's rather difficult."

"It is, however a verity extremely facile to discover. Shut the room you inhabit in such a manner as only to let a single beam of sunlight pass through a hole that you've made in your shutter. You'll see that ray illuminate the place where it falls, on the floor or against the wall, but you won't perceive it during its trajectory from the hole in the shutter to the bright spot."

"That's true."

"Thus, the ray isn't luminous in itself. In order for the fluid that forms it to become so, it needs to come into conflict with a material surface, and for it to combine chemically with it. In this instance, in your room, the ray will emit a little diffuse light, because it will be in contact with the material atmosphere that fills your apartment. But do otherwise to avoid all doubt; take a glass box hermetically sealed, empty the air from it by means of a vacuum pump and cover it with opaque black paper. Make two holes in that cover opposite one another and place two short tubes therein to avoid refraction by the glass; pass a luminous ray from a lamp through the two holes across the box, without the light falling on a single point on the walls, and its interior will remain in complete darkness, although traversed by a ray of light.

"Now, my dear, the fluid generator of light doesn't combine in the same manner with all species of matter; there are some—for instance, water, glass, air and gases—with which it combines very little, and that matter is what is called transparent, or with which it does not combine at all, and that matter is invisible. It is no less matter for that, and, as you have just seen in the Pallasians, capable of organization. The beings that it forms are necessarily invisible, at least for humans and animals whose vision is analogous."

"Well, that's something that appears to me to be demonstrated, and yet I've never heard mention of it."

"If light were luminous in itself, it would inundate infinite space, and no mortal eyes would be able to sustain the glare—but far from it; the universe is plunged in an obscure and eternal night, and light only appears where its fluid generator has an atmosphere to traverse, matter to strike with its contact."

"Tell me, do those spirits floating on that ocean of air have passions and needs?"

"One cannot exist without the other, and they're the two essential conditions of life.

"Do they eat?"

"Certainly, but in the manner of vegetables. They take their nourishment from the matter that bears them, through the feet, for their heads are in the void, and it's by respiration. Their souls and their thoughts are in their heels, while their head only has the eyes for a sense organ."

"Do they love?"

"That's another of the primal conditions of life, but their kind of love has no relationship with yours. When two Pallasians please one another, they dissolve into one another, like two different liquids mixed in the same jar, or, if you prefer, like two light mists mingling in the sky to produce a single cloud. That double being no longer has but one life of its own, until the gases composing it become too condensed, and separate into three or four parts to form three or four new beings. Here, as you can see, and by a method of nature that cannot be simpler, fathers are as young as their children, and children as old as their fathers."

Chapter XII
Jupiter

After having traveled for some time in space, we began to discover Jupiter and its four moons. Although we rested for a while on one of the latter, I shall not say anything about it, for the reason that the moons of Jupiter, Saturn and Uranus offer no remarkable difference in their physical constitution from Earth's Moon, about which I shall tell you in due course.

We entered the atmosphere of Jupiter, and as the genius abandoned his attraction momentarily, we fell with such a frightful rapidity that, in our fall, we traveled 42 feet per second, while on Earth we would only have traveled 16. We were then dragged away violently by the regular winds that reign constantly on that globe and which blow in a direction perpendicular to its axis. As they draw with them the clouds by which the sky is almost always covered, those clouds, seen from Earth, resemble bands or dark zones that vary in their width and position on the disk, but never in their general direction. Sometimes, but very rarely, one sees them break up and disperse over the entire planet.

"The violence of these constant winds," the genius told me, "comes, according to your astronomers, from the rapidity with which Jupiter rotates on its axis. In fact, the globe in 1,470 times larger than Earth—which is to say that it is about 33,000 leagues in diameter—but the Earth, which is only 3,000, rotates on its axis in 24 hours, while Jupiter only takes 9 hours 56 minutes to make the same revolution. Judge from that the speed of its rotation. Its diameter, near the equator, is 107% of its diameter measured from pole to pole, which proves that it's even more flattened at its poles than the Earth. If its nine-hour days are much shorter than Earth's, by way of compensation its year is considerably longer, for it's no less than 4,332 of our days."

We came down next to a wood almost entirely composed of pines, larches and other resinous trees, and we rested on the grass. The weather was superb, but a trifle somber, because of the distance from the sun, which appears to us five times larger when seen from Earth, and sends us twenty times more light. I thought on arrival that it was autumn, as the daylight was as gray as it usually is in Paris during that season; but the demon told me that Jupiter's axis is so slightly inclined to the plane of its orbit that the variation of the seasons is scarcely perceptible there, and its nights are always almost equal to its days.

"The consequence of that," he added, "is that the inhabitants of each latitude, only ever experiencing the same temperature, very nearly, have an organization adapted to their climate, and can hardly ever leave it."

We walked along the edge of the wood for a few minutes, and suddenly. emerging from a mountain gorge, we discovered a magnificent castle in the middle of an open plain, of unimaginable beauty, grandeur and richness, comparable with the most marvelous palaces of the Thousand and One Nights.

Apart from the genius and the Solarian, we all stood there stupefied by admiration, because we had never seen anything like it, on the Sun or even in the courtyard of the Louvre.

"That," said the inhabitant of the Sun, "announces a civilization that is making progress, but is nevertheless still not far removed from barbarity. Its several thousand years since we Solarians were there; we believed then that one could never pile enough stones one atop another, or built palaces big enough to house creatures five feet tall. Let's go in; the ridiculous prerogatives that the owners must have will certainly amuse us."

We went in, and thanks to the magic crutch, we were not put out of the door as good-for-nothings and vagabonds, which would certainly have happened otherwise.

I remarked immediately that the master of the castle was a small man four and a half feet tall, with crooked feet, squinting eyes, red hair and a wan white complexion; he was slightly hunch-backed and rather uncouth, but clad in a rich embroidered coat whose weight overwhelmed him. He was surrounded by a host of busy domestics, the smallest of whom was a head taller than he was, and who all seemed more distinguished in their build, beautifully proportioned, with ebony black skin.

"That's because the nobility here isn't the same species as the commoners," the demon told me. "The wives of these valets could pass for beautiful negresses in Algeria, and you can judge with your own eyes what their mistress is."

We went into a kind of boudoir, where we found a small creature, pink and white, nonchalantly lying on a sofa, with some resemblance to a woman and a great deal to a wasp. Although she could not stand upright because her delicate feet were so tiny, it was evident that she was about three feet tall. Her waist was so thin that it could easily have been surrounded by an eight-year-old child's bracelet, and as she had a torso as large as a five-year-old child and enormously developed hips, one could have believed that her body was composed of two short squat cones, one of which was stuck by its point to the base of the other by means of a little sealing-wax. Her head was very small, but she could scarcely carry it even so, for she supported it constantly either with one of her hands or on a soft cushion. Whenever her frail body was raised up on her settee, that pretty head remained tilted slightly over one shoulder, which was not without a certain grace.

The face of that "celestial angel"—that is the name given to the women of Jupiter—was made to turn the head of a romantic poet, for it had a fantastic and consumptive expression of suffering that it would be impossible for me to describe, but of which I can give some idea by returning to the vignettes of Monsieur ***. Her arms were a trifle weak, but white and round, her hands very small and her feet shod in slippers into which I would not have been able to plunge two fingers. In sum, she was a little creature so frail, so delicate and so debilitated that one would not have dared touch her with the tip of

241

one's finger for fear of breaking her—and yet, she was in the flower of youth, for she was no more than one and a half years old, which is equivalent to seventeen or eighteen years on Earth. She passed for one of the most beautiful and lovable women on Jupiter, and her husband was desolate because, he said, she had too much intelligence.

"Madame," I said to her, bowing profoundly, "permit strangers to present their respectful homages to you."

"Strangers? What's that?"

"They're sages, curiosity-seekers or idlers who travel the world to kill time, under the pretext of educating themselves."

"Ha ha ha! You find me pretty, don't you?"

"Charming."

"I have a very nice waist, feet and hands, haven't I?"

"Admirable."

"I'm an angel, a celestial woman, aren't I?"

"A divinity."

"You seem to me to be rather well brought-up, for some-one from another world, but are your companions mute?"

The Solarian approached her then and said to her, in a slightly pedantic tone: "Permit me, Madame, to congratulate you on advantages more precious than those of grace and beauty, on..."

"On my intelligence, my genius, my talents, no? On all the brilliant qualities that make me adored in society, on..."

"No, Madame, but on the virtues you possess, I'm certain, on the qualities that make you a good wife and mother..."

He was at that point when the celestial angel seized a bell-cord, which she agitated with all her might, shouting for help and calling her servants to throw out that boorish scholar, that brutal moralist who had just insulted her in her own boudoir. She had an attack of nerves and ended up fainting.

The demon took advantage of the opportunity to place her in a large box lined with cotton, which he put under the Pongo's arm, and we all departed through the window and headed through space toward Saturn.

242

"The lord of the fine castle that we've just left," I said, "thinks his wife has too much intelligence, but personally, I think she tends too much toward imbecility."

"And you're both right. This is how it is. At the beginning of their civilization, the Jupiterians perceived that their wives, along with the same physical and moral strength as themselves, also had beauty, grace and, above all, the mental delicacy that men lack. They were afraid of being dominated by them, and in order to ensure their permanent tyranny over the sex they feared, they resolved to brutalize it mentally and physically; they found nothing better for that purpose than vanity and ignorance. It was from the day that women consented to be called 'celestial angels' that they began to be a little less than men. Flattery, idleness and toilette have completed their descent into the state of stupidity in which we found the chatelaine whom the Pongo is taking to Parus, where the Solarian will exhibit her as a curiosity—for in Paris, as you know, nothing similar can be seen."

Chapter XIII
Saturn and Uranus

Saturn appeared to us at first like a nebulous star, having a dull and leaden light. That is because, being so very distant from the sun, at 329 million leagues, it receives seven times less light than the Earth; but as it is constantly illuminated by its seven moons, there was a soft daylight there, very convenient for a thirty-five-year-old coquette. First we approached the singular ring that serves it as a girdle, but we did not descend there because the genius said to us, very nearly in these terms:

"Saturn's ring is a solid, opaque body, a land, which you can see by the shadow that it projects on the body of the planet on the side nearer to the sun, and by the shadow the planet casts on it on the opposite side. That marvelous girdle is composed of two flat rings, broad and very thin, which both have the same center as the planet and are set in the same plane; their thickness is scarcely 36 leagues but their breadth is considerable; the first—which is to say, the exterior ring—is 3,828 leagues wide; between it and the interior ring there is a gap of 648 leagues, through which you can clearly see the sky and the stars. That interior ring, much wider than the first, is no less than 12,438 leagues in extent, and the gap between it and the planet is 6,912 leagues.

"That girdle, carried by the planet's movement of rotation, opposes to it a slight resistance that suffices to maintain its equilibrium, for Saturn's diurnal rotation is completed in 10 hours 18 minutes and that of the ring in 10 hours 29 minutes 17 seconds."

"I'm curious," I said to the demon, "to know whether these rings are inhabited."

"Since they're composed of solid matter," he told me, "you can't doubt that the matter in question is in part organized; but also, as the center of gravity of the rings is the same as that of the planet, the surface of the ring is, in consequence, perpendicular relative to the animals that populate it, like the surface of a wall on Earth, or at least very slightly oblique, so those animals are organized as they need to be in order to live on an almost vertical plane; they all have wings, or suckers on their feet. Like the flies that are so inconvenient on Earth, they can walk perfectly on a surface from which they are suspended by the feet, body downwards, in the same fashion as a fly walking on the ceiling of an apartment. The plants have an organization analogous to that of our climbing plants, but their trailing stems are directed constantly toward the exterior rim of the ring to seek the light of sun, in an inverse direction to the force of attraction."

"From that, I take the inference that there are only flies and birds on Saturn's sings."

"Not at all; there are analogue of all the beings there are on Earth, with the exception of apes and humans. As they all have wings, or suckers or pincushions on their feet, and hence unable to obtains perfect knowledge of external objects by touch, their intelligence has not been able to develop much, and in general, does not surpass that of fish."

We soon arrived on Saturn, a very beautiful globe, almost 900 times larger than the Earth—which is to say, being 28,664 leagues in diameter at the equator. As I have said, the days there are only ten hours long, but the year is 29 years 5 months 11 days.

The rings offered a magnificent spectacle seen from the illuminated region where we were; they appeared to us as vast arches dividing the sky from one horizon to the other and maintaining an invariable position relative to the stars. For the regions situated on the dark side and on which the shadow of the ring fell, however, there is inevitably an inconvenience, which is to occasion an eclipse of the sun for half a Saturnian year—which is to say, nearly fifteen years. The inhabitants are not plunged into total obscurity by that, however, for they enjoy the light of their seven moons. You can easily understand how they have a slightly etiolated complexion when they emerge from that, but that is not a reason for being unable to live there, as some people think. And in fact, why should not the organization of beings on Saturn be adapted to it as well as on our Earth? Do we not know that the tenebrous caverns of La Carniole are populated by animals, eel-like proteans, that can only live in profound obscurity and which the slightest ray of sunlight kills almost immediately? Do we not have our bats and owls, which flee the daylight and are only at home in the pale light of the moon?

But we were not there, because we came down in an il-luminated part of the globe, toward midday. The first thing I did was to sit down on a shard of rock, which I recognized as the hardest granite, and I leave you to imagine how astonished I was to feet it yielding softly under the weight of my body, as if I were sitting on a sack of wool like a peer in the English House of Lords.

The fact appeared to me so singular that I got up with a start and stated walking along a road so flat that it might have be the one between Paris and Versailles. Further astonish-ments: I sank into the soil to my ankles, as if I were marching on quicksand. I was bewildered by surprise, and no longer knew whether I ought to go forward or retreat, when the de-mon said to me:

"If you take the trouble to reflect, my dear, the astonish-ment will cease. You know that the density of Saturn is scarcely an eighth of the mean density of the Earth. In conse-quence, the constitutive materials of the large planet are each eight times less dense, and granite here has the same density as cork in Paris. On Earth you weighed 150 pounds, on the Sun 4,050, on Mars 50; here, in order for you and the others to be in harmony with the surroundings, it's necessary for me to reduce your weight to 15 pounds—which is to say that I'm abandoning you to the laws of gravity of the planet where we are.

He touched me with his crutch, and my companions as well, and the ground suddenly solidified under our feet—but another inconvenience resulted from that which was nearly deadly to me. This is how: the Solarian had decided to make a collection of Saturnian minerals, and in consequence, not only was he laden down with specimens of all sorts of stones, but he was also making all our companions carry enormous loads, with the intention of studying their mineralogical characteristics at the first halt, and making notes. He also wanted me to carry some, but nature had not created me sufficiently obliging for me to allow myself to be beaten and loaded like a donkey, and I refused.

To avoid his persecutions and to avoid him slipping a few pebbles into my pockets, as he had tried to do on the sly, I increased my pace and drew some way ahead of our little caravan. I had reached the summit of a picturesque plateau and was about to sit down to wait for my companions when a little breeze got up, which soon degenerated into a strong wind, which I felt lifting me off my feet. I clung to the branches of a bush in order not to be blown over, but alas, all my efforts were in vain; the wind caused me to turn like a weather-vane around the branch on to which I was holding with both hands. It was engulfed in my trousers, making me let go and carrying me away like an autumn leaf, sometimes skimming the ground, sometimes flying at a height of five or six feet. At other times I rolled on the ground like a bear turning fifty successive somersaults.

For more than ten minutes it was impossible for me to stop and to progress other than on my head or on my back. Fortunately, Pongo and the Venusian set off in pursuit of me; they had a great deal of difficulty reaching me, for every time they were about to lay a hand on me, a gust of wind would carry me further away, just like the pointed hat of a fashionable estaminet taken by surprise by a gust of wind of the Pont-Neuf. Finally, they succeeded in catching hold of me; they set me back on my feet, and I eventually succeeded in conserving sufficient aplomb when the Solarian had filled my pockets with stones.

If the genius had not alerted us we would have passed over a Saturnian village without perceiving it, for the inhabitants are all troglodytes and live in holes in the ground, like foxes. The demon's power gave us courage, so we all entered with a firm tread into a hole that seemed to us to form the entrance to a profound cavern, and by the most fortunate chance, we found ourselves in the abode of the prince of the region.

I shall not describe our host's vast subterranean palace to you any more than the celestial angel's castle; it will suffice for me to tell you that it closely resembled what you have seen in or heard about the grottos of Antiparos, but with the difference that the shiny stalagmites and stalactites that formed the principal decoration were all in the elegant and regular forms of columns, pilasters, girandoles, etc., as if they had been carved in diamond or rock crystal by the most skillful sculptors.

At the very back of the hole, in a remote cabinet, we found the royal family, consisting of the father, the mother, a young damsel and a young man with the greatest expectations. As the palace was only illuminated by a few glow-worms attached to the walls at intervals, I was unable at first to make out the individuals perfectly, and I confess that at first glance I mistook them for four white rabbits of an exceptionally large species; but they got to their feet as we approached, and started to make a throaty hissing sound, like baby owls surprised in their nest, and I was then able to distinguish them perfectly.

The father and the son were rather handsome fellows, of an ordinary height, but by and muscular. Their hair, smooth and two feet long, hung down over their shoulders, and as a very bright white. The skin of their faces and hands was also white, but a milky mat white, and very singular.

I thought at first that they were enveloped in Angora goat-skins, but I did not take long to perceive that their entire bodies were covered with thick fur, as white as snow, which I had mistaken for animal fur.

What was most curious of all were the eyes and ears; the former were red, like those of a white rabbit, large and round, and the pupil, instead of being round, was linear and transversal, like those of our owls and other nocturnal animals; that pupil as susceptible of a very large dilation, so that the Saturnians, on our terrestrial globe, would have been able to see perfectly by night, but not by day.

The women had fur much whiter and silkier than the men, more delicate limbs and more gracious figures, but otherwise resembled them closely. They all had ears nearly eighteen inches long, forming a kind of funnel bordered with long, stiff hair arranged in a row like lashes. When they were listening to what we were saying to them they advanced their mobile ears toward us, like those of a hind, and closed their eyes, fearful of distraction, which gave them an air of charming amiability.

"Here," said the Solarian, "are people perfectly adapted to a cold and tenebrous climate, but I'd like to know whether they would cease hissing like snakes in order for us to ask them a few questions."

The genius touched them with his crutch; they never stopped hissing, but we could understand their language and they replied to all our questions very affably. This is the substance of what we learned:

The Saturnians live in caves in order to protect themselves not only from the cold but the wind, which is capable of lifting them up and dispersing them all over the surface of the globe when they least expect it. Their history cites one example of an entire nation that was transported eight thousand leagues from its native soil by a fortnight-long storm. Sunlight fatigues their sight greatly, so they only ever go outside in daylight with their eyes closed and their ears open; the latter, which they direct forwards, warn them of the slightest sound, preventing them from bumping into one another, and is sufficient for them to direct their steps.

They live entirely on mushrooms, morels, black truffles and other cryptogamic vegetables, because their climate does not produce any others. The people have a morality, because the young boys there are brought up in great modesty, have a strong sense of decency and live in virtual seclusion, under the surveillance of their parents. It is true that the education of girls is not as closely supervised by the families, who allow them to go to estaminets where they spend their days talking nonsense, drinking, smoking, fighting and indulging in all kinds of extravagances that often ruin their health and their purse, but all that appears charming, because it is customary— except that good houses close their doors to them for fear that they might seduce their young sons or ruin their reputation by abusing their inexperience to compromise them.

All that only piqued the curiosity of a Parisian like me very slightly, so the genius gave the signal for departure, and after having put a pair of blue-tinted spectacles on the nose of our host, we took him with us.

We were a little more than 662 leagues from the Sun when we descended on Uranus, or Herschel, which we had seen from afar under the appearance of a globe whose clear-cut disk was bluish-white.

That little planet is only eighty times larger than Earth, and in consequence, its diameter is only twelve thousand leagues. As we only stayed there very briefly, I cannot tell you how many hours its days last, and I do not think our astronomers can tell you anymore, because in spite of their telescopes, they have not perceived any patch whose disappearance on one side of the disk and reappearance on the other can allow them to calculate the time of its axial rotation. Nevertheless, however long its nights might be, and although the Sun only sends it a three-hundredth of the light that it sends to Earth, it is bright enough there thanks to its six moons and its slightly phosphorescent atmosphere.

The latter phenomenon astonished me greatly, because no astronomer has mentioned it, but the genius observed to me that a body that receives three hundred times less light than the Earth would not be visible from our globe if it did not have a gleam of its own, since it requires one luminous ray to be sixty times more powerful than another to extinguish it in our eyes, according to our astronomers.

"Besides," he told me, "You'll see from the Paris Observatory that the brightness of Uranus has much more analogy with the phosphorescence of rotten wood or putrefied fish than with a ray of light emanating from the Sun."

For want of anything better, I contented myself with that reasoning.

Uranus is only slightly inclined on its axis, from which it results that the seasons there are almost uniform, and the inhabitants, at least near the equator, enjoy a perpetual spring, neither too hot nor too cold; thus one does not see there, as on Earth, migratory animals obliged to make long journeys annually in order to seek their nourishment in others climes. That has to be the case, for, the year being 84 years long, a poor swallow would be obliged to absent itself for 42 years, and would have died of old age before completing a quarter of its journey.

We fell very gently on Uranus, for we only traveled four feet per second in our fall, while on Earth we would have traveled sixteen.

I saw, in spite of what the genius had told us about the relationship that exists on the planets between the sum of their own caloric and the quantity of light that the Sun ends to them, that Uranus is in general a cold country, for among its vegetables I recognized species analogous to our birches, firs, larches and other northern trees, and among its animals, blue fixes, white bears, martens, ermines and other inhabitants of our polar circles.

After having crossed a rather dismal plain without encountering any other inhabitants than animals, we arrived on the edge of a vast pond, where I thought I could see in the distance a flock of white geese frolicking over the water. I thought that they might be domestic geese, for I saw a quantity of cabins on the shore resembling the lodges of beavers, although larger. As we approached I saw that the geese differed from ours by virtue of the size of their head and the absence of a long neck. But good God, what did I divine when we got much closer?

They were all flying and chattering in the air, with the exception of one, which had its foot caught in a clump of

251

reeds. I ran to it and was about to take hold of it when I recoiled in astonishment; it raised toward me a white head decorated with a magnificent tuft of long plumes, and showed me the prettiest young woman's face that I have ever seen in my life.

By means of the virtue of the crutch I understood her chatter immediately, and she said to me with a supplicant expression:

"Strange monster, I beg you in the name of Heaven not to do me any harm. I'm a poor little goose, very innocent and very young, for I'm only two months"—scarcely sixteen years—"old and I haven't yet emerged from under my parents' wings."

Then she extended two white wings, brought them together very gracefully and joined the two little hands that terminated them

"You'll take pity on me," she added, weeping, "for even though you're very ugly, you appear to me to be good, and you won't put me in a cage. Besides which, I'd love you; I'd make feathers grow on your head by dint of caresses and cares; in sum, I'd devote my entire life to you, even if I were to find your society extremely tedious."

Those sweet words delighted me to the depths of my heart, and I could, I believe, have spent my life watching her talk. I was about to fall at the feet of the charming goose when the Solarian seize me by the arm, prevented me from throwing myself to my knees and said:

"What are you doing, my poor terraquean? Are you falling in love with a goose?"

"Well," I replied, brusquely, "I wouldn't be the first."

"That's certain—but my dear, that doesn't make it any better. Besides which, without embarrassing yourself with a foreign goose, you'll find enough of them in Paris, for its said that there are a great many in that region."

That discourse caused me to open my eyes. I thought, in fact, that I had seen plenty of them, just as pretty, in many other places.

In consequence, I came to an immediate decision; I let go of the one I was holding, and we all resumed the spatial route, heading for my homeland, reflecting that in a cold country like Uranus, nature had done well to cover the human species with feathers.

Chapter XIV
The Moon

We were near the Earth, which already appeared to us as a ball fifteen or eighteen feet in diameter, when its satellite, the Moon seemed to emerge, radiant, from behind its disk. We descended on to that night star, as the poets say, and that was our last station.

As you know, the Moon is eighty thousand leagues from the Earth; its diameter is only 782 leagues—which is to say, a little more than a quarter of that of our globe, and in consequence, it is 49 times smaller. That does not prevent it from being a very curious country, even though one does not find flying humans there or oxen with sails, or pigs with ruffs, as a very modern author claims who has written about that matter with the same gravity as me. [94]

One of the first singularities that I remarked there was that its atmosphere is extremely diaphanous and so lacking in height that it only surpassed the summits of the highest mountain by a few feet. I deduced from that fact, which I have verified with my own eyes, two consequences of the greatest importance for science. The first is that on the Moon, falcons cannot fly as high as on Earth; the second is that our scientists are mistaken in alleging that the Moon has no atmosphere. In fact, they all recognize that it has or has had volcanoes, and how can one comprehend fire without air to aliment it, for fire is extinguished in a void.

But, they might say, it might be the case that there is air or oxygen, or some other gas favorable to combustion, under-

---

[94] The reference is to the New York *Sun*'s "Moon Hoax" of August 1835, reporting discoveries allegedly made by John Herschel with the aid of a new telescope at the Cape of God Hope, which was equally successful when translated for French newspapers.

ground and not on the surface. To that I reply that it is impossible, for the reason that gases, whatever they may be, always being lighter than solid matter, necessarily come to float on its surface by virtue of the laws of weight, and form an atmosphere there. Thus, in order to admit that the Moon has no atmosphere, it would first be necessary to admit two things: firstly that, combustion not being possible on the Moon, there has never been any elevation of mountains or volcano there; and secondly that the mass of the planet does not include any gaseous matter—which appear to me to be inadmissible.

The astronomers say: "If the Moon had an atmosphere, when it passes in front of a star, that star would appear increasingly nebulous before disappearing behind the disk, as it was immersed in that atmosphere." That would be true if the layer of air approached the thickness that it has on Earth, but if the latter did not rise more than a few toises above the mountains, it would be impossible to see it even with our largest telescopes, for there is none that brings the Moon closer that one would see it with the naked eye if it were eighty leagues away—but where is the eagle eye that could distinguish a few feet of gas at a distance of eighty leagues?

On landing, I could not help laughing at the opinion of some of our geologists, who regard the Moon as an icy globe, because, they say, it has been incandescent like our globe and is extinct. And by the way, it would not be a bad thing if our geologists, before building these beautiful theories into which they want to introduce, continually and for no good reason, frightful revolutions, terrible cataclysms, horrible abysms of fire, and immense seas of molten platinum, gold and lead, would take the trouble to learn a little chemistry, physics, astronomy, natural history and many other things beforehand; that would put a bridle on the leaps of their imagination, but they would still be able to tell us fine tales. Let us return to the Moon.

As you know, however little you read Mathieu Laensberg,[95] the Moon rotates around the Earth in 29 days 12 hours 44 minutes 2 seconds; but what is very singular is that it also rotates on its axis in exactly the same space of time. The result of that is that we only ever see the same side; that only the inhabitants of that side can see the Earth, and that they are never in darkness because our glove sends them thirteen times more light than it receives from the Moon. One very remarkable particularity of astronomy is that the satellites of Jupiter, Saturn and Uranus are in exactly the same situation, and only ever present the same face to their planet. By reason of hose two movement, therefore, the Moon has, as I said, one face that has almost no night, and the opposite side very dark nights a fortnight long, succeeding days of the same duration.

The heavenly body in question has two years: its terrestrial year, comprising a revolution round the Earth, which is what we call a lunar month; and its solar year, the great revolution it makes around the Sun, drawn by the Earth. During that solar year, it makes its revolution around our globe thirteen and a half times. The combination of those various movements gives rise to its phases—which is to say, the different aspects in which it presents itself to us.

We had landed on the Moon in a country of which you can form a very precise idea if you have seen the volcanic mountains of the Puy-de-Dôme or traveled in the Phlegraean Fields. Herschel has described the same country very well, except for a few details that distance prevented him from perceiving in spite of the perfection of his telescope. This is what he says about it:

"The physical constitution of the Moon is better known to us than that of any other celestial body. With the aid of telescopes we can distinguish inequalities on its surface that can

---

[95] The fictitious Mathieu Laensberg was credited with authorship of the annual *Almanch de Liège*, published almost continuously from the early seventeenth century to the present day, with a brief gap during the Terror.

only be mountains and valleys, since se see that the former project shadows whose length corresponds precisely to the inclination of solar rays in the regions of the lunar surface where those inequalities are observed. The convex edge of the limb turned toward the Sun is always circular and almost smooth, but the edge opposite the illuminated part, which ought to offer the appearance of a clear-cut ellipse of the Moon were a perfect sphere, always exhibits profound inter-ruptions or indentations, which indicate cavities and promi-nences.

"The mountains neighboring that edge project long shad-ows, as one would expect if one reflects that for the points of the Moon his positioned, the sun is at the moment of rising or setting. When the illuminated edge passes these points, or—which comes to the same thing, when the Sun gains in height—the shadows shorten, and when the Moon is full, and the direction of all the rays corresponds with that of our line of sight, one can no longer perceive any shadow at any point of the surface. In accordance with micrometric measurements of the shadows, taken in the most favorable circumstances, it has been possible to calculate the heights of several remarkable mountains; the highest rises up to a vertical height of about 2,800 meters. The existence of similar mountains is further confirmed by the appearance of dots or little luminous islets placed outside the illuminated edge, which are the summits of mountains gradually illuminated by the Sun's rays before the intermediate plains; as the light advances one sees these lumi-nous dots connect with the edge and form projections there.

"The majority of lunar mountains present a singular ap-pearance and a striking uniformity. Their number is astonish-ing; they occupy the major part of its surface, and almost all of them are circular or take the form of cups whose interior sometimes has an elliptical curvature toward the edges. For the largest ones, the bottom of the excavation is ordinarily a flat area in the center of which a small conical eminence rises steeply. In brief, they offer to the highest degree a truly vol-canic character. One can even succeed with powerful telescopes in distinguishing on some definite marks of volcanic stratification or successive deposits of dejections.

"What is very singular in the geology of the Moon is that although its surface does not offer veritable seas anywhere—for the dark patches to which that name has been given present, when they are examined closely, appearances irreconcilable with the existence of deep water—vast regions can be observed there that are perfectly level, and which definitely have the character of alluvial terrain.

"It is necessary to observe that, by reason of the low density of the materials that enter into the mass of the Moon, and given that the force of gravity there is considerably weaker than on the surface of the Earth, the same muscular force would be able to lift a mass six times as great. Furthermore, it seems impossible, for lack of air, that living beings analogous in their organization to those populating our globe, can be found on the surface of the Moon; nothing there indicates the appearance of vegetation or any modification of the surface that might be attributed to a change of season."

The sage Solarian, to whom I quoted that passage of Herschel's, made a few observations that I found quite just:

"The Moon," he told me, "to judge by what we can see of it, cannot have any seasonal changes with regard to vegetation, because its agricultural year, if I might make use of that expression, is fifteen days and fifteen nights. Now, during that short lapse of time, no vegetable can go through all the phases of its vegetation; in consequence, they must take several years for that; if they succeed one another gradually, and the ground is perpetually covered by a sum of vegetation equal at all times, Herschel could not hope to recognize vegetation by modifications of the surface occasioned by the seasons.

"As for what animals there are on the Moon, although we have not yet encountered any, I'm sure that there are some; but because of the rarity of the atmosphere, and also because the Moon appears to me to be in its third geological period, those animals can only be lizards and other reptiles, and beings belonging to those inferior classes; and by reason of the slight density of the globe they must be enormous in size.

"Herschel, in my opinion, is also mistaken when he says that there are alluvial deposits on the Moon and not seas, which is incompatible, for where are those streams and rivers going that we can see descending from the mountains? Then again, how can the volcanic eruptions be explained, and the formation of this lava that we are treading underfoot, without the collaboration of water?"

As he finished, we came around a small hill that had masked an immense plain from us, dotted here and here with small salty lakes. It was evident that all those lakes owed their existence to a sea that had retreated, and which, the genius told us, now occupies the other hemisphere of the Moon.

The vegetation exactly resembled that which the Earth presented in the third geological period: there were lichens, mushrooms, ferns and cycads, but there were no dicotyledonous trees as yet, and monocotyledons were very rare. It was the class of cryptogams that was immensely dominant. We were plunged in a pretty forest of horsetails and ferns, the smallest of which were no less than a hundred feet high, when frightful whistling sounds became audible on the edge of a small lake not far away.

Immediately, we ran to a small hill to see what was happening, and we discovered two horrible monsters: a plesiosaur with a serpentine neck and a pterodactyl with a scaly body and wings like a bat. They closely resembled the similar animals that the demon had shown me in *Paris Before Humans*, but they were six times as large—which is to say that the plesiosaur was fifty feet long and the pterodactyl had a wingspan of ninety feet. The latter was fluttering around the other in a hostile manner, and a terrible combat as about to commence when the genius took a Bréguet watch from his pocket, looked at the time and said to us:

"My good friends, it's after midnight; that's an honest hour to send people to bed, so sleep well. Perhaps we'll meet up again another day, if the voyages I've enabled you to make have amused you.

As he finished speaking, he disappeared, and we all found ourselves on the boulevard in Paris, as astonished as people fallen from the Moon.

Celestial Angel, who had been sleeping tranquilly until then in her box, stuck her head through the carriage window and perceived the sprightly rig of a dandy coming back from the Opéra; immediately, she made a diabolical noise, crying murder, rape and arbitrary detention.

The elegant rig stopped; curiosity-seekers assembled in a crowd and surrounded us. The people picked up stones, and a riot broke out, in a manner that seemed likely to turn out badly for Pongo, because he did not want to let go of the box in spite of the demands of a Commissaire de Police and the shoving of the National Guard.

As for me, I succeeded in slipping through the midst of the tumult, and went back as fast as my legs could carry me to my little house in Montrouge, from which I did not emerge for a fortnight.

I learned then that the sage Solarian had been lodged and nourished at government expense at Charenton, in the lunatic asylum. Celestial Angel was about to make her debut imminently as a dancer at the Opéra. Pongo, the Venusian and the Saturnian had been claimed by the owner of a traveling menagerie, who asserted brazenly that they had escaped from his establishment. They were handed over to him, and he exhibits them for two sous to curiosity-seekers who want to see an orangutan, a chimpanzee and a savage woman from the albinos of the Arctic seas. As for the Martian, he was the most fortunate, because he obtained the succession of the Ethiopian who looked after the giraffe.

SF & FANTASY

Adolphe Alhaiza. *Cybele*
Alphonse Allais. *The Adventures of Captain Cap*
Henri Allorge. *The Great Cataclysm*
Guy d'Armen. *Doc Ardan: The City of Gold and Lepers; The Troglodytes of Mount Everest/The Giants of Black Lake*
G.-J. Arnaud. *The Ice Company*
André Arnyvelde. *The Ark; The Mutilated Bacchus*
Charles Asselineau. *The Double Life*
Henri Austruy. *The Eupantophone; The Olotelepan; The Petitpaon Era*
Barillet-Lagargousse. *The Final War*
Cyprien Bérard. *The Vampire Lord Ruthwen*
S. Henry Berthoud. *Martyrs of Science*
Aloysius Bertrand. *Gaspard de la Nuit*
Richard Bessière. *The Gardens of the Apocalypse; The Masters of Silence*
Chevalier de Béthune. *The World of Mercury*
Albert Bleunard. *Ever Smaller*
Félix Bodin. *The Novel of the Future*
Louis Boussenard. *Monsieur Synthesis*
Alphonse Brown. *City of Glass; The Conquest of the Air*
Émile Calvet. *In a Thousand Years*
André Caroff. *The Terror of Madame Atomos; Miss Atomos; The Return of Madame Atomos; The Mistake of Madame Atomos; The Monsters of Madame Atomos; The Revenge of Madame Atomos; The Resurrection of Madame Atomos; The Mark of Madame Atomos; The Spheres of Madame Atomos; The Wrath of Madame Atomos* (w/M. & Sylvie Stéphan)
Félicien Champsaur. *Homo-Deus; The Human Arrow; Nora, The Ape-Woman; Ouha, King of the Apes; Pharaoh's Wife*
Didier de Chousy. *Ignis*
Jules Clarétie. *Obsession*
Jacques Collin de Plancy. *Voyage to the Center of the Earth*
Michel Corday. *The Eternal Flame*

André Couvreur. *Caresco, Superman; The Exploits of Professor Tornada* (3 vols.); *The Necessary Evil*
Camille Debans. *The Misfortunes of John Bull*
Captain Danrit. *Undersea Odyssey*
C. I. Defontenay. *Star (Psi Cassiopeia)*
Charles Derennes. *The People of the Pole*
Georges Dodds (anthologist). *The Missing Link*
Charles Dodeman. *The Silent Bomb*
Harry Dickson. *The Heir of Dracula; Harry Dickson vs. The Spider*
Jules Dornay. *Lord Ruthven Begins*
Alfred Driou. *The Adventures of a Parisian Aeronaut*
Odette Dulac. *The War of the Sexes*
Alexandre Dumas. *The Return of Lord Ruthven*
Renée Dunan. *Baal; The Ultimate Pleasure*
J.-C. Dunyach. *The Night Orchid; The Thieves of Silence*
Henri Duvernois. *The Man Who Found Himself*
Achille Eyraud. *Voyage to Venus*
Henri Falk. *The Age of Lead*
Paul Féval. *Anne of the Isles; Knightshade; Revenants; Vampire City; The Vampire Countess; The Wandering Jew's Daughter*
Paul Féval, *fils. Felifax, the Tiger-Man*
Charles de Fieux. *Lamékis*
Fernand Fleuret. *Jim Click*
Louis Forest. *Someone is Stealing Children in Paris*
Arnould Galopin. *Doctor Omega; Doctor Omega and the Shadowmen* (anthology)
Judith Gautier. *Isoline and the Serpent-Flower*
H. Gayar. *The Marvelous Adventures of Serge Myrandhal on Mars*
G.L. Gick. *Harry Dickson and the Werewolf of Rutherford Grange*
Raoul Gineste. *The Second Life of Doctor Albin*
Delphine de Girardin. *Balzac's Cane*
Léon Gozlan. *The Vampire of the Val-de-Grâce*
Jules Gros. *The Fossil Man*

Edmond Haraucourt. *Daah, the First Human; Illusions of Immortality*
Nathalie Henneberg. *The Green Gods*
Eugène Hennebert. *The Enchanted City*
Jules Hoche. *The Maker of Men and His Formula*
V. Hugo, P. Foucher & P. Meurice. *The Hunchback of Notre-Dame*
Romain d'Huissier. *Hexagon: Dark Matter*
Jules Janin. *The Magnetized Corpse*
Michel Jeury. *Chronolysis*
Gustave Kahn. *The Tale of Gold and Silence*
Gérard Klein. *The Mote in Time's Eye*
Fernand Kolney. *Love in 5000 Years*
Paul Lacroix. *Danse Macabre*
Louis-Guillaume de La Follie. *The Unpretentious Philosopher*
Jean de La Hire. *The Fiery Wheel; Enter the Nyctalope; The Nyctalope on Mars; The Nyctalope vs. Lucifer; The Nyctalope Steps In; Night of the Nyctalope; Return of the Nyctalope*
Etienne-Léon de Lamothe-Langon. *The Virgin Vampire*
André Laurie. *Spiridon*
Gabriel de Lautrec. *The Vengeance of the Oval Portrait*
Alain le Drimeur. *The Future City*
Georges Le Faure & Henri de Graffigny. *The Extraordinary Adventures of a Russian Scientist Across the Solar System* (2 vols.)
Gustave Le Rouge. *The Dominion of the World* (w/Gustave Guitton) (4 vols.); *The Mysterious Doctor Cornelius* (3 vols.); *The Vampires of Mars*
Jules Lermina. *The Battle of Strasbourg; Mysteryville; Panic in Paris; The Secret of Zippelius; To-Ho and the Gold Destroyers*
André Lichtenberger. *The Centaurs; The Children of the Crab*
Maurice Limat. *Mephista*
Listonai. *The Philosophical Voyager*
Jean-Marc & Randy Lofficier. *Edgar Allan Poe on Mars; The Katrina Protocol; Pacifica 1, 2; Robonocchio; Return of the*

Nyctalope; (anthologists) *Tales of the Shadowmen 1-12; The Vampire Almanac* (2 vols.)

Ch. Lomon & P.-B. Gheuzi. *The Last Days of Atlantis*

Camille Mauclair. *The Virgin Orient*

Xavier Mauméjean. *The League of Heroes*

Joseph Méry. *The Tower of Destiny*

Hippolyte Mettais. *Paris Before the Deluge; The Year 5865*

Louise Michel. *The Human Microbes; The New World*

Tony Moilin. *Paris in the Year 2000*

José Moselli. *Illa's End*

John-Antoine Nau. *Enemy Force*

Marie Nizet. *Captain Vampire*

Charles Nodier. *Trilby and The Crumb Fairy*

C. Nodier, A. Beraud & Toussaint-Merle. *Frankenstein*

Henri de Parville. *An Inhabitant of the Planet Mars*

Gaston de Pawlowski. *Journey to the Land of the 4th Dimension*

Georges Pellerin. *The World in 2000 Years*

Ernest Pérochon. *The Frenetic People*

Pierre Pelot. *The Child Who Walked on the Sky*

Jean Petithuguenin. *An International Mission to the Moon*

J. Polidori, C. Nodier, E. Scribe. *Lord Ruthven the Vampire*

P.-A. Ponson du Terrail. *The Immortal Woman; The Vampire and the Devil's Son*

Georges Price. *The Missing Men of the* Sirius

René Pujol. *The Chimerical Quest*

Edgar Quinet. *Ahasuerus; The Enchanter Merlin*

Henri de Régnier. *A Surfeit of Mirrors*

Maurice Renard. *The Blue Peril; Doctor Lerne; The Doctored Man; A Man Among the Microbes; The Master of Light*

Restif de la Bretonne. *The Discovery of the Austral Continent by a Flying Man; Posthumous Correspondence* (3 vols.)

Jean Richepin. *The Crazy Corner; The Wing*

Albert Robida. *The Adventures of Saturnin Farandoul; Chalet in the Sky; The Clock of the Centuries; The Electric Life; The Engineer Von Satanas*

J.-H. Rosny Aîné. *Helgvor of the Blue River; The Givreuse Enigma; The Mysterious Force; The Navigators of Space; Vamireh; The World of the Variants; The Young Vampire*
Marcel Rouff. *Journey to the Inverted World*
Marie-Anne de Roumier-Robert. *The Voyage of Lord Seaton to the Seven Planets*
Léonie Rouzade. *The World Turned Upside Down*
Han Ryner. *The Human Ant; The Superhumans*
Frank Schildiner. *The Quest of Frankenstein*
Pierre de Selenes: *An Unknown World*
Norbert Sevestre. *Sâr Dubnotal: Vs. Jack the Ripper; The Astral Trail*
Angelo de Sorr. *The Vampires of London*
Brian Stableford. *The Empire of the Necromancers (1. The Shadow of Frankenstein; 2. Frankenstein and the Vampire Countess; 3. Frankenstein in London); Eurydice's Lament; The New Faust at the Tragicomique; Sherlock Holmes and The Vampires of Eternity; The Stones of Camelot; The Wayward Muse.* (anthologist) *News from the Moon; The Germans on Venus; The Supreme Progress; The World Above the World; Nemoville; Investigations of the Future; The Conqueror of Death; The Revolt of the Machines; The Man With the Blue Face; The Aerial Valley; The New Moon; The Nickel Man; On the Brink of the World's End; The Mirror of Present Events; The Humanishere*
Jacques Spitz. *The Eye of Purgatory*
Kurt Steiner. *Ortog*
Eugène Thébault. *Radio-Terror*
C.-F. Tiphaigne de La Roche. *Amilec*
Simon Tyssot de Patot. *The Strange Voyages of Jacques Massé and Pierre de Mésange*
Louis Ulbach. *Prince Bonifacio*
Théo Varlet. *The Castaways of Eros; The Golden Rock.; The Martian Epic* (w/Octave Joncquel); *Timeslip Troopers* (w/André Blandin); *The Xenobiotic Invasion*
Pierre Véron. *The Merchants of Health*
Paul Vibert. *The Mysterious Fluid*

Villiers de l'Isle-Adam. *The Scaffold; The Vampire Soul*
Gaston de Wailly. *The Murderer of the World*
Philippe Ward. *Artahe ; Manhattan Ghost* (w/Mickael Laguerre); *The Song of Montségur* (w/Sylvie Miller)

Victor Margueritte. *The Bacheloress; The Companion; The Couple*

NON-FICTION

Stephen R. Bissette. *Blur 1-5. Green Mountain Cinema 1; Teen Angels*
Win Scott Eckert. *Crossovers* (2 vols.)
Georges Grison. *The Heads that Fell in Paris*
Jean-Marc & Randy Lofficier. *Shadowmen* (2 vols.)
Randy Lofficier. *Over Here*
Brian Stableford. *The Plurality of Imaginary Worlds*